On the Run with Dick and Jane

Praise for
One Hundred Dollar Misunderstanding:

"Gover writes like a Salinger with guts."

- Los Angeles Times

"Gover has created a tart as remarkable as any to be found in recent literature."

- Joseph Heller

"So exuberantly different from the common run of novels that the celebration should be loud and long."

- Atlantic Monthly

"Gover has written a 'special' book, a freak of a novel; he has farced up the race, sex and money issues in American life by caricaturing two amorous antagonists in a series of burlesque monologues, extended exercises of style."

- New York Times

"In the early sixties, this novel which mixed sex, race and money shocked America. Now, 40-some years later it still has readers turning pages."

- Writers World

"The book was hot stuff for us children of the 50s."
- Bob Dylan, from a Studs Terkel interview

"A college sophomore spends a weekend with a pretty 14-year-old black prostitute under the manly misapprehension that she has invited him because she finds him irresistible. Outraged when her guest resists payment, Kitten steals her rightful $100 fee...."

– Time

Books by Robert Gover

One Hundred Dollar Misunderstanding
Here Goes Kitten
J.C. Saves
The Maniac Responsible
Poorboy at the Party
Getting Pretty on the Table
Going for Mr. Big
Tomorrow Now Occurs Again
On the Run with Dick and Jane

Nonfiction

Voodoo Contra:
Contradictory Meanings of the Word

Time & Money:
The Economy and the Planets

Get the latest information at:
www.RobertGover.com

On the Run with Dick and Jane

Robert Gover

Hopewell Publications

ON THE RUN WITH DICK AND JANE
Copyright © 2006 by Robert Gover.

Published by Hopewell
Publications, LLC
PO Box 11, Titusville, NJ
08560-0011 (609) 818-1049

info@HopePubs.com
www.HopePubs.com

International Standard Book Number: 1933435127

Library of Congress Control Number: 2006927864

First Edition

Printed in the United States of America

For my beloved and very much alive wife, Carolyn.

<u>Editors' Note</u>:

When this manuscript first came across our desks, it had been collecting dust in the author's drawer, virtually unseen by anyone for fifteen years. We were immediately struck by the timeliness of the story, even though it was set in pre-cell phone, pre-9/11 America, circa 1990. Gover writes with prophetic insight about characters involved in the burgeoning American health care crisis, child abandonment, and the child sex slavery trade that moves silently over borders throughout the world. We understood that this book was more relevant now than ever.

1

This all began eight days after my wife, Mae, died. The urn containing her ashes now sat beside me in my Dodge van. I was leaving North Carolina for California where my two sons and their families would scatter Mae's remains on the waters of the Pacific. After that, I had no idea what I would do with the rest of my life, or even why I should go on living now that I was sixty-three years old, financially ruined, alone, and homeless. Together, Mae and I had been a cornucopia of bountifulness and joy. Alone, I was a puddle of self-pity and pain.

Official cause of death was heart failure, after a series of increasingly critical heart problems during recent years, beginning just after I took early retirement. I could not return to the company, un-retired, so my world was blizzards of bill collectors and depressingly bleak prospects. I could have kept my job at Grandmother's Home but without Mae, it would only amplify the hurt. Her absence pained and haunted me like an amputated limb. I needed time alone to grieve, make peace with her absence, commune with her shade or whatever—the Mae that filled my heart. And I needed my family, the familiar people and places of my homeland, California.

Then, my second night on the road, I discovered I was not alone. I was overnighting in the parking lot of a shopping mall on the outskirts of Houston. I'd turned off the overhead lights, climbed up to the bunk over the front seats and was on the brink of sleep when I heard scratching noises. Maybe rodents have taken up residence in my van, I thought; I'll check it out tomorrow. Then the scratching turned to shuffling, thumps and bumps and heavy breathing—coming from the rear of the van.

A streetlight illuminated where I'd stacked some stuff too big for boxes, like my two-man tent and winter clothes, and suddenly I saw this pile move, rise up, undulate, tilt. In a panic, I jumped down from the bunk and opened the glove compartment and grabbed my can of Mace and flashlight. Pointing both at the moving pile of stuff, I yelled, "Who's there?"

A girlish voice squeaked, "Don't shoot, Dick, it's me."

"Who the hell is 'me'?"

The pile rose higher then flopped over against some boxes, and up from this mess rose Jane Doyle, one of the kids I'd worked with at Grandmother's Home in the mountains of North Carolina.

"What the hell?" I said, the can of Mace still aimed her way.

"Hold it, Dick, let me explain!"

Jane was twelve going on forty. According to her Department of Human Services records, her biological mother had abandoned her when she was eight, and thereafter Jane's life had become one long litany of probable incest, truancy, juvenile detention, suspected rape, probable rape, child prostitution, promiscuity, and so forth, as she was sent from her biological father to one foster home and another, until she wound up in Grandmother's Home. They had assigned her to West Cottage, where Mae and I met her.

Now Jane shielded her eyes and smiled up at me. "I couldn't stay there no more," she said, stressing the word *stay* and running the words *no more* together.

"You've been hiding in my van for two full days and one night and I didn't know it?"

"Yeah," she said with her usual disarming smile and coquettish tilt of the head. Brushing a curl from her forehead she added, "We're going to California, right? I been listening to you talk to yourself while you drove."

I turned on the van's two overhead lights, and put the flashlight and Mace back into the glove compartment.

"You picked the wrong way to run, Jane. Don't you know you're forcing me to have you arrested?" Which came out sounding like a boozy "A-reshdid" since my dentures were overnighting in a cup.

"I won't be no trouble, Dick. I just got to get out of the system. They're planning to sell my ass to an Asian prostitution ring."

I rolled my eyes and sighed. "Jane, when are you going to quit making up wild stories like that?"

"Okay, I know you don't believe it, but anyhow, I got to get out of the system, it's killing me. Take me with you to California."

"Jane," I said calmly, "I'm going to get back in my clothes and drive you to the nearest—"

"Oh, no you ain't!" she shrieked, anticipating my intentions. "You do and I'll tell the police you *raped* me."

"They'll call in a doctor and find out you're lying."

"I'll tell 'em you forced me to give you a blow job. Two days ago. How they gonna find evidence of that? Be my word against yours."

"Jane," I said, straining to remain calm, "why are you doing this?"

"I told you, I gotta get out of the system. I want to go to California. With you, Dick," she added in a soft, appealing, please-help-me little girl voice.

"Sweetheart, they have social services in California, the same as everywhere else in this country."

"So? They don't have me on record there."

"No, I don't suppose they do. But I can't let you do this. It's wrong and it's against the law."

Abruptly she switched from the appealing little girl to the harassing shrew: "The law!" she sneered. "You just set yourself up for a kidnapping rap, Dick!"

That hit hard. I had learned during my brief stint as a child-care worker at Grandmother's Home that if a child accuses a grownup of rape, the police are legally obliged to assume the grownup is guilty until proven innocent. We've been on the road two days and I haven't turned her over to the police. My only excuse is that she hid out in my van and I didn't know she was aboard—who is going to believe that? Jane had already thought this through to the conclusion the police would believe until proven otherwise: I'd kidnapped and raped her.

I was mulling this over when she climbed up out of the pile of tenting, blankets and winter clothes, and crawled over the boxes to the van's side door. She opened the door, pulled down her jeans, "mooned" the parking lot, then squatted, and let go a loud stream of urine.

She glanced up to see if I was watching, then smiled fetchingly and said, "Ain't peed since the last time you stopped driving."

I looked away and said nothing.

When she'd finished and was pulling up her jeans and fastening her fancy red belt—I'd been with her since she'd shoplifted that belt at Wal-Mart—I said, "Okay, look. Let's call it a day and get some sleep. Tomorrow we'll decide what to do. Have you had anything to eat?"

"Oh, sure. I brought a whole bag of stuff. You hungry?"

"Not right now, thanks. I thought maybe you were." Then, out of curiosity: "What did you bring?"

"Stuff from the dining hall. Fruit and cookies, mostly. Two jugs of Koolaid. I got plenty. Want some?"

"No, thanks. Why don't you curl up on top of that pile of stuff you were under. And I'll get back into my bunk and we'll work on this problem tomorrow."

"I'll just crawl in with you," she said, moving toward me.

"No no, Jane, you sleep back there!"

"What're you afraid of, Dick?" she asked with a smirk. "Ain't nobody here but us."

I replied with a frown that projected a warning threat, turned out the overhead light and climbed up to my bunk over the van's front seats. She lay down on the pile of stuff. Tomorrow, I decided, I'll figure out something, some way to get her sent back.

As I was drifting toward sleep I remembered that she'd won an essay contest just a month ago with a few pages entitled, "Why Don't They Arrest Psychological Abusers?" I'd helped her put it together on a word processor, donated by a well-meaning lady from the local Baptist Church, who never guessed what was behind the charming "thank-you-m'am" smile she'd gotten from Jane Doyle, who had, a few moments before this, stolen the lady's credit cards.

This reminded me of another incident: Jane had seduced one foster father, then called the police and sent that man to prison and destroyed what had been his life. She later bragged that she'd engineered the crime scene to get back at the guy for trying to discipline her. The police arrived to find the guy reeking of booze and asleep in his easy chair with his trousers down around his ankles. A dab of his semen on her cheek sealed his fate.

On the edge of sleep, I hallucinated Mae's presence beside me. It really is like losing an arm or a leg. I know she's gone, but my emotions or subconscious or autonomic nervous system or whatever keeps reproducing the sensation of her presence. I had known other women before Mae but, for reasons beyond my comprehension, I'd been so deeply mated with Mae that I knew she'd be an invisible presence till I followed her into the great mystery. I've never been a depressive type, but the situation I suddenly found myself in—the seeming impossibility of explaining why I had not turned Jane over to the law back in North Carolina—had me tortured.

Then I remembered a kitten Mae had taken in many years ago. This poor little kitten had been kicked around by kids who had been kicked around by parents who had been kicked around by... what? Their parents? Fate? Society? Life? I don't know but Mae had patiently healed that kitten and it grew to a most affectionate black and white cat—we'd named him Sir—who shared life with us till overwhelming medical bills forced us to sell the house in Santa Barbara. Sir refused to be coaxed into the cat carrier. His home gone, Sir disappeared himself. Well, Mae had been my home. Once I've fulfilled her wish to scatter her ashes on the Pacific, will there be any reason not to follow Sir?

A fleeting dream image of Jane holding Sir disrupted my search for sleep. I put myself under with deep breathing and a self-hypnosis technique I learned years ago.

2

Before, see, the kids in Group used to say, You're always running away, but you *know* you're only coming back. You ain't for real, girl!

Well, I knowed I had to get gone from goddamn Herb Williston and his slimy ways, from the whole dam system. Only question was how.

It got so bad I almost called this dude in Memphis, Johnny Hooper. He'd of come got me without fucking Herb and them others making a dime off my ass. But then I found out Dick was taking off for California and decided he was my way out.

Once we get gone from Grandmother's Home, maybe I can tell Dick what was really going on with Herb Williston—what a big-time hypocrite he is. Maybe out in California he can believe what I say. Nobody would believe the truth if I just blurted it out. Herb and them are good church-goers.

Knew I could get to Dick first time I laid eyes on him. We kids was swimming when these two new staff came by, Dick and Mae. He looked at me and I looked at him, and I knew I could get to him. Had the *feeling* in my heart of hearts. Our eyes connected and I knew he knew that I knew that he knew. Know what I mean?

Went back into the locker room and took off the t-shirt over my bathing suit, which is not allowed at Grandmother's Home, see, cause girls got to wear t-shirts over our bathing suits, or there's *consequences*. I figured the consequences was worth it this time.

Come strutting out of that locker room, wearing this sexy scanty I snitched from the mall last month, just to let him see what I got. That got his attention.

Well, then, fat old Emma Williston jumped up screaming and told me to get back in there and get fully dressed and not to come out till I was. She's a Bible thumper. Us kids call them Hurt and Enema. They think Yoga is Devil Worship, but the truth be told, the pair of them are real devils. They can go to church of a Sunday morning, eat the body and drink the blood of Jesus, and an hour later be harassing your ass, telling you you're a worthless piece of shit.

Dick has sparkly white hair and wears granny glasses and has a little paunch. Everybody puts out messages through the eyes, right? Message Dick puts out is, Hey, I love you but I don't know what to do about it. Me, I decided first time I met him, I could oomph it out of him, what to do about it.

His wife Mae—she died from a heart attack—was kind of skinny and had nice curly dyed-black hair hanging down her back. I liked them both, and they was easy on us kids, too, just like I knowed they'd be. See, this other pair, the Murphys, was leaving, so Dick and Mae was taking their place. That was a long time ago, maybe a year.

After Mae died, Dick didn't want to be there no more. Yesterday afternoon the word come down he'd quit his job and was leaving the next morning for California. He has this van, see, and he was packing it up with his stuff that evening after dining hall. I watched him from the window of my room. Carrying stuff out and putting it in his van.

It ain't easy to hide food in your room at West Cottage, but I done it—I smuggled out a whole shopping bag worth of food. Cookies wrapped in tin foil—you can always get all the tin foil you want—and apples, oranges, a couple bananas, some grapes, buns, and two big jugs of cool aid I got from Betsy the kitchen staff.

Lights go out at nine thirty. Herb didn't come for me that night. I set my mind for three in the morning and snoozed, woke up right at three, got up, dressed, packed my suitcase and overnight bag with as much clothes as they'd hold—we get tons of clothes from the church basement, see—sneaked across campus to the staff apartments and Dick's van, parked outside his door.

I was worried I'd have to pick the lock of his van to get in but the side door was unlocked. It squeaked when I opened it. Inside, he had clothes hanging from the roof and boxes, boxes, boxes. I sneaked in and squirmed over the boxes to the back of the van and found a place to hide there, under a pile of camping stuff. Smelled like wet ground. That smell meant I was on my way out of the system.

Slept till the next morning when I woke up with the van's engine va-rooming, and pretty soon we're moving. With Dick driving, his eyes on the road, I could sit up a little and peek at the scenery flying by. I could tell what road he was on from the treetops and mountains.

I could even sit up and look over the top of his boxes and watch him drive. It's kind of fun watching Dick drive. He don't just sit there with both hands on the wheel, he's always doing two or three things at once. Like lifting a cup of coffee with one hand, lighting up a cigarette, folding a map, unwrapping a candy bar, or just waving one hand around while he talks to himself. I seen a lot of staff drive and none of them does it any busier than Dick.

But the one thing got on my nerves was the music he plays. Pity party music. Like, What is this thing called love, why should it make a fool of me. You know, all that two-step shit-kicking music. And when that tape runs out, he plays classical da-da-da-daaah music. Even snug to the bottom of his van, I can feel the vibrations when it's loud, boom boom booming through my arms and legs and belly.

I ever get a hold of that radio, we're gonna have nothing but country and crossover.

Along about ten o'clock our first day out, I had to pee something awful. I thought he'd never stop, but finally he did, at a gas station. So when he went into the men's room, I shot into the lady's room. When I come out, he was talking to an attendant and I thought for sure he'd catch me. But he just kept talking as I scooted back into the van slick as a Miss Priss Pants from California in the movies.

So he gassed up and took off again, and I ate and slept some more. Around the middle of the afternoon he stopped at one of those roadside rest areas. I peeked out and saw him get out, looking like he was going to take a little walk about. So I hopped out again and made it to the lady's room for another pee and this time a shit too.

Second day went by pretty much like the first. Whenever he stopped to gas up and pee, I sneaked out and did mine.

I thought, man, I'm home free! I'll be in California before he ever knows I'm along for the ride.

Then I heard him talking and crept closer to hear. He was saying, like, *God damned Willistons ought to be keeping pigs and cows, not human children! And, Oh, Mae! How you would have loved this beautiful spring morning in the mountains.* Stuff like that. Talking to himself. I almost laughed out loud and blew my cover.

But the second night, just after he stopped to catch some shut-eye, I had to pee so bad my back teeth was singing Anchors Away. This time, when I tried to sneak out, he heard me and put a flashlight on me.

Said he was gonna take me to the police, turn me in. I told him, no way! He did that, I'd holler rape and they'd believe me.

18

It's the law. That slowed him down. Said we'd talk it over tomorrow.

Found out a long time ago it's either or. If it's or, then I can yell rape and they got to listen cause it's the law. If it's either, then he owes me cause he done sinned with jailbait.

So the next day I just sat down next to the driver's seat and put on my shades and got set to travel like a tourist, you know. Like we're doing just what we're supposed to be doing, leaving the system behind, going to California.

He shook the sleepers out of his eyes, put his teeth back in his mouth, made a cup of coffee and revved up the engine, drove to a Dunkin' Donuts.

Sitting at this little table in the shop, he told me he had to turn me in. Said he had no choice, I had to grow up *safe*, not out on the road with a man old enough to be my grandfather.

I had to tell him again that if he took me in, I'd holler rape—and kidnap—and how's he gonna squirm out of that.

Looked me over hard through his bifocals awhile, then says, Well, suppose you make it to California. You'll still wind up in a group home or juvenile detention or, if you're lucky, foster care. You know that, don't you?

No such thing, I said, let's hit the road. Later for what to do in California. When we gonna get there?

Not for days, he says.

He's a softy, ain't gonna turn me in. And I ain't gonna turn *him* in, long as he don't drive to no police station or social services office. I'm out of the system now and I'm gonna stay out.

A few miles on, I ask what he plans to do, now that he lost his job and his wife's gone. Said he didn't know but he didn't have enough money to support himself, so he couldn't support the two of us, if that's what I had in mind.

I said, Hey, don't worry about it, Dick, I can take care of us both.

He laughed and said I was an impossible *child* and didn't know what I was talking about.

Hell, it's him don't know what I'm talking about. I'm young but I got street smarts.

One time I run, back when I was eleven years old, this dude picked me up, took me home to his trailer, told me, Girl, you got the most magnificent ass, the cutest ass, the most glorious ass in ten counties. No, a hundred counties!

That dude laid me out on his bed and rained down dollar bills all over me. Tens, twenties. Sprinkled all over and around me. More money than my Mom ever made in a year waitressing. That's when I knowed I don't need no more group homes or foster parents. I can make it on my own. I was so busy scooping up all them dollars, I couldn't care less where he stuck his wiener. Came to over five hundred dollars I found out the next day. I was rich!

I'd have stayed with that dude forever except, the next day, he went weird. Woke up looking at me like he was gonna kill me! Like he thought he didn't get his money's worth. Maybe his downers were kicking in over his coke, or maybe he felt guilty. I don't know. But I got myself out of there *fast*. Had no place to go but back to Grandmother's Home, back into the system.

But for a couple of months, I was Queen Tittycaca. Forget Miss America, as Hurt and Enema kept harassing me, I was like a secret fountain of money. Everybody in West Wing ate, drank and partied on my money. On the sly, which made it all the more fun.

In Grandmother's Home when we give the staff a bad time, they say, Please help me understand... this or that. The staff's way of telling kids they is full of shit. Well, I had a mind to say that to Dick now. Please help me understand why we shouldn't be going to California where we can start a new life, me and you. You lost your wife, quit your job, so why don't we help each other? Something wrong with that?

Herb Williston, the senior staff—he was always telling me one thing, doing another. Says he don't like my vagina, don't want to put his penis in my vagina, don't like me wearing tight jeans and featuring my ass, don't like nothing about me and my ass and my vagina, and yet he'd force me to give him head, after lights out, in the dark. A couple of times when Herb was talking that harassing trash at me, I seen Dick's face, like it pained him to hear it.

If *I'd* made faces like that, Herb Williston would have jumped me and put me in the legal restraint hold and squeezed me half way to Hell.

Me and Dick, we'll be okay, once he knows he can't turn me back into the system without I holler rape and get him in trouble with the law.

3

I awoke with the thought, when in doubt, procrastinate. Impossible situations often have a way of resolving themselves.

I really couldn't blame Jane for running away. Soon after taking the job at Grandmother's Home, I realized it made big bucks *holding* kids. There was no real effort made to help them. Supposedly, we staff were using a method called Positive Peer Culture to *treat* them, but that was hogwash. In reality, what we were doing was holding them for the money involved. It was a profit-making prison for children I was duty-bound to return her to.

On the other hand, Jane showed a self-destructive streak foreshadowing a life of prostitution, addiction, prison. Many an afternoon, after the kids had come home from school, Mae and I had dutifully conducted group sessions designed to help them avoid that kind of fate—only to have Jane Doyle make a mockery of it.

Jane's best friend, a black girl named Yoni—she was also twelve going on forty, but could pass for eighteen or older—would ponder long and hard over her problems and how to deal with them. But Jane persisted in telling the group she had no problems, everything was fine, and then she'd deliver another of her triple X-rated tales, with the rest of the group hanging on her mix of autobiography and fantasy, demonstrating she had more problems than anyone else, plus the imagination of a pint-sized Marquis de Sade. Her tales were more compelling to her peers than Arnold Schwartzneger movies.

The Willistons and Murphys, being "good Christians," had squelched those stories, but Mae and I let Jane talk them out, which had the effect of letting her lie her way into a corner, giving the group opportunity to separate the biography from fantasy by badgering the truth out of her... or at least a new version the other kids could accept.

Her biggest problem was that sexual manipulations of all kinds had become her main means of coping. Hardly a week went by that a teacher or school principal didn't call the cottage with news that Jane Doyle had misbehaved, again, and this time they wanted no more of her. The socio-babble for this was "sexual acting out," and covered a multitude of "sins," from de-pants-ing a rival in a ball game to reaching around from behind a male teacher to brazenly fondle his private parts.

We had other inmates at Grandmother's Home who were liable to do worse. What made Jane such a fearful case was her seductive powers. She looks like a dark-haired Shirley Temple and fully appreciates how serious she has to be taken when she cries rape. She can manipulate the law better than many lawyers.

But no one at Grandmother's Home knew, for certain, which accusations were true—that was the problem. A close reading of her Department of Human Services records revealed merely a medley of accusations and counter accusations. Never mind, the law took hers seriously, and holding her made a profit for Grandmother's Home, a money mill masquerading as a charitable institution. Don't get me wrong: I'm keenly aware that social services are needed for the growing number of discarded kids in our society, it's just that I hate it when profits are made from the misfortune of others, especially helpless children.

About six months ago, Mae and I had done what in the jargon of Grandmother's Home is called "family work," by paying a visit to Jane's biological father. We were unable to call him because he had no phone, so we'd asked Jane's social worker, Maude Jennings, to alert Sam Doyle of our impending visit.

We found him in a small Appalachian crossroads, Elk City, near the border of North Carolina and Tennessee, in a rundown trailer littered with dirty dishes, strewn-about clothing, newspapers, empty whiskey bottles and such. Apparently Maude hadn't been able to convey our message, for Sam had no idea who we were, and was in the process of drinking his brunch while reading his Bible. He wore a baggy pair of blue jeans that hadn't been washed in a long time, and a t-shirt in worse condition.

Sam wanted us to know what a diligent parent he had been. "I done everything I could to make Jane behave. I slapped her mouth when she took the Lord's name in vain. I beat her with my belt for other stuff, and if that didn't work, I beat her with the very same buggy whip my daddy used on me and his daddy before him used on him. I even brung it from Viet Nam to have her kneel in a box of raw rice with her hands and feet in the air. Sir, there just ain't no way to make that born-bad girl behave."

About fifteen minutes into our visit, I asked him pointblank if he had raped Jane, and he said, "No, sir, never. She says I did, but it ain't so."

Mae, always more diplomatic than me, said, "Did you ever play around with her... you know?"

"She used to crawl in bed with me during the night, especially when it was storming out—this was after my wife left."

"But you were arrested for rape and incest," I pressed him, holding Jane's DHS records in my lap. "What the record doesn't show, though, is whether or not you were convicted."

Sam was sitting at his small formica kitchen table, his chair tilted back, one hand resting on his Bible and the other holding a glass of whiskey. Mae and I had declined his invitation to drink with him and were on his broken down couch, squirming to avoid the snapped springs.

"Sir," he said with the authoritative rumble of a self-righteous preacher, "I found Christ! Now I'm proud to say I'm Assistant Preacher at the House of Prayer to Our Savior—right yonder where you make the turn into Elk City."

In other words—or so I thought at the time—his religious conversion had saved him from prison.

After we left Sam that day, Mae and I drove to the hamlet's police station and asked the young lady we found alone there if she could enlighten us as to the outcome of those charges against Sam Doyle.

"Oh, that must be Jane Doyle you-all's talking about, huh. Yeah, well, see, Jane's a *problem.* Everybody here abouts knows she lies like a *rug.* Nobody takes what she says *serious.* You her new foster parents?"

The glint in her eye as she asked that question led me to believe she was sure we were in for hellish times, trying to deal with Jane Doyle.

That was so. Wild enough were her tales of whips, rape, madness and revenge. She also had a light side. She entertained the group one afternoon while playing baseball by wielding the bat like a giant dildo as she stepped up to the plate. The Willistons maintained she'd be putting on sex shows in a couple of years, doing her acts for money and drugs, on her way to an early death. That was her fate and we could only delay it, not stop it.

Roger Murphy, who I replaced, was of a like mind: "Most of these little girls'll end up drug addicts and hookers. Our job is to keep 'em alive in the meantime."

And the boys? He thought he knew their destinies too. "They'll turn up drug addicts and pimps or thieves," he proclaimed, "like most of their kind."

Jane, as we continued along the interstate, had been grooming herself. Her hands had been busy brushing and combing her luxuriant curly hair, of a dark chestnut so deep and pure it seemed unreal. She used Mae's mirror on the back of the sun visor to apply a light blue eye shadow and an orangish-red lipstick.

Indeed, Jane's hair and eyes and lips were, in a sense, her tools, the items she used to manipulate the sexual desires of those she targeted. Even the other kids in West Wing used to make fun of her by imitating the way she tossed her head to bounce and twirl her hair, the way she projected that startlingly violet-blue-eyed come-hither look, the way she licked and pursed her lips while listening to, say, a male visitor to West Wing. I recall one staid young gentleman from the Baptist Church who almost did not get out of her allure uncriminalized.

Now she sat quietly gazing out at the road through sunglasses with flowery frames. I recognized those glasses—they belonged to Yoni. Had she stolen them or been given them? I asked her.

"She *give* 'em to me," said Jane, sounding as cool and natural as you please, a good indication she was lying.

How could I—so recently widowed, in my sixties, wondering what I was going to do with the rest of my life—handle such a child as this? I had no choice but to hand her over to whatever authorities I could find, as soon as possible—without allowing her to criminalize me.

4

Past Houston, Dick pulls off the interstate into this truck stop, the Iron Skillet. I was hoping there'd be some kids my age inside so I could make new friends, but there were no kids. They're all in school except you, Dick told me.

Going in, some people stared at us. Probably wondered why I wasn't in school, or what a kid my age was doing with such an old fart as Dick. I turned and stuck out my tongue at one old biddy for staring. I said, What you staring at? Her eyes got big and round and she turned away, like she couldn't stand the smell.

When I caught up to Dick, he asks me why I was lagging behind. I said it was cause I have to go to the rest room. He said for me to go and hurry back. See, he thinks I'm gonna pick up some trucker and run. But hell, I'm already on a run. He got nothing to worry about.

When I come back I could see that Dick was bothered, cause he wrinkled his forehead and chewed his teeth while we sat in a booth and looked at menus. Then he mumbled something about this being the biggest mistake he'd ever made in his whole life. I thought he meant coming in here where people was staring, and I said, Don't let them bother you, Dick. They can't hurt us.

And he said, I'm not talking about them. I'm talking about you! Look, I really have to take you in and have you sent back to Grandmother's Home.

Bullshit! No way! Hey, I'm miles away from there and I mean to put more miles away together as we go.

And he says, Jane, you always came back after you ran away. What's different this time?

For just a second, I thought of telling him I was running not just to get out of the system, but so's old Hurt Williston can't sell my ass to the Chinaman. But then, how could Dick believe this, even though it's true? So all I says is, This time I'm with you and we're going to California and we're about to eat, right? Why should I go back?

He gives this nasty laugh and snorts awhile, then he says, This is trouble.

How come?

They'll pick you up in California and ship you back to North Carolina. Why not go back now?

Won't get me identified in California.

Oh yes they will.

If you don't want me I'll find some man who does. He'll take care of me and I'll take care of him.

Yeah, says Dick, like that guy you found last winter when you ran. A drug addict with the clap and head lice.

So? I healed, didn't I? Anyhow, that guy wasn't an addict, he only did drugs now and then. Trouble with him was, he didn't have no job. I'd still be with him if he did. I'd be out of the system and living free.

We ordered sandwiches and didn't talk no more till we finished eating. Then Dick heaves this big sigh and says, Jane. He hems and haws a time, and says, I just can't in good conscience bring you with me. Got to take you to the nearest police station and let them handle it.

Thought we got that settled last night.

No, he says, it's not right, I'm not your legal guardian. Come on, he says, let's go. And he stands up.

You ain't gonna turn me in, Dick. Know why? Two reasons. First, I ain't walking in no police station. And second, if you drag me in, I'll scream that you kidnapped and been raping and abusing me.

They won't believe you, he says.

We'll see who they believe. I know cops. They'll believe the worst. It's the law. And you know from what I told in group that I can come up with more worst than anybody else.

In those groups, he says, nobody believed you, Jane. You used to give purple descriptions of being tied up and beaten with a belt, then repeatedly raped by a dozen grown men, and left to die. But after you told stories like that too many times, nobody believed it any more because you kept changing it. First it was your own daddy who did this, then it was this foster parent or that. Why do you lie so, Jane?

You're making me mad, Dick. I lied and I didn't lie. How can I tell you? The Willistons were calling me Princess and Miss America, and making fun of how I did my hair and took good care of my clothes and was always neat and upbeat. That's why I told that story—part of it I made up but part of it was true.

That made him look sad and regretful. And after that, he shut up. We ordered and ate and left the restaurant and hit the road again.

It was hot and sunny, big clouds in the sky up ahead. I sat with a map of the United States on my lap, and helped Dick keep track of where we was and what was up ahead along this interstate, and if we should cut over to another interstate, stuff like that.

Then I remembered this auntie I got.

5

Somewhere past Houston, she asked me about what it was like when I grew up. Knowing Jane, I should have kept my mouth shut or changed the subject, but I bit. I told her I was raised during the nineteen thirties and forties in a place called an orphanage, which in today's world would be called a group home, a place like Grandmother's Home, a campus of group homes.

"Was there abuse?" she asked.

"Those were different times," I said. "Nobody called it abuse back then. It was called punishment, and punishment was supposed to be good. 'Spare the rod and spoil the child,' they used to say."

"What kind of rod did they use?"

"They used belts, mostly. One housemaster used to line us boys up against our washbasins nude and smack all our asses, one at a time, with his belt. That's if someone talked when he'd ordered silence and nobody would own up to who it was. In fact, sometimes he just imagined someone talked—so he could strip us down and smack all our bare asses. That was abusive. He was a ghoul."

"Yeah!" she said, glowing with a nasty glee. "Hey, Dick, maybe we should go back to Grandmother's Home and do a video of that one—we could make a million dollars, split fifty-fifty."

I gave her a sour look.

"Sure! You beat all our bare asses, I sue Grandmother's Home, and we split fifty-fifty."

"I'd wind up in prison," I said.

"Yeah but you'd get out soon. Good behavior. The jails are overcrowded, they'd have to let a nice old guy like you out real quick. You know, to make room for the dopers and thieves. They always let out the rapists and killers and old men like you."

I was missing Mae. And adult conversation. The thought of spending hours on the road with this child and her inane banter and mad conspiracies depressed me. In her DHS report, her first social worker had written that Jane had stated that her mother had abandoned her along a roadside when she tried to run off with her mother and her mother's new boyfriend. The social worker had noted that there was no verification of this, and that she was deemed abandoned because her father could not support her and had committed incest, and her mother could not be located; she had no other known living relatives and had become a behavior problem at school. Somewhere, somehow, I had to find a way to get her sent back to Grandmother's Home. Things were far from ideal there—I could sympathize with her woes about being "in the system"— yet what else could I do?

I was pondering this problem when she blurted out, "What does I. C. U. P. spell?"

"Eye cup," I said, distracted by my own grieving.

Jane burst into laughter. "I see you pee!" She'd had me. A twelve-year-old's notion of a dirty joke.

"Now you tell me one," she said, jumping out of the shotgun seat and, with one hand on the back of my "captain's" chair, dancing in the crowded van's limited aisle to my music tape.

"I can't think of any. Besides, you're still a child."

"Yeah? How come the staff says I'm twelve going on forty?"

"Actually," I said, "you're really a good kid, just a little—"

"No I'm not. I read my report. I sexualize everything! I'm nasty nasty nasty!"

Dylan's "Mr. Tambourine Man" began on my homemade tape. "You think sex is nasty?"

"My daddy told me long ago, back when I was only eight years old that sex is *ungoldly*. Sure sex is nasty. Ain't it?"

I huffed with frustration and kept my mouth shut. She danced around, holding onto the back of my chair to stay on her feet in the moving van. It was nerve-wracking, her being out of her seat belt, but I was in no mood to do battle over this as I drove.

I thought of a possible solution. I got out a tape of The Doors and shoved it into the tape player. Jim Morison's voice conjuring spirits as he sang "When You're Strange" put Jane into a different mood. It was wonderful to behold. We shared music from the sixties, that crack in the marketing culture when some meaningful new art had slipped past corporate control.

After awhile she tired of that and sat down again, and said, "I have an auntie in California, you know."

"Oh? Whereabouts in California?" This was bound to be another of her famous whoppers, I thought, but I played along.

"Southern California."

"What's your auntie's name?"

"Something like... Fills or Fillus, I think."

"Is that her last name?"

"No, that's her first name, only that ain't quite her name neither. I forget. She's my mother's sister but she married a few times, and I don't know what her last name is now."

I glanced at her with a look that said I did not believe this story, and she quickly replied, "But I can find out."

"How?"

"Call my Daddy."

"He didn't have a phone, last I knew."

"I call the liquor store down the street and when he walks in, they tell him and he calls me back."

Maybe she wasn't lying. This got me thinking. My original plan had been to overnight mostly in the van, and take motel rooms every other night or so, to shower and shave and get a good night's sleep. If we stopped at a motel, we could call her father's liquor store and have a number for him to call back. "We have to be near a phone to get his call."

"What's the number of the liquor store?" I asked.

"Hell, I don't know. Wrote it down on a scrap of paper but I didn't bring that scrap."

"What's the name of this liquor store?"

"Discount Liquors," she said matter-of-factly.

"What's the name of the street this discount liquor store is on?"

"Right down the road from where my Daddy lives. You know it, you been there. The road through Elk City."

"Okay," I said, "tonight we'll stop at a motel and we'll put through a call to that liquor store and give them the number where we are, so your daddy can return the call."

After a sizable silence, she said, "I don't think he can do that. They won't let him make no long distance calls from there."

I went the whole nine yards. "We'll leave a message that he can return the call collect. How's that?"

"Great! Then I'll find out who this auntie is and where she lives now."

"So when we get to California, you'll have a relative to be with."

"Yeah," she replied, her ballooning enthusiasm suddenly punctured.

6

D on't know what made me think of this auntie. Ain't seen her for years and years, not since I was six. But I can still remember my daddy saying, Jane, this here's your auntie, your mama's youngest sister, and now she lives in California.

She was rich, too. Drove a big old Lincoln, wore brand-spanking new store-bought clothes. That made my Daddy a little crazier than usual.

See, Daddy loves two things: his Bible and his bourbon. Hates black people, fast women and rich people—not necessarily in that order. But this auntie—I wish I could remember her name—brought out another kind of craziness in Daddy. He couldn't decide which he wanted to do most: whop her ass or drive her car and spend her money.

This auntie had a man with her when she come visiting, but he drove off somewhere for a couple of days—went to Florida, I think they said. And this auntie and my Dad and Mom sat up late one night drinking and talking, and she told them they ought to up and move to California.

Remember laying awake on my bed listening to them talk about this. Moving to California. Daddy didn't like the idea half as much as Mom. She was ready to take off in a New York second.

But then, Mom was like that, ready to go anywhere, anytime. Anywhere but work, Daddy used to say.

Next day I asked my auntie what was California like and she said it was warm and dry most of the time, and there was tons of money out there. Then my Mom fussed at me and told me to shut up and get out, and my Daddy fussed at her, and pretty soon they was drinking again, and then I heard my Mom crying and my auntie moaning and my Daddy huffing and puffing. I guess he fucked her.

After my auntie left with her man in their big old Lincoln, Daddy put another whooping on Mom and read from his Bible, then Mom tried to take my head off with a broom handle and I grabbed the cat by the tail and sailed him over the balcony onto the street. We had days like that where Daddy's bashing and Bible thumping rippled down to the cat, Chester, who usually got the worst of it all.

Anyhow, leaving the truck stop, I told Dick I had this auntie in California. Over breakfast he'd been talking about turning me in again. This auntie give him another way to think. Maybe he can dump me off on her, he thinks—I can read him like a book.

So along about sundown we pulls into this motel somewhere around El Paso. Flopped down on one of the king sized beds and said he was worn out cause Texas was such a big state to drive across.

I went into the bathroom, took a shower and changed to some fancier clothes. Well, fancier than blue jeans and sweatshirt. Then I took a walk around the motel, saw the swimming pool and where you buy the junk food and soft drinks. It had a restaurant and bar, too. I wanted to go in there and hang out, but they chased me away for being too young.

Back in the room, Dick was awake and watching the news on TV, laying back on his pillow with his hands behind his head. Says, Okay, now, let's track down that liquor store and put through a call, leave a message for your dad.

Elk City is such a little place—couple of gas stations, couple of grocery stores—it wasn't hard to find the only liquor store in town. Discount Liquor, it's called.

Dick dials the number and hands the phone to me, and pretty soon some man comes on and I say, I'm Jane Doyle, Sam Doyle's daughter.

And this man says, Oh yeah, I remember you. How you doing, Jane?

I'm doing real good, sir. Real good. On my way to California.

And he says, Does Grandmother's Home know about this?

No, and for God's sake, don't you tell 'em, I says. See, I'm gonna visit this auntie I got out there in California, and if my social worker knew that, she'd slam my ass back into the system. So don't you tell nobody, for God's sake.

Okay, Jane. You want for your daddy to call?

Yeah, that's why I'm calling now. I want him to call me here, right here, soon as he can. Collect.

Well, where you at, Jane?

Where we at, Dick?

He puts a hush-hush finger on his lips and with the other hand points to the number and whispers it in my ear as I count it out, room number included. Old guy on the other end says he'll have my daddy to call soon as he comes by. Collect, call collect. And Dick whispers, Call *this room collect,* and I repeat that, and hang up.

After that, Dick looks a little happier. He grins and stretches and says, What would you like for dinner?

I want to go out to that restaurant and bar, but he says no, we have to stay in the room, wait for my daddy to call.

So we order from a menu and wait and wait and wait till I'm ready to eat my fingernails down to the elbows before some cute dude come by with a tray and lots of food. I swear, I ate so much that night, I liked to burst. Ate this humongous hamburger with French fries, tomato salad. This thing was so big and thick and round, it made three or four McDonalds.

Next thing I knew, it was morning and Dick was shaking me awake, saying come on, we have to get back on the road. I ask did my daddy call and he says, No, not at all. You think he's ever going to call?

Dick was back in his thundercloud mood, makes his silver hair turn gray. Tossing our overnight stuff back in the van, he says, That's it, kid. I'm not going to believe any more of your lies. Who'd you really talk to last night on the phone?

I talked to the guy in the liquor store.

Well, he says, I'm starting to think you don't have any auntie in California, and maybe your daddy left town too.

Hell, Dick, maybe my daddy did leave town last night. So what? Don't worry, he'll call when he gets back. Sometimes he just gotta go out alley-cattin'.

And Dick turns and gives me this real dirty look and says, Don't you understand? We're leaving this motel. We're not going to be here if he calls.

Well, that's okay. Next time we stop, we'll call again.

That didn't make Dick feel better. I was starting to worry. If I don't get my daddy to call soon, maybe Dick really will turn me in and I'll have to holler rape and start all over with a new social worker.

At Grandmother's Home, old Herb Williston used to say, Jane, don't you want to be normal? Get adopted by nice people, have a nice home, go to a nice school, grow up nice and marry a nice man?

Sarcastic son of a bitch. I knew he was just taunting me so I used to say, Herb, I don't wanna be normal. My Daddy's the craziest dude you ever hope to see, and my Mom's worse. Why should I wanna grow up to be normal? That wouldn't be natural, now, would it?

Old Herb, he'd pretend to be pissed off at that, but shit, everybody knows he got a bigger lying problem than any kid there. If the law knew half of him, they'd roast his balls. But he gets away with it cause he works through the Chinaman. I got two girlfriends in Bangkok, sold to there by Herb. It don't sound like a bad deal, really, the way they tell it, but I ain't gonna give old Hurt the satisfaction of making money on my buns. I'd rather die than do that.

Which reminds me: I want to call my social worker, when I get the chance. Wanna ask her if she knows the name of this auntie of mine in California. She likes to think she knows every-thing about me—every time I ever had sex, every time I run away, every Bible passage my Daddy said he taught me. She ought to know where my auntie is and what's her name now.

A couple of weeks ago, while I was doing a plan of care review with my social worker, I was doodling on this sketch pad while she was asking questions, see. I was doodling her getting her ass banged by my Daddy's big old dick.

So after she was done with them silly questions, she says, Jane, what you drawing? And I shows her. I got *Maude* wrote below the buns bent over a table, and *Daddy* under the big-footed dude who's shoving it to her. She freaked so bad! Broke down and cried and fussed at me and carried on.

I was supposed to feel real bad about it, but I really didn't. That's what come to mind while she was throwing them questions at me. And my psychologist *wants* me to doodle what comes to mind while we're talking. So I did. Big deal!

Still, I like Maude. She's the best social worker I ever had. Most of 'em, they ain't got time to give a damn. Maude, she took time out to care about me. I really didn't mean to hurt her feelings, and I want to tell her that. I was only having fun.

7

I thought it was worth a shot, this auntie in California she was talking about, so outside of El Paso I pulled into a motel that advertised rooms for $19.95 a night. Of course they never have that one available; we managed to over-night for a few cents under $40.

I helped Jane put through a call to the liquor store in Elk City and heard her end of the conversation. She left our number for her dad to call, then we ordered and ate. I lay awake waiting for the call, watching the prime time sitcoms.

The next morning, the auntie in California had evaporated like an apparition, for her daddy in Elk City had not called. I was showered by 5 A.M., had us checked out by 5:15 and was shaking her awake by 5:30, ready to roll. I was irked with myself, thinking of all the times I fell for her lies back at West Cottage and now out here on the road.

An hour or so down the road, as I was thinking of stopping for breakfast, she came up with another idea: "How about if I call my social worker and ask her to track down my daddy and give me the name of my auntie."

If I let her make this call, I reasoned, her social worker, Maude Jennings, would trace the call, alert the nearest lawmen to capture Jane, and return her to North Carolina, ending my dilemma. I knew, too, that Maude would never buy the idea that I had kidnapped Jane.

So I said, "Sure, Jane. I wonder how much change it will take to make that call from here?" We had just crossed into New Mexico.

"Oh, I call her collect. She says always call collect."

I turned off the interstate at the first sign of civilization and put a quarter in her hand. We walked into a restaurant with a Wild West theme, a tourist trap half developed but already attracting enough customers to look promising. She headed for a bank of pay phones, I went to the men's room.

A few minutes later, sitting across from each other at an imitation Wild West table, her eyes sparkled brightly and she peered up at me coyly. "Everything's taken care of," she said. "Maude says she has this auntie's name and address somewhere in her records. She's going to find it and give it up next time I call, and she's gonna call my auntie and tell her I'm coming."

This was startling news. "Doesn't Maude want you to come back?"

"Told her I wasn't coming back."

"Oh. Where did you tell her you are?" I asked, tensing up.

"Just crossed into New Mexico from Texas, right? Ain't that what you said?"

"Did you tell her what interstate we're on?"

"Yeah! I had to ask some lady. She said, I-10. Is that right, Dick?"

"That's right." So Maude the social worker now knew that Jane Doyle was on I-10 just into New Mexico. What else did she know? I said, "And did you tell her who you were with?"

"Yeah, but don't worry, she likes you. She said so. She said I was in good hands with you."

"Good hands, huh. Aren't you afraid she'll alert the police to pick you up?"

"She'll try. But we'll be long down the road before them cops get around to looking for another runaway." She flashed me a wry-cynical smile.

"What's her number? I'd like to talk to her about this."

"I don't *want* you talking to Maude. I'm afraid *you'll* try to send me back."

She was right about that, but not till I found out what Maude had in mind—surely not dispatching Jane to her auntie in California. But then, with social workers, you never know. They work with such a thick batch of regulations it becomes like a kaleidoscope. They can turn the regulations to whatever rationale suits them at the moment and "go by the book," confident that they've done the right thing, as in the old bureaucracy game of "cover your ass." Well, if Jane didn't want to tell me Maude's number, I'd have to hunt through my things for my own address book. I decided to have breakfast first.

Our breakfast was served by a slender young woman who looked like she'd been molested as a child. I'd developed an eye for the symptoms: self-loathing coupled with hyperactivity that is self-defeating. The young woman was obviously new on the job; she almost spilled the tray and then, once she got it settled, did drop the little pot of coffee. Had to go back to the kitchen for another.

Finally we ate. Ham and eggs with coffee for me, Danish pastry with a milkshake for Jane. I was focused on feeding my face when she said, "Be right back, Dick." And was suddenly gone like quicksilver through the fingers.

I thought little of this sudden departure at the moment. Jane, since I'd known her, had always been given to fits and starts as various moods moved her. I finished my ham and eggs, left the fried potatoes, took one last sip of coffee, and got up to pay the bill, locate Jane, collect a doggie bag and go on.

That's when I saw two hulking guys in uniforms and dark glasses. They cruised up and stationed themselves on either side of me at the cash register, and after I'd paid the bill, the taller one said, "Sir, would you mind stepping outside with us? We'd like a word with you."

And as we moved toward the door, the other said, "Where's your traveling companion, the girl?"

"I'm not sure where she went," I said, looking around the large dining room. "Try the ladies room."

"She went into the ladies room," said the beefy one as he opened the screen door for us, "but she's not there now. We had someone check on that."

"Yeah," said the other, "she must have gone out the ladies room window. That's the only explanation."

"Anyhow, we just want to have a look inside your vehicle, if that's all right with you, sir."

"What choice do I have?"

"Well, you could force us to get a search warrant."

"I won't do that. Have your look." It did not take a clairvoyant to surmise that these two had been dispatched by a call from Jane's social worker, and it was Jane they were after.

It quickly became apparent that there was nothing inside the van suggesting the presence of a girl. All of Jane's things had vanished. How did she know these lawmen were coming for her?

"Well," drawled the taller one, "we're going to ask you to come down to headquarters for questioning. I'm pretty sure we aren't going to hold you. It's that young girl you're with we want."

"I realize that, sir. And her things were right back there in my van, last I knew."

"Want to lock up your van in the meantime?"

8

I never should of called that damned social worker. Maude. What a dumb mistake that was! How could I a-been so stupid? I thought I could get her to give me my auntie's name and address in California, and she said she'd look it up and all, and she asked me where I was, and I told her I-10.

Now here come these two highway patrolmen, walk into this restaurant while we was having breakfast, take off their dark glasses and look all around, hunting for somebody. Damn that Maude Jennings! But I didn't come this far to get hijacked by no fucking lawmen and shipped back like store merchandise. Not now, no way! Damn! How could I a-been so god damn dumb?! Before them cops eyeball me, I drop my fork and take off.

From inside the ladies room, I open the door a crack and peek out, and them two cops is staring right at me. I looked around inside and saw this open window half way up to the ceiling, and went for it. Climbed up a crapper partition and went through that window head first, caught the window frame so I could get my feet under me and landed running.

Went to the van, grabbed my suitcase and duffel, stuffed everything of mine back in 'em real quick, and pretty soon they was coming out the front door, Dick between them. I was behind the tires of an eighteen-wheeler when they got to the van.

Searched the van. Took Dick away but left his van, so I climbed up into the overnight bunk of this eighteen-wheeler and lay there, waiting. This was still morning, maybe half way to noon. I hid out there in that sleeper till a driver come out and got behind the wheel, fired up the engine and was shifting into low when I hollered, "Hey, you ain't Johnny!"

The old guy looks back up at me like he's seeing a ghost.

I fling my legs over the edge, plop down on the seat and bounce out the passenger door, hauling my luggage with me. Then I scoot across the parking lot—and it's a big one, a truck stop—and around the side of the restaurant, then under it. There's this opening under the building, which I duck into.

It's a pretty cool place, once my eyes get used to it. Wires and pipes all over. This is where they go to fix stuff, I guess. And I can see Dick's van from here real clear cause it's parked on the near end of a line.

They got to bring Dick back to his van, don't they? I mean, they can't just keep him wherever they took him to, not forever! He ain't done nothing wrong. It's me they're after, so they can send me back to my social worker and Hurt Williston's stinking wiener. Ain't going. Kill myself first.

Cars and trucks and campers and such come and go all day long, parking and leaving, people getting out and getting back in, and still no Dick. Oh Lord, please help Dick get out of this, I pray. So we can go to California and stop being hassled.

I was so nervous I ate my trail mix and drank half a jug of Koolaid. The sun got low and the shadows of the eighteen-wheelers looked like dinosaurs. I started to cry. I felt Dick was gone forever. Why they keeping him?—I mean, what good could he do those thug cops? I'm the one they looking for.

Then I thought, maybe they're gonna try to pin an abuse rap on him to hold him. Could they do that? But I remembered what my social worker told me, they can't do that unless they have evidence, and your word is the evidence they need.

Well, neither of us sinned. Yet.

Near dark, I come out from under the restaurant and go to the van. I seen Dick locking doors before they drove him away in the patrol car, but knowing Dick, he maybe missed one door.

In West Wing, he always seemed to miss locking at least one door, every night. It was a joke among us kids. If Dick and Mae was on, we knew he was gonna miss locking at least one door, and we'd take bets which one. Sometimes it was the walk-in cupboard where they kept the snacks, and we'd go raid the place along about midnight when the staff was all asleep.

Missed the back door this time. I tried both front doors and the side, all locked. My heart was down around my toes when I tried the back door, and wham! Open!

I crawled into the back of the van and scrunched down under his tent and camping stuff, blankets, what all. Smelled like wet ground, so I could daydream I was out camping.

It was starting to get real cold but I was fairly warm and okay down there, right where I'd started this trip. I fancied a campfire right outside my tent, and Dick here beside me, nice and warm.

I was asleep when I heard something—Dick just outside the van yelling, "Jane! Yoo Hoo, Jane, where are you?"

I lay like I was dead. He could have them cops standing by, waiting to see if I'd show.

Then, finally, he gives up calling for me, and unlocks the driver's door, climbs in and starts talking to himself some more. Says, Son of a bitch! What did I do to deserve this? Oh, Mae, I miss you—I may join you soon. He turns on the engine, but then he suddenly gets out of the van. I stick my head up and look out the back window. He's walking to the restaurant. Oh well, he'll come back. He's just looking for me. And I ain't gonna show till we're on the road again.

Finally he comes back and gets in, the engine varooms and pretty soon we're moving, bumping over this truck stop parking lot—got pot holes the size of baby elephants—and then onto the interstate, where the engine settles into this hum I like.

I go to climb out from under this stuff and say hello to Dick, but the steady hum of the engine lulls me back to sleep. I'll pop up on him tomorrow.

9

I decided, as I rode in the back of the highway patrol car, that I would have nothing more to say, unless they provided me with a lawyer. Although I wasn't guilty of abduction, I should have had her sent back to the agency as soon as I'd discovered she'd stowed away in my van. And there were certainly people back at that agency that would love to see me hang on a kidnapping charge. What I was guilty of was foolishly sympathizing with her. Because I'd have wanted to flee from Grandmother's Home too, if I'd been in her shoes.

The jail was a clean, well-lighted block of cells made of tile, and I was its only occupant this fine spring day. Twice they called me into an interrogation room, and twice I demanded the help of a lawyer before I would divulge any information.

Between interrogations, I lay flat on my back on tile flooring with my arms under my head, staring up at the beige ceiling and around at the beige tiled walls. It was a modern version of the old drunk tank, I guessed, for it contained no furniture or plumbing, only a drain in the exact center of its square floor. An enclosed space designed to be hosed down quickly and easily.

There is no place like jail for reevaluating one's life, taking stock of where you've been and charting a course into the future. But what had happened to me during the past six months or so left me feeling I had no further destinations or goals to reach in life. How long would Mae's absence feel like a huge hole in my existence? A lingering shadow limb, as when a person loses an arm or leg. Except I'd lost a whole body and mind, a living presence. I kept talking out loud to her in thought-less moments, imagining her responses.

But landing in jail seemed something like a punctuation in that discussion with her ghost. Her lingering presence seemed unable or unwilling to follow me here, and I was completely alone to face the huge debt her series of illnesses had left, and my loneliness as I endured the inevitable aging process. I wondered if I could endure this, or even if I should endure it.

In some remote part of my heart, I wished they would find me guilty of kidnapping or something and put me away, and then perhaps I could persuade a prison doctor to prescribe a bottle of sleeping pills strong enough to send me to the other side.

Yet when I thought of taking my own life, checking out of this realm of hell, I balked. There are the grandchildren to love and nurture, to teach and tease and thrill to the smiles of. There are my sons and their wives to enjoy, to encourage when things go wrong for them. And there are glorious sunsets and sunrises to ponder, realizing as I stare up at a starry night sky that I am composed of a universe of molecules and atoms too, and savoring the mystery of it all. If you could magnify the mole-cules composing a human, would it look like the night sky? Would it tell you anything about the mind and motives of the great creator of it all? How remote that Divine Intelligence seems from the prides and pains of we humans, and yet all the ancient religions speak of the creator god being involved in our personal lives, our limited dimension of the vast night sky reality. Is that master of the vast cosmos the master of our atoms and molecules too? Are our souls somehow comparable to those so-called black holes into which disappear the planets way out there? Is our sense of time and space a blindfold that will be removed when we depart this reality? One thing for sure: I don't think this human shitbag existence is all there is, all there ever will be. I can't help feeling we're part of something beyond our comprehension, and it, whatever it is, is very much part of us.

Shortly after four that afternoon, someone unlocked my cell door and asked if I would like to speak by telephone to Maude Jennings, Jane's social worker. I said yes. Here was my chance. I'd make arrangements with her to have Jane returned to North Carolina—if these lawmen could find her—and continue on my journey unmolested by the long arm of the North Carolina DHS. Or so I thought.

They led me to a wall phone. Maude said, "Dick! So sorry to hear about this. I know you're no threat to the child, and I've told those officers that. What we need to do is recover Jane. She shouldn't be out there on the highway, so far from *home*, you know."

"I agree," I said, "and will be more than happy to return her to you. *If* we can find her."

"Yes, that's the problem right now, isn't it. Apparently she's slipped away again."

I'd met Maude Jennings half a dozen times, yet still didn't have a clear image of her physical being in my mind. She impressed the senses—mine, anyway—by her *sound*. Her voice was her stamp of personality. How to describe it? It was the kind of voice that might advise a brain cancer patient to imbibe a wee pinch of bird shit in order to survive, recover, revert to age eighteen and live those most important years all over again. I often thought she'd missed her calling; she should have been selling her own herbal concoction back in the eighteen hundreds. In today's world there was nothing left for her talents but this: social work. Gathering up society's abandoned and attempting to reconstitute them into functioning human beings, of value to themselves and others. And the economic system. If you were to measure her success by those she'd sent off to function in the economic system, you'd come up with a

big question mark. No one kept track. But, if you were to measure her success by how many kids she had on her "case load,"
she was doing very well indeed. She had a huge caseload, and
worked with amazing energy on behalf of each kid. Still, I could
only wonder what became of those kids after they left her care.

She was waiting for my reply. "You know Jane. Maybe she's
hitched a ride with a trucker and is off for parts unknown.
What's your guess?"

"Sounds reasonable to me," said Maude's excited, trilling
voice. She was one of the best social workers we at Grandmother's Home dealt with, owing to her ability to bend the
regulations to permit a bit of common sense to shine through. I
urged myself to keep that in mind.

"Perhaps you could persuade these gentlemen that if I go
back to where they picked me up, that restaurant, Jane might
return, if she's still around there."

"I'll suggest that. And if you don't find her, they should let
you go on your way." Then she hesitated before adding, in a
surprisingly low, conspiratorial voice: "Be sure to call me again,
from the road, after you're released. There's something urgent I
need to talk to you about, but not now, not on this line. Let me
talk to that sergeant, or whoever."

I handed the receiver to the first hand that reached for it. The
shorter of my captors got on the line with Maude, and within
two minutes the deal was done.

After hanging up, the taller one looked me over with a critical
squint to his eyes, and said, "We're not sure who to believe.
But you don't have no little girl with you and the social worker
says you're okay, so you're free to go."

Waiting for the return of my personal items, I felt like one of
our kids waiting for the same kind of paper shuffling—often for
weeks, months, years. At one point I asked anyone who would
listen: "How am I supposed to get back to my van from here? I
don't know where I am."

"We'll drive you back," said an anonymous voice.

It was dark outside now. This entire, pointless detention had eaten the day. Driving back to the restaurant I could see the vast landscape of desert and mountains, with humanity's vehicles and headlights confined to the interstate as though to emphasize that we mortals are no more enduring on this landscape than fire flies on a summer lawn. Could Jane have fled to those mountains? Most unlikely.

We talked a little on the way. I told the two officers I'd been a childcare worker at the facility Jane had run from, and that I'd left after my wife's death. I told them I was bringing my wife's ashes to the Pacific Ocean so my two sons and their families could join me in laying Mae's spirit to rest. That seemed to move them toward a modicum of sympathy for me, now that they had Maude's word that I was not a known sex offender, smuggling his prey across the continent.

When we arrived in the parking lot, I explained that Jane would never show herself if they remained here. But I would turn her over to their care if she did show herself. They said their goodbyes with stiff cordiality, like they had accepted me as one of their paramilitary allies, then drove off.

I cupped my hands and yelled into the night, "Jane! Yoo hoo, Jane Doyle! It's okay now, Jane, you can come back. Nobody's going to hurt you."

Patrons of the restaurant, walking toward the front entrance, stopped to gape at me and wonder. Maybe they thought I was crazy, or that I'd just had a fight with a daughter. Their stares were the only response I got.

I unlocked the driver's door and got into the van. I turned on the parking lights in the hope that Jane, if she were hiding within sight of the van, would see this and come. Then I turned on the engine so the lights wouldn't drain the battery and dozed. If she were within sight of the van, surely she'd see the parking lights and come back. Wouldn't she?

Then I got out and went into the restaurant, looked all around there for her. I circled the outside of the building, stuck my nose into a trucker's laundromat, checked out a few hookers who were hanging about, asked if they'd seen a teenaged girl about five feet four inches tall, dark curly hair, pretty. None had.

Supposing she'd probably hitched a ride with a trucker, I gave up and drove west, determined to leave it all behind like a bad dream. I might have wound up behind bars for the rest of my life, especially if the highway patrol had contacted the Willistons instead of Maude. They would have enthusiastically suggested the worst.

I remembered with bitterness how the Willistons, and before them the Murphys, had smirked about the fate of these children: they were doomed to become whores, pimps, thieves, drug addicts, and either die young or spend the rest of their lives in prison. "Mae," I said aloud as I drove, "if you have any power from that other realm, please help Jane to safety."

What was so ironic, in retrospect, was how much I had liked the Willistons when we first met them. It was about a year ago, a bright May day in the North Carolina mountains, intoxicating aromas and all. Herb was wearing old army fatigues, Emma dressed more formally in standard department store blouse and slacks. I felt sorry for her; she obviously had a weight problem. About five feet tall, around two hundred or more pounds. Yet Herb had no problem showing adoration for her, which I found... well, nice. Comforting. A sign that the man was genuine.

Herb impressed me as an affable old soldier with not a mean bone in his body. Emma came off as dour but hard working and dedicated to the kids. They invited Mae and me into the West Wing kitchen for coffee and talk that first time we met. Mr. Sinclair, the administrative director, had sent us over to, as he put it, "see how the chemistry between you two couples is."

Over coffee, we talked about why we all found ourselves in this job. I said that Mae and I were caring people in need of a job—I didn't mention our need for medical insurance—and these kids were in need of caring people. Herb, who has the kind of jaw made famous during the 1930s by Italian dictator Mussolini and now sometimes called "lantern," said he and Emma didn't need the money but did need the job, some way to be of value in their golden years. Besides, he said, dealing with these problem children kept them alert and on their toes. I said that sounded like an extra perk to me.

I found no reason to doubt the Willistons were "independently wealthy," as Herb put it. He drove a large BMW sedan and told me at some length how he had to pay the IRS twenty thousand dollars a year. "From the business I sold but retain an interest in," he said.

Later, I told Sinclair the chemistry felt fine to me. Mae said nothing. I said I thought the Willistons were neat people. Willing to work hard at a thankless job—for the inner satisfactions it brought. Sinclair grinned broader than ever and said he was glad we got along with the Willistons, for other couples had found them "difficult" to work with. I said I didn't see any problems working with them.

Mae didn't agree. She didn't tell Sinclair that. She waited till we were alone later, after we'd been assigned to work with the Willistons. Then she said she found them devious and false, said they had something to hide and were working hard at hiding it, whatever it was. I asked what they could possibly have to hide. She didn't know. I asked why she hadn't said something before, instead of letting me get us lined up to work with them. She said she didn't know, that it was something intuitive she felt and how could she explain it to Sinclair? I hoped she was wrong, but feared she wasn't. Mae could read new people a lot better than I. And I had to keep relearning that the hard way.

Oh well, I thought, I've been sprung from jail. There's always something to be thankful for. Several hours down the road that night, arriving at another small crossroads town, I pulled off the interstate, parked in a shopping center's lot, shed my clothes and climbed, exhausted, into the upper bunk. Blessed sleep took me quickly.

Sometime between midnight and dawn, I awoke from a nightmare, and forgetting where I was, sat up in bed and banged my head on the van's roof. It was pitch dark. For about a minute, I was utterly disoriented. Gradually, I came to my senses and remembered where I was.

I also remembered that I had a habit of forgetting to lock the van's back door. I got down from the bunk, slipped on my jockey shorts and, rather than struggle through the piles of boxes and things inside the van, got out the driver's door and hustled through the chilly air around to the back. Sure enough, the back door was open. I locked it, got back in the van, locked the driver's door, checked the other two doors, then climbed back up into the bunk and slept.

But lightly, slipping in and out of dreams and half-dreams. I had to admit to myself now that I felt rotten about Jane's disappearance. What would happen to the child? Where did she go? I imagined her flagging down some trucker with the morals of a tomcat, the sort who eat their young. He kept a library of kiddie porn and snuff videos in his rig. He was a serial child killer whose lust for blood knew no limits. A whole scenario spun itself out in my mind: Jane forced at knife point to sexually service this slimy, ugly, fat slob, after which he slits her throat with his knife, leaves her lying in a corn field off a secondary highway, where her remains won't be found till harvest time. He walks back to his rig and pulls away from the scene. Next autumn, a farmer is horrified when his combine almost runs over her decomposing remains.

10

It got damn cold that night, so cold I decided to hatch a plan. Dick don't know I'm here, and I'm so damn cold my teeth are chatterin', and Dick just got arrested on my account. He's gonna try harder than ever to get rid of me now. Unless...

Cold as it is, I get up out of that pile of smelly old camping stuff and take off my jeans and sweater, put on my teddy pajamas, then climb up the ladder to Dick's bunk and slip in beside him. It's good and warm under the covers with him. He's sleepin' with no clothes on. Good.

Real careful, I slip down under the covers and real slow and gentle I get my hand on his cock, and it's about half up and semi hard. He's laying on his back so I gotta straddle his legs to get at it.

If I can get him to come before he knows what happened, he'll be talking to me different from here on out. But about the time I get his cockhead swelling up good, he pops awake, throws off the covers and says, Jane! What the hell? And what the hell do you think you're...

He grabs my head but I just keep workin', cause I know he's near the brink of can't-hold-back. I feel him shudder, then he lets go with a loud moan.

I look up and he's got his head back on his pillow, chin in the air, hands holding my head. I nail him! I say, Gotcha.

He twists onto his side and sort of throws me off. I can hear him moaning and groaning and cussing.

Jane, Jane, Jane, he says. What in the hell did you do that for?

So you'll quit trying to turn me in or get rid of me. Didn't I make you feel good? Come on, admit it.

That's not the point, he says, sounding like he's about to cry.

What is the point, Dick?

What you did was wrong, unnatural.

Oh bullshit! I just give you a blowjob, what the hell's wrong with that? What's unnatural about it? It felt good, didn't it? So what's your problem?

You're too young, I'm too old, it's not something I'd ever do with you—you're too young. That's why it's against the law.

Oh sure it's against the law, but what ain't?

It's just plain wrong and unnatural for a man of my age to have sex with a girl your age.

If it's unnatural, why do so many men your age do it with girls my age? You ain't talking to some twit never been around the corner, you know.

I'm laying beside him now and we got the covers over us. So what're you gonna do, Dick? Accuse me of old man molesting?

He puts a hand over his eyes and moans.

Don't worry, I ain't gonna report you. All I want is for you to know I gotcha. So you'll want to keep me around, stop trying to get rid of me.

Jane, I am in no position to become your legal guardian. I'm sixty-three and broke.

Don't worry about money, I can always go out and bring home money.

Please, stop that talk. You're not going to prostitute yourself. Come on, let's get up and make coffee and put the rubber to the road. And, he says, as he's climbing over me and going down the ladder, don't you ever, ever do that again! From now on, you stay in your own bed and—

Ain't got no bed, Dick.

Well, you stay out of mine. I'm not going to allow myself to be seduced into an affair with a twelve-year-old.

You just did! I nailed you! You can't undo what's done.

He hisses and mumbles as he pulls on his shorts and pants and a sweater. Then puts the key in the ignition and starts the engine. Good. Now we'll soon get some heat in here.

Don't worry, Dick. It's our secret.

You know very well it's not how to grow up as a normal girl.

I'm grown up the way I'm grown up. What's normal got to do with it?

He doesn't say nothing for a time, just gets out the coffee pot, puts coffee in it and water, and then puts it on the stove to heat. Sits down on a box and looks up at me. Says, You know that sexually acting out is what keeps getting you into trouble, don't you.

Hurt Williston done sexual acting out on me, and he never got in no trouble, and I sure didn't want him nowhere near me.

Dick looks away, like he don't know whether to believe me or not. I don't care what he wants to believe.

Sexual acting out, I say, only gets me in trouble when somebody in the system finds out about it. Don't make no never mind to any of them if I done it for money or enjoyed it or was forced, or even if I'm lying about it.

You're a child! Twelve years old! There's so much you don't know yet.

I know what I know. And I ain't no child! Look, I got tits! And my ass, tell me it ain't gonna draw eyes when I put on tight pants. Gonna draw more than eyes, and I damn well know it.

You are quite beautiful, he says, but you're not ready.

Ready as I'm ever gonna be, I says. Besides, this body is my money—our money. You take care of me and I'll take care of you. What's wrong with that?

Dick just shakes his head and mumbles some more. Then he lifts the coffee pot off the stove and pours himself a cup. Looks up at me and says, You want coffee?

Yeah.

Pours me a cup and hands it up. I sit with my legs dangling over the bunk, sipping. I'm not really wild about coffee but I want him to know I ain't a kid no more.

You don't understand the consequences, Jane. Sex is powerful. You've got to use it very carefully or you'll wind up suffering.

You think I don't know that?

He shakes his head and groans. Says, I'm gonna forget this ever happened. Let's drive on to California and see if we can get you placed with a relative.

Okay for driving on, but I like relations with you better than any other relative. Just keep that in mind, Dick.

He gets behind the wheel, shaking his head and mumbling, and pretty soon we're back on the interstate, leaving all this behind. I get up and put on my best slacks and sweater and my warmest boots, then sit in the shotgun seat.

So, he says, like he's talking to the empty road up ahead. It's just dawning. What I hear you saying, he says, is that you're trying to do anything you can to keep me from turning you back into the system.

That's right.

I didn't turn you back into the system when they arrested me in that restaurant, did I?

How could you? I hid out.

But this morning—I could drive you in the other direction and turn you over to those highway patrolmen, let them take it from there. But I didn't do that either, did I?

No. It was my social worker put them cops on us back there. The bitch, I ain't calling her no more.

It was Maude that alerted those patrolmen, true. But you've got to understand, she's just doing what she feels is best for you, Jane.

Well I'm doing what I knows is best for me, Dick. I'm partnering up with you.

Honey, I'm an old man. My wife just passed away and I'm lonely. But I can't take care of you indefinitely. I have no money, just big piles of medical bills. More than I can pay if I live to be a hundred, and I don't even have a job any more.

You got me!

So you think I should pimp a twelve-year-old girl for a living? What kind of person do you take me for?

You don't gotta pimp nobody, Dick. Just watch out for me so I don't get fucked up by no crazies. I'll do the rest. How many times I gotta tell you I got something men will pay good money for.

Why would you rather do that than go back into the system? What's so horrible about Grandmother's Home?

It's like living in a suburb of hell, that's what's wrong with it.

A suburb of hell, he repeats.

Yeah, with old Hurt Williston as the devil.

After that, he drives a long way without saying anything.

11

A s if I didn't have enough trouble.

Sometime before dawn, while I was in a deep sleep, I dreamed or half-remembered that Mae was in bed with me and felt comforted. Or maybe it was the missing limb sensation. Anyway, I was aware of someone in bed with me but I clung to sleep, lost between memory and dream.

Then, I gradually became aware that this someone was under the covers astride my legs manipulating my penis. This awareness sneaked up on me as if emerging out of a chaos of dreams, and it took a moment to realize that someone was having oral sex with my penis.

I whipped back the covers, unable at that moment to imagine who in the world it could be. When I realized it was Jane, I was relieved and, almost simultaneously, terrified. Her manipulations and the shock of my discovery combined to trigger an ejaculation. It was a sickening sensation for I instantly realized I had just joined the ranks of those I detest, even as I realized I'd been had by Jane. She'd just made me another victim of her famous sexual conquests.

Now she had me in her blackmail box. But that couldn't ease my conscience, for on some unconscious level I had allowed it to happen. Or been too far gone to stop it. I lay there thinking of what I should have done: pushed her away, rolled out of the bunk and dumped the both of us on the floor. I was full of self-loathing and fear. Now she could go the police if she wanted to, get her stomach pumped and put me in prison for the rest of my life. For a moment I felt loathing, disgust, repelled, nausea-ated. I hated her passionately.

Soon she was lying beside me as I stared up at the low-slung ceiling of the bunk, aghast at what had just happened, roiled with disgust. I glanced at her and she was grinning, giggling. "Got ya," she said. I forced myself to take three long, slow, deep breaths before I replied.

"That was a nasty, dishonest thing to do, Jane."

"Oh, bullshit," she said. "You can't tell me you didn't like it."

"You should not have done that."

"What's should got to do with it. You liked it. Don't say you didn't."

I knew, of course, that sexuality is her means of coping, or as she called it, her money. The word *should* was not in her vocabulary. Told what she should not do, Jane will do it.

"I want you to become my legal guardian," she said.

Her legal guardian and she would prostitute herself to support the two of us. If I were coming from a different back-ground, my moral reflexes wired differently, I might take her up on this proposition. As it was, I hated to just turn her back into the system. I'd hate even worse to lose her out on the road somewhere. But I could not live with myself if I gave into her manipulations. I reasoned that the best hope I had was to place her with her relative in California. With that in mind, I got behind the wheel and drove on.

"What's so wrong about us having sex?" she wanted to know as we got onto the interstate by the gray light of dawn.

The months of group sessions with the kids devoted to "working on problems"—Jane's sexual manipulations being her main problem—crowded my memory. Was she serious, or toying with me?

"Jane, you know how much trouble you've gotten into by being sex driven, don't you?"

"Yeah, but I don't know why, Dick. Why is it such a big deal to *enjoy* sex?"

She was suddenly serious but I was hard pressed to come up with a serious answer, at dawn out here on this vast expanse of landscape in New Mexico where our sudden assignation seemed so meaningless? At least to her.

"Well," I said as the van's heater began to ease my tension, "sex is what bonds a husband and wife."

"I know that," she said impatiently, "but what's the problem with doing it just for fun. Don't you like it?"

"The joy of sex is sacred because it's what makes babies. What perpetuates the human race. What keeps all species recreating themselves. On the other hand, yeah sex is fun, it's awesome, it's deadly dangerous and the most wonderful pleasure our creator gave us."

Where am I going with this, I asked myself. Well, the coffee hadn't kicked in yet. I sighed, wondered how I could change the subject. Sex is such a multifaceted subject, where does one begin? Especially when trying to discuss it with a girl on the brink of womanhood and most especially with a sexually damaged child. I was perplexed, confused, and kind of scared.

"Dick," she said, "come off the preaching and get real. I want to know what's the trouble with doing it for fun?"

"Careless sex can have some horrible consequences," I said. "AIDS, sexually transmitted diseases, slavery."

"Slavery?"

"Yes. You could be kidnapped and used by someone to make money on you as a sex object."

She gave me a coy smile. "You gonna kidnap me, Dick?"

"My point is," I said as sneeringly as I could at this moment, "you just can't go doing it to blackmail me or make a few bucks out on the streets without winding up in a house of horrors. But

61

I realize you're not yet aware of that. You don't yet know the downside of promiscuous sex."

"We just passed a sign," she said. "This way leads to Los Angeles. Stop trying to put me back in the system and I'll be good."

"You're going to have to obey me, or else."

"Or else what? My word against yours, you try to turn me in. Guess who the law gonna believe."

"You liked my wife, Mae, didn't you?"

"Sure. Everybody loved Mrs. Sweet."

"Well, her urn is in this van with us. Do you want to dishonor her memory?"

"What are you talking about? Would Mrs. Sweet want you to never have no more fun?"

"My wife would want me to enjoy myself," I said, "but she wouldn't want me to be blackmailed by *you*. After I scatter her ashes on the ocean, I very well might meet a lady closer to my own age and fall in love."

I didn't believe a word of it. Oh yes, Mae had said she hoped I would remarry and not allow her untimely death to destroy my libido. But she was my libido.

"You don't like doing it with me?" smirked Jane.

"You got it."

"Bullshit!"

"Don't you ever do that to me again."

"You ain't my boss."

"And you ain't my woman."

"You're weird."

She abruptly stood, set her cup on the console beside Mae's ashes, and let go with a big stretch and yawn. Then: "I already feel weird about myself. So now you feel weird about yourself, too, don't you."

"You have a lot to learn."

She rubber-necked her face around in front of mine and, with a big theatrical wink, said, "Teach me."

"Sex is the only way you know how to cope. And it's already gotten you in trouble and put grown men in prison. But you'll learn the hard way."

"You say hard, Dick?"

"Cut it out."

"Why? Because some uptight stupid people are scared of sex?"

"There's that, sure. But sex is like nuclear energy. It can destroy or it can enlighten. All depends on how you use it. It's the alpha and omega of existence. It's—"

"If God didn't want us to do it, why did He make us *love* it so much?"

"Well," I said, stumbling, "if God wanted us to do it with everybody or anybody, why did he create sexually transmitted diseases, including AIDS? I believe our Creator is saying we must handle it with the greatest respect and caution."

"Take the fun out of it?"

"No, take the poison out of it."

She seemed to think about that a beat, then:

"The sun's coming up."

Then she crawled over the boxes to her nest in the back and changed out of her nightie into some clothes.

A few miles later, she was in the shotgun seat wearing a sweater and a pair of slacks she'd selected from the church give-away bin, rose-colored and smoothly ironed. They were the kind of tight-fitting slacks we at Grandmother's Home discouraged as "featuring my ass." She had the visor flipped down and was going through her elaborate grooming ritual.

I suddenly remembered telling the police at our last stop that I'd turn her in if I found her. That was no longer a possibility. She'd scream rape and be able to "prove" it, and there's no way I could talk my way out of it. She did indeed have me between a rock and a hard place.

After a long silence, she said, "I don't think I'll ever understand it."

"Understand what?"

"Why people make such a big deal over sex. I mean, I just want to pleasure you so you'll keep me around."

"Tell you what: I'll promise to keep you around till we get to California and find your auntie—if you promise to not try to... to do that to me again. Just don't mess with my private parts and ... I'll take care of you until we get to California and get you hooked up with your relative. Deal?"

Her violet-blue eyes flashed in the early morning light as she smiled. "Dick, you're the best relations I got."

"Help me."

"Help you what?"

"Help me bring my wife's ashes to the Pacific Ocean with dignity, and I'll help you get a better life."

"It's a deal. Dignity, Mae deserves that, she was a wonderful woman. You were lucky to have such a great wife, you know that?"

"I know that way better than you ever will. Another reason I don't want to mess around. Understood?"

She gave me her a down-under fetching look and said nothing.

But there was another reason I had to evade her wiles. A reason having nothing to do with morality. Long ago I learned that if you have sex with a gal who is happy and healthy, you'll come away feeling the same. Fuck with a gal who is a cauldron of self-loathing and distress, you catch it from her by some strange form of osmosis. Even if Jane were of legal age, I'd want to avoid catching the spirit that had her in its grip.

And I wondered, as we continued across the continent, if an exchange of emotional traumas happened with what we'd just had. Did I share my angst with her and catch my own version of hers?

Well, we'd made our deal. I was keeping her aboard, heading West, the sunrise behind us, and I was trusting to fate. I really did want the best for her.

As I drove on, I remembered how Mae and I had used the names of foreign countries so we could discuss the kids in our own code. Wesley was Poland, Yoni was Nigeria, and so forth. We had trouble pegging Jane till we decided she was like Native America and called her Injun. Abused and abandoned, bitter and cynical, fragmented and scattered. An emotional wreck inside a perfectly gorgeous body, trying to hang on as best she could.

Can I help her? Can I afford not to try? Could we ever have a father-daughter kind of relationship? As the parents of two sons, Mae and I had often wondered what it would be like to have a daughter. And if Mae had lived, and if some other elements had fallen into place—financial elements, mostly—we might have adopted Jane, we'd been so taken by her spunk and vitality. How would that have worked out? Could we have overcome the damage she'd suffered emotionally, psychologically, and nurtured her into a woman who loved and respected herself, and therefore had love and respect for others?

That was the message I really wanted to deliver to her. But how? She's like a frightened animal using sex as her only weapon. How can I convince her that I have her best interests at heart?

12

I got him to promise he won't try to turn me in no more.

But I don't know, staffers don't always keep promises. Back in West Wing, Hurt and Enema used to promise this and that, and when they broke their promise, they'd just laugh and say, We lied! Sweet and Sour used to say that was a way they had of making fun of how us kids lied or forgot our promises. Bullshit.

And old Hurt Williston, he's a retired army something or other, he used to drive me nuts by calling me Miss America. Like we'd be lining up early in the morning to go to dining hall for breakfast and old Hurt would say, Oh look, children, look what Miss America is wearing today. Then he'd make everybody wait while I had to go back to my room and change clothes. He didn't like it when I wore featuring my ass pants.

I bet old Hurt's fit to be tied, now that he can't sell my ass to the Chinaman. I know that's what he was planning to do.

Hurt wouldn't let us watch the music videos neither. Said it was too suggestive, meaning it looked like the people dancing around was having fun. And Emma Williston's the one made us girls wear sweatshirts over our bathing suits. What stupid shitheads. Us down and outs can't hurt nobody when we're dancng. And if we give up dancing, where them high-falootin's gonna be?

You ever saw the Willistons, you couldn't imagine them getting it on together. She's built like a cartoon fire hydrant and he's got a pot sticks out so far you wonder how he can see to take a stand-up pee. Always got a verse or saying to prove whatever they're trying to prove at the time, a knock-knock joke for every occasion.

One day I asked how long ago the Bible was written, and old Herb looks over the tops of his glasses and says, The word of God was given to the Israelites two thousand years ago. Then I says, Did God speak this weird old-fashioned English way back then? And the Group cracked up laughing and I wound up having to mop both the kitchen and laundry room six times over.

Dick, he's different. In a way, what he says makes sense. I know I shouldn't try to mess with a grownup man, especially one whose wife just died and he's still got her ashes. But it would make it better for both of us if he'd just relax and enjoy it. Then he'd know there's no way he could turn me back into the system.

Anyhow, we got the interstate pretty much to ourselves this morning, till we get near Albuquerque. It's such a funny word for a city, me and Dick have a good laugh, looking at how to spell it.

And as we're going through Albuquerque on the interstate, Dick says, I know what you need!

What?

A pet. A puppy.

A puppy?

Yeah. Pets weren't allowed in Grandmother's Home. I'll bet you'd love to have a puppy.

All my own?

Yes, exactly, all your own.

Then he turns down this off ramp and we're in the middle of this city, and he drives awhile to a shopping mall, a big one. We park and walk in, and find this store called Pet Doctor. And in the window, they got this pile of puppies climbing over each other in a box, looking so cute you could cry.

Dick says, Pick one. Come on, we don't have time to dawdle.

I pick one with black and white spots, big floppy ears and eyes that just beg you to hold him and cuddle him and make him all warm and feel-good.

I really don't have the money to be doing this, Dick says, whipping out his wallet and buying this puppy, along with some food and a box and some other stuff. Then he carries the stuff and I carry Mindy, the name I give my puppy cause she's a girl. Back to the van, and we're on the road again.

Sitting up front with Mindy in my lap, riding along, my heart feels different. Feels like its bursting with love, you know? Makes me darn near want to cry—for happiness, see—and I says, Oh Dick, thank you so much! I love Mindy.

And he says, Yeah, well, you're gonna have to take care of Mindy, too. She's liable to wet on you pretty soon—which she done about the time Dick said it—and you're gonna have to clean it up. Look under the seat, there's some rags under there. Then fix Mindy's box in the back somewhere. Make sure she don't pee on my valuable books.

After that the time went by fast. I played with Mindy all over the van, and I fixed her box so it's her own little house, and tried to teach her to pee outside, when we stopped for a rest. I fed her and stroked her and let her know not to be scared when we're moving down the road. Got her to sit up and watch the scenery go by.

That night we stopped at another motel somewhere. Dick says, We're gonna give your Daddy another chance to call us. To find out your auntie's name and address in California. Cause we just crossed into California, you know.

When did we do that?

Remember that bridge we went over? That was the Colorado River. Took us from Arizona to California.

Inside the motel room, with Mindy sleeping in her box, Dick got out the map and showed me where we was—on the California side of the Colorado River. Put me in mind of them old black and white movies on TV, you know. Driving covered wagons across this big puddle and up the other side with Indians attacking.

Dick got me to put through another call to Daddy's liquor store in Elk City, then we got dinner sent to the room. He looks at his watch and says, It's six o'clock here, which means it's nine o'clock back in North Carolina. Think that's too late for your Daddy to get the message?

No. If Daddy worked today, he won't get home till around nine o'clock, which is when he stops by the liquor store to pick him up a fifth of something.

Okay, but remember—don't tell him you're with me. Understand? Cause if you do, we're liable to get stopped again by police, and this time they're liable to catch you and send you back.

What do I tell him?

Tell him you are thinking of going to California to visit your auntie, and you want to know her name and address. And telephone number, if she has one.

Okay, I put through the call, talk to somebody in the liquor store, leave a message. Give 'em the phone number and tell 'em to get my Daddy to call collect.

A little after nine, dozing off with Mindy beside me, the phone rings and Dick motions for me to grab it. I say, Hello?

Collect call for anyone from Sam Doyle. Will you accept charges?

Yeah. Daddy?

Hello, little darling, how you be?

69

Well, we talked awhile. Daddy was back working and he had the address of auntie Phyllis with a y, whose new last name now is Angelica. Not only that, he had a phone number where my Mom is now! In California! My mom!

It took me a time to write it all down, what with trying to hold the phone to my ear and all. Dick finally took the pen and wrote down all these names and numbers Daddy was giving me. My hand was shaking.

Then Daddy wanted to know when he was going to see me again. I said, Hell I don't know, but I'll call you when I get set up in California. You can count on that. And he says, Call collect if you have to, I got a promotion, gonna soon have a phone.

And that's how this day ended. I got auntie Phyllis's name and number, along with my Mom's.

Which I don't know if I want to look up her. See, Mom's pretty crazy. Last time I seen her, she bashed me over the head with her pocketbook, on her way out the door with her newest man. Knocked me down so I couldn't follow, like she'd won the lottery and didn't want to cut me in. Oh well. Maybe she's calmed down.

Curled up with Mindy and went to sleep, with Dick sitting up reading a book. Him in his big double bed, me in mine. I felt real good. Got me a puppy, a bed, some auntie to look up in California, and Dick to take care of things.

Out of the system at last.

13

Buying my pint-sized seductress a puppy was the best move I could have made. This I did during a quick stop in Albuquerque, in an air-conditioned shopping mall, at a Doctor's Pet Shop, from a lovely female clerk who blessed the transaction with her heartfelt enthusiasm, and after that the trip went smoothly. Jane's attentions focused on her puppy—she quickly named it Mindy—and I was free to drive and ruminate about life, where I was coming from, my missing better half, what the future might hold.

We crossed the Colorado River late that day and stopped at a motel in Blythe, where we put through another call to the liquor store in Elk City and this time her father returned the call only a few minutes later. In the mountains of North Carolina there was once an abundance of elk, thus Elk City, Banner Elk, Elk Ford, Elk this and Elk that. Now the elk were gone but the names lingered on. Seems that's what a lot of rural America has become, names with vanished meanings.

Between trying to hang onto Mindy and handle the phone, Jane had her hands full. So as her father gave out names and addresses, she repeated aloud and I jotted down each on a motel notepad.

I took hope from learning that not only did she really have an auntie in Southern California, but also her biological mother was here. Surprise, surprise! Jane was awed. She hadn't expected to ever see her mother again. "My *Mom*," she said several times, "is pretty crazy."

The former Mrs. Doyle was now named Helen Bixbe and had an address in Oxnard. Her auntie's name was Phyllis Angelica, with a more upscale-sounding address in West Hollywood.

We now had two options for her final destination. If Mom didn't want her, she'd go to auntie, and vice versa. And yet even as I thought this, I wondered if I were being overly optimistic. Ever since I found her in the van, Jane had me in a damned if you do, damned if you don't situation. Well, that will change, now that we're in California, I decided.

Supposedly, I was going to California for several very legitimate reasons. I say *supposedly* because suddenly I was having second thoughts. Cold feet. Scattering Mae's ashes on the ocean, visiting my children and grandchildren, solving the world's problems in late night discussions with my old friend Malcolm Knor... these paled to the flimsy excuses of a lonely old man who has nothing left to live for and nowhere else to go. And has taken on a totally incongruous traveling companion in the meantime.

Late this afternoon as we drove across the Colorado River, it occurred to me that I could have scattered Mae's ashes anywhere, for now that she had departed her physical being, what difference would it make?

And showing up on the doorstep of my son Hampton (my wife's maiden name and this son's middle name, by which he preferred to be called) could be traumatic all around. Hampton was money motivated, a product of "trickle down" ideology. His wife Charlene had several hundred million bequeathed her in a trust fund. I suppose Hampton had somehow used that trust fund as collateral, and pursuing good old American know-who, had created a small fortune of his own. He'd been far too busy to notice that his parents had gone through their nest egg paying medical bills. For his father to show up with a twelve-year-old waif... well, this would definitely not sit well with either Hampton or Charlene.

His younger brother by two years, Kent, was of an entirely different nature. Kent knew my circumstances, for he always asked about our finances and we never lied. Kent, however, had majored in Liberal Arts and now scraped by on two salaries, his own and his wife Anna's. She taught grade school, he installed electronic security devices in cars, and together they coped with their three young offspring.

Unless I was going to turn Jane in when we got to the Coast, I'd have to tell Kent and Anna the story. How will they react to it? If I arrived alone, they'd insist that I move into their already crowded house and stay till I insisted on leaving. But with Jane along...?

Much as Hampton and Kent resembled each other physically, their outlooks and values were so drastically different that they rarely spoke any more. This evening, for the first time, their estrangement did not pain me. My plan was to confide in Kent and Anna, knowing they would understand.

I called Hampton first. His wife Charlene answered and told me he was working late as usual. I detected a note of strain in her voice as she conveyed this, and wondered if all was well with the two of them. But I didn't ask; I knew from past experience that I was far down on her list of preferred guests. I said, "Will you talk it over with Hampton and decide which date would be best for the scattering of Mae's ashes, then call Kent and Anna and coordinate?" Her vague reply indicated she really didn't know what I was talking about. Did she even know her mother-in-law had died? Or was she just too self-absorbed to care?

Kent and Anna knew. I'd called them right before leaving North Carolina and promised to call from the road to let them know I was all right. When I reached him this evening, I laid it on the line. "Kent, one of the girls at that agency stowed away in my van. She's still with me."

"Dad, you're such a pushover for helpless kids. Tell her welcome to California for me. How old is she?"

"Twelve. Chronologically twelve but..."

"A volatile age, eh? I'll bet you have your hands full."

"I do, and I won't burden you and your family with either of us—I want you to know."

"Nonsense! You'll come straight here and we'll make room."

"You and Anna don't have any room to make," I mildly protested.

"You come straight here, Dad. You must be mighty tired from the road."

After that conversation we climbed into our separate king-sized motel beds.

Jane had reverted to another side of her nature: playing mama to her puppy, and she'd suddenly become quite modest about undressing in front of me. Good! This night she took Mindy—who went everywhere with her—into the bathroom to disrobe and get into her shortie nightgown, then made sure the lights were out before slipping from the bathroom to her bed.

Whereupon, Mindy felt a sudden, nocturnal urge to romp and frolic about the room. Jane gave chase, naturally. With only outside lights filtering in, Jane had a tough time catching him—the puppy was a male, even though Jane insisted it was a "her." I had to exert some self-control to keep my mouth shut about their romp through the room, but I couldn't bring myself to insist that she leave Mindy in "her" box in the van. The vixen seductress of early this morning had become a little girl enchanted with her live puppy dolly.

I soothed my jangled nerves with visions of reuniting Jane with her natural mother, ignoring the nagging suspicion that this might not be possible.

Tomorrow I planned to drive through Los Angeles and up to Carpenteria, but overnight at a campground before showing up at Kent's house.

Finally Mindy wearied and went to bed with Jane, and I fell asleep noting that I thought of Kent and Anna as living in a *house*, while I called the mini estate owned by Hampton and Charlene a *home*. This was ironic because Kent and Anna were settled in their place, while Hampton and Charlene were merely stopping over on their way to a dramatically increased net worth. Kent and Anna produced things for people, Hampton and Charlene multiplied their money.

Around ten o'clock, with Jane and Mindy sleeping soundly in the other bed, I thought of Maude's words and got up, found my address book, looked up her home phone number and dialed. Ten o'clock here meant one o'clock there. I should have called earlier but had forgotten. Better late than never, I reasoned.

As I waited for her to pick up, I remembered her sincere expression of sympathy during the brief funeral service for Mae, held in a chapel next door to where she'd been cremated. Maude had asked that day what I planned to do and I'd said I had no definite plans, just to fulfill Mae's request to scatter her ashes on the waters of the Pacific. And Maude had then said she hoped I'd keep in touch. I nodded but without any conviction. Little did either of us know then that Jane would keep us in touch.

Maude was a single mother with three little ones, whose loud presence had often been evident when she answered her phone at home. Tonight, the din was absent. I'd wakened Maude out of a sound sleep.

"It's Dick, calling from Blythe, California. Please forgive me for calling so late, but you wanted to tell me something else?"

"Yes," she said, struggling to wake up. "Dick, I don't know exactly how to get at this, so I'll just be blunt. Seems someone in law enforcement has come up with the idea that the

Willistons may be mixed up in some kind of white slavery business."

"Who do you mean, white slavery, someone in law enforcement? What's going on?"

"I'm not at liberty to say. Not yet. I've been sworn to secrecy about this. I'm sure you understand how sensitive it is. Anyhow, the latest development is that Herb Williston... There have been no formal charges, no arrests. But I want you to know that Herb Williston has suddenly decided to take off for a while. He has sick days and vacation days coming. I tried to track him down at his farm and through Emma, but can't locate him."

My throat went dry. "Well, is Emma still working?"

"Yes, but she will only tell us that he's gone fishing, that he's out of contact." After a lengthy hesitation, Maude said, "You should also know that the state prosecutor's office suspects the Willistons collected payments on some of those little girls before they turned them over to some kind of prostitution thing. Now that's just a suspicion, mind you. No charges. They're investigating and they keep asking about Jane."

"Williston collected money on who?"

"Some girls who'd been in Grandmother's Home."

I swallowed hard and said, "Do they think he could have, or might have collected money... on Jane?"

"They didn't say, just kept asking questions about her."

"Sounds very suspicious."

"I guess so. They sure are working hard on it, whatever it is."

"And Williston is missing."

"My hunch is he's trying to find Jane. Or maybe I should say that's my suspicion."

"Maybe," I ventured, "he promised her to this ring, or whatever it is."

"That's the impression I got last time I was questioned by the police. I asked, but they said they could not yet speak freely about it, just to let them know if I heard where Jane might be."

"Seems a lot of people are hunting Jane."

"So, that's what I wanted you to know. I need sleep. Call me at the office tomorrow, maybe I'll have more for you by then."

What *other* girls was she talking about?

Before I turned out the light and sought the solace of sleep, I made one more call, this one to my old pal Malcolm Knor. Malcolm and his wife Winnie bought a house from Mae and me, just before we packed up and left California for North Carolina. His parting words were, "If you're ever by this way again, my house is your house."

Malcolm, before his retirement a couple of years ago, published and edited a weekly financial newsletter called *Ups and Downs*. You weren't likely to see him on the TV show *Wall Street Week in Review*, but he had a loyal following, especially among the "economic experts" you *were* liable to see on *Wall Street Week in Review* and other fiscally "informative" television shows.

Many's the night Malcolm and I sat up late over an after-dinner drink or two, exchanging opinions, cussing out politicians, that sort of thing. I'd called him from North Carolina to let him know about Mae's passing, and to say I might be returning to Santa Barbara, and he'd been adamant about my staying with him. "We have more room here than we know what to do with, you know."

Tonight I heard a Chopin sonata in the background when he picked up the phone. "Malcolm, it's me, Dick."

"Hey! Winnie and I were just talking about you. Where are you?"

"A motel in Blythe. With complications."

"What complications?"

I sighed, not sure where to begin. "I have a runaway teenaged girl with me, for one thing. And where she's running away from—they may have a big legal problem, something to do with selling teenaged girls into prostitution."

"Well, we have room for her too, you know. When can I look for you? Oh, my! Winnie and I are leaving day after tomorrow for Hawaii. We've been offered big money for our house there. Three times what we thought it was worth. Japanese buyer. But no problem. I'll leave the key hanging on a nail under the eave of the back door. The key is to the front door, though. It won't open the back door. You and your young friend just put in and make yourselves at home. Winnie and I will call from Hawaii."

"Thanks, Malcolm. I appreciate that."

"I know you would do the same for me, my friend. See you when we get back." But he sounded strangely nervous.

About ten years ago, I had saved his newsletter by investing in it. Best investment I'd ever made. Trouble was, last year I had to withdraw the principle to pay medical bills. He understood, and by that time it didn't matter. The newsletter was generating a magnificent cash flow and he was going to sell it and retire. That's when he and Winnie bought the mountain house from us. One of half a dozen houses they now own.

With that port in the storm secured, I relaxed and went straight to sleep.

14

California wasn't at all how I pictured it. Once, when we stopped by the roadside so Dick could check a back tire, I got out and kicked some dirt, and it was so dry it just went *poof* and became dust.

Well, like my daddy said when I talked to him on the phone last night, you can't even grow a decent tomato in California unless you pipe in water and dump chemical fertilizers on the ground, cause it's desert.

Yeah, California in the movies sure is different from California on the interstate. Don't seem to be no people except them sitting in cars in the next lane over.

Along about early afternoon, Dick says, Want to see some movie stars, maybe? I said, Sure. So he pulls off the interstate into Palm Springs, which I know something about from the soaps on TV. But there weren't no movie stars. Weren't no room either, it was so mobbed with college kids on spring break. We wound up doing takeouts at the McDonalds.

Then we got back on the highway and kept going, and pretty soon there's buildings, then more and more buildings, and pretty soon there's houses too. That had me feeling better. I'd hate to be stuck out there in the desert.

Is *this* LA?

Part of it, he says.

Gee, what do people do here?

That's what I'd like to talk to you about, Jane. The first thing you gotta be able to do, he says, is support yourself. Then you can find a man to share your life with. So, how would you like to support yourself? What are you gonna be doing when you're twenty-one years old?

You want me to plan my old age? Right this very minute? Man, I'm lucky to be making it from one day to the next. How do I know what I'm gonna be doing when I'm twenty-one? Give me a break!

Says he's not asking me to plan my old age. Says twenty-one ain't old age, it's the bloom of youth. How are you going to become a worthwhile member of society?

I don't want to be no worthwhile member of society. I just want money. I don't have to go to no school to learn what I already know, and I can make a lot more money, faster, doing what I know. Okay?

Not okay, he says. You gotta have a *plan* for your life. Being a hooker is a dead end.

So is being a waitress, I say.

Then he pulls into a gas station to fill up and make a phone call, and I take Mindy for a walk. We cross this busy highway at the red light and walk over to a park so Mindy can go poo in the grass.

Guess I kind of lost track of time, playing with Mindy down under the trees in this park. Next thing I know, here's Dick, yelling and scowling and telling me to get my butt back up there to the van.

I told him I was sorry, lost track of the time, and he says, Forget that for now. Says, I'm trying to call your social worker, but she's out.

Yeah, I know what you mean. She always says, Call me, let me know how things are. But when I call, she ain't there. Out in the field, they say.

Well, who would you like to look up first, your mom or your auntie?

That gives me a pain in the stomach, trying to answer that question. If I had my druthers, I'd just hang in with Dick, take it day by day. Cause there ain't no telling what my mom's into, and I really don't know this auntie Phyllis.

He says, Well? Answer me!

Going seventy miles an hour, we got to yell over the engine noise.

I say, Dick, I can't think straight now. Can we talk about it tomorrow?

Okay, tomorrow, he says. But I got one more question for today. You ever hear anything about the Willistons making money on you girls? You know, he drives a new BMW sedan. Where did he get the money to buy that thing?

I say, Remember a couple of months ago when this post card came from Bangkok?

No, he says, I guess I wasn't on duty that day. What about it?

Oh, I remember what happened. You were on, you just never knew about it. We got little Johnny Monroe to act up so you was fussing at him. Us girls fooled you and Mae. That's how we got to read this post card. Anyhow this post card was signed Peaches, right? And it says, The Bellies got me sent here. Been tootin' and hootin' and living in a big hotel. Signed Peaches.

Tooting and hooting? What's that?

Prostituting and doing hooters, cocaine and heroin, you know. Speedballs and stuff. Pot, Ecstasy, who knows?

Oh, says Dick, trying to keep a straight face. What's that got to do with the Willistons?

Peaches is the pet name we give Wendy Miller. Remember her? She was there when you and Mae come on.

Yes, I remember Wendy. She was adopted by a wealthy family in Boone.

Right, and then she was sent away to school.

Yes, so I heard. In Phoenix, Arizona.

Right, and then she wound up in Bangkok.

I don't think he heard me, cause he says, What's the name of that school she was sent to?

It was just a front, Dick, the name don't make no never-mind. She ain't there, she's in Bangkok, tootin' and hootin'.

He's quiet awhile, then he says, You know any other girls that happened to?

Three. Yoni knows about it too.

Which three?

Wendy Miller, the one we called Peaches. Nancy Gardner, the one we called Wildflower, and Pamela Striker. She was kind of skinny and we called her Tennis Balls cause that's what her tits looked like.

Do you know where those girls are now?

I guess Peaches might still be in Bangkok. Wildflower was in Tokyo, but that was a couple of months ago. And Tennis Balls sent us a card from Hong Kong—a long time ago, sometime last winter. Sent 'em to the school so we'd be sure to get 'em.

And were all three of these girls adopted by those people who live in Boone.

You got it!

And does your social worker know about this?

The adoption? Sure she knows. About Bangkok, not likely.

Indeed, not likely, he says. So how do you suppose they got from Boone, North Carolina, to Bangkok, Tokyo, Hong Kong? And how do you feel about this?

The Chinaman in Boone? I visited two Sundays ago. Had my hopes sky high they'd adopt me right then, but they didn't say anything about it. I asked 'em, and they just said, We'll see.

Then I decided fuck it, I don't want the bellies making money on my buns, so I run with you.

So, says Dick, it appears that the Willistons have these young ladies adopted by this family in Boone, who sends them to a school in Phoenix—

That's just what they tell Maude—a private school, very fancy.

Yes, and from this private school, they go to Asia. What's the name of this adopting family in Boone.

Mr. and Mrs. Woo Chin. They own the Chinese restaurant there. You ever ate there? Pretty good food, nothing great. And it ain't what makes 'em rich, for sure. I don't mention Johnny Hooper. He's my ace in the hole.

And what's the name of this private school in Phoenix?

Don't waste time wondering. It's just where you change planes.

And you stowed away in my van because Mr. and Mrs. Woo Chin didn't say whether or not they were going to adopt you?

Hell, I ain't hanging around Grandmother's jail another six months to find out—not when I can go to California with you.

He says, I've got to get to a telephone and check this out with Maude Jennings.

Shit, Dick, she don't know nothing. After a girl leaves North Carolina, they ain't Maude's business no more.

No? We'll see. And is that why the Willistons have so much extra money?

Ask *them!* They's into free enterprise.

That's not free enterprise, says Dick with a frown on his forehead and his jaw sticking out. That's white slavery.

Huh! Slavery is when you're in the system. You can't travel, you can't go hootin' and tootin', you're just stuck there like a zombie, shuffling from West Wing to the dining hall and the school and the playground and back again to West Wing. I couldn't even have Mindy with me there. Huh, Mindy.

15

West of Palm Springs, as we drove, Jane opened up with some startling information that dovetailed with Maude's suspicions about the Willistons.

Somewhere around San Bernardino, I got off the interstate and went to a pay phone, put through another call to Maude Jennings. It was around one o'clock in the afternoon here in California, which made it around four back East. Maude was out, again, but her assistant, Jenny Hatfield, was there, so I decided to pass on the information I'd picked up from Jane.

Which came to the following: according to Jane's account, three girls from West Wing were adopted by a Mr. and Mrs. Woo Chin of Boone, about twenty miles from Grandmother's Home. And it seems the Chins then sent the girls to a private school in Phoenix, Arizona, name unknown at this time. From there, they wound up in places like Bangkok, Tokyo and Hong Kong. Apparently, what we have here is a ring of child prostitution.

I remembered Jenny Hatfield as a bright young gal fresh out of Appalachian State with a degree in social work. She distinguished herself in that DHS office by being from an affluent local family. Her response now to what I'd just outlined was this:

"Okay, Dick, I'll relay this message to Maude, but..."

"But what?"

"Did you get all this from twelve-year-old Jane Doyle?"

"Yes! She said these girls sent back post cards."

"Well, Dick, as you know, the incoming and outgoing mail at Grandmother's Home is monitored."

A euphemism for censored. "Yes, I know that. What's your point?"

"Well... don't you think we ought to allow for childish imagination here?"

"No, I think what we ought to do is get the police to check out this story, get the name of this school in Phoenix and find out what happened to those girls."

"Okay," she sighed, impatient with what she perceived as my naiveté, "I'll relay the message to Maude."

"And tell her Herb Williston is the one gets them adopted by the Chins."

"He's on sick leave. I tried to see him yesterday, but he's gone."

"Sick leave, eh. Well, tell Maude I'll call her later this evening, after she's home."

"She's got a meeting at seven."

"I'll call her at four in the morning if I have to."

"Take it easy now, Dick, Rome wasn't built in a day."

I left the phone booth fuming. Apparently Jenny Hatfield had not yet heard the suspicions about those two "seasoned child care workers," Herb and Emma Williston. I was kicking myself in the butt for talking to her the rest of the way to the Coast.

When we got to Carpenteria, I headed for the state beach where Mae and I used to overnight now and then. It was only a few blocks from Kent's house, so I thought it would be a perfect place for the time being. Jane and I could cook hamburgers over a fire pit, and call Kent and Anna and the kids. We could invite them to our cookout. That way we wouldn't be imposing on their hospitality.

The same friendly face at the campground gate that used to smile at Mae and me was still there. But now he said that campsites were by reservation only, and you'd best call months ahead. And when I looked around, I realized that the place was jammed with campers.

Turned away from that option, I parked near a phone booth and called my son and his wife. Anna answered, and when she learned where we were, demanded we come right over, that they were waiting dinner on us. Reluctant though I was to impose Jane on them, we went.

They gave us a warm reception. Hugs all around for me, smiles and younger children to play with for Jane.

Kent's and Anna's three are ages four, six and eight. They quickly adopted Jane as their new heroine, showing her all around the back yard, yanking out toys they thought she would enjoy.

Jane, who had been forbidden at Grandmother's Home to have anything to do with children younger than eleven, was presented with very different expectations here. She was soon down on her haunches with the others, playing with the doll-house, remote control cars, and a large beach ball, which kept getting blown over the fence by the late afternoon wind.

She had again reverted to a little girl, and seemed joyfully lost in the kind of play she'd probably not gotten much of in her previous years. Her puppy Mindy pranced happily amid the children, while we grownups kicked back with beer and hamburgers, and I told my story. Or tried to. Actually, I wasn't sure what was happening. Only glad to be back on the West Coast among my kin.

And by eleven o'clock I was tired. Very, very tired.

16

Y ou sure could tell it was Friday evening in this beach town called Carpenter something. People coming in loaded down cars for the weekend. Campers and trailers all over the place.

Dick drives up to the entrance to this campground on the beach, saying we're gonna stay here this night before going on to see his son and daughter-in-law and their kids. I get the idea that this son is another day's drive away, but when Dick finds out from the guard that they ain't taking no more campers today, he says, Oh shit, and drives to a pay phone to make a call.

After the call, he looks like he's feeling better, and we drive on. He says, Change of plans. We're going to stay with my son and his family.

Drives only a few blocks and then pulls into this driveway, beeps the horn and here come a flock of people running.

I can't tell who's who for awhile, but soon I know the tall guy with the long blond hair in a ponytail is Kent, Dick's son, and the nice looking lady with the dark tan is Anna, Kent's wife. Three of the kids are theirs, and the rest are neighbor kids. I climb out of the van and go off with these kids. They want to show me stuff.

Even though they're a lot younger than me, I like 'em. Ruthie is about eight, and Dick is six and his little brother Bruce is four. Their last name is the same as Dick's, Steel. Ain't been around three kids with the same last name since I can't remember when. They all like Mindy and she likes all of them.

The grownups sit around watching us kids play and cooking hotdogs and hamburgers, and when the sun gets low and we get hungry, there's plenty to eat, and we can keep playing while we eat. That's cool.

Later that night, when I went to bed, I was so dead tired I couldn't keep my eyes open to see where they was putting me. Woke up the next morning in a big room, inside a sleeping bag, on a mattress, on the floor. Crawled out of the sleeping bag and looked around, and there's the two boys in one bunk bed, and Ruthie in another bed across the room under a window. Looked out the window and find we're on the upstairs, and I can see the ocean from here if I squint through a couple of houses on the other side of the street.

Downstairs, Anna's cooking breakfast for everybody, and Dick's up having coffee, talking to her. When I come in they shut up, so I guess they was talking about me. Anna asks if I want orange juice, and I say, Sure.

I look outside to see that Mindy's okay. Her leash is tied to the van and somebody put a bowl of food near her.

When everybody else is up, we all eat a big breakfast a-round this humongous table, then start talking about going to the beach. Pretty soon we're loading up Kent's Toyota pickup with blankets and beach chairs and stuff, and putting on our bathing suits.

We spent a great day at the beach, but the ocean was so cold nobody went swimming. Mindy had the best time of all, running around from this kid to that, jumping on sand castles, making everybody laugh.

Around the dinner table that night, Dick says, Well, Jane, I talked to your mom on the phone today, and she'd like to see you as soon as possible.

Don't want to see her, I tell him.

Maybe she shouldn't go straight back to her mother, says Anna. Who knows what's going on in her life?

Tell you what, says Dick. Tomorrow, I'll drive over and have a talk with her, check out her place, make sure you'll be safe. I'm certainly not going to drop you off there and never know what becomes of you. It'll just be an overnight to see how you and your mom get along.

The next morning, Monday, the little kids all go off in somebody else's van to their school, while Kent and Anna drive away to their jobs in Santa Barbara. Anna is a schoolteacher and Kent puts radios in cars.

Dick and me clean up the dishes and straighten up the house and feed Mindy, then he says, Let's drive to the post office, see if they've forwarded on my mail yet. I left this forwarding address, Kent's post office box.

I tie Mindy to the back porch and let her know I'll be back soon.

You can't help notice what a pretty little town this Carpenter something is. It's right on the ocean and just big enough to have lots of places to go without getting lost.

The post office has a big flagpole in front of it. Dick parks right at the bottom of this, and I sit in the van and wait while he goes inside. And then is when I get the shock of my life.

Cause walking over toward me, staring right at me, comes this old man, belly hanging over his belt, a shit-eating grin on his face. Takes me a couple seconds to see it's—Herb Williston!

My eyes must have opened to the size of saucers when I seen it was that scum son of a bitch. I get the same sick feeling I got them nights he stood over my bed in the dark playing with his thing. Call me Princess and Miss America in the daytime, and tell me he didn't like my vagina and didn't want to put his penis in it, didn't like my ass, didn't like me, didn't think I had a snowball's chance in hell of ever getting placed with a decent family and making a go of it. All that shit he used to run by me every day, the hypocritical son of a bitch, and here he comes— what the hell's he doing way out here?

I quick dive for my old nest in the back of the van. Dick ain't unpacked yet so all that stuff is there, the tent and heavy coats, and I dig my way down into 'em and hide out, hoping he don't find me—but hell, I know he seen me sitting there with my eyes wide as saucers when I seed it was him!

Pretty soon I hear him call my name, Oh, Jane... Jane, come on out, Jane. This is Herb, Jane. I've come to take you back where you belong.

I stick my head up and yell, I ain't going back with you, Herb. You get the hell out of here. I'll kill myself before I go back there with you! Got his head through the open window.

I come to get you, Jane. Come on now, don't make it difficult. Don't force me to restrain you or call the police.

I duck down under again and wonder when's Dick coming back? How long can I hold this son of a bitch off? All the doors in the van is unlocked, cause me and the other kids was playing in it yesterday.

While I'm stalling for time, I hear him walk around to the back of the van to try the back door. He has to give it a couple of tugs before he gets it open and by that time I'm diving over the boxes for the front seat, thinking I'm gonna jump out and run like hell.

Then I remember that can of Mace Dick keeps in his glove compartment. I know Mace. Got sprayed with it by a cop in Durham once. You ever get hit by Mace, you don't forget it.

I yank open the glove compartment and grab that can, lift up the top and got it aimed at Hurt Williston by the time he comes around to the front door again. I don't think twice about it, I just point it straight at his face and push the button.

It lets out a stream like cat spray, only further. Old fat belly Herb yells like he been hit with buckshot. He whirls around and goes down on his butt, then rolls around on the ground, holding his eyes and face. Yelling like hell!

I jump out of the van and run over and give him two more shots just to make sure. He's got it all over his face and in his ears now. Great! I wish to hell it was a gun—I'd pump every bullet I could through his sick brain. Some people begin to crowd around. Old people, mostly. One says, Call an ambulance. Another says, What happened to this poor man? And some lady says, That little girl, she sprayed him with something. I palm the can of Mace and move backwards toward the van.

Just about now, Dick comes out of the post office carrying this big stack of mail. He does a double take at Herb laying there on the parking lot pavement moaning and groaning and holding his face, and this crowd standing around. Then he sees me backing up toward the van, holding the Mace behind me. He runs to the van and gets behind the wheel. Get in, he says while I'm climbing in the passenger side. Hell, I'm in before he gets the words out.

He drops the mail between the seats and revs up the engine and we're out of there. Half a block down the street, Dick says, Look back and tell me what's going on.

I look, and say, Herb's up on his feet now. Bent over, holding his face.

Anybody else?

Sure. Big crowd.

Oh shit. They probably got our license number. If he tries to follow us, let me know.

No, he ain't following. Some old Asian man's holding up Herb and watching us. Telling that crowd of people something.

Dick says, Asian! It's not Mr. Chin, is it?

No, Dick, it ain't Mr. Chin. He's back in Boone.

Are you sure?

Well, I'm sure this guy ain't Mr. Chin.

But he's Asian.

Yeah.

He floored it back to Kent's house and this time he backed up the drive and into the backyard, and swung the van around so you couldn't see it from the street.

Going in the back door, he says, If Herb got the forwarding address at the post office, he probably has this address too. Jane, we've got to get you out of here fast. Pack an overnight bag, we're gonna visit your mom.

17

The next morning, up popped the devil in the form of "good Christian" Herb Williston. While I was in the Post Office collecting my mail from the forwarding address I'd left—Kent and Anna's box number—Williston turned up and tried to nab Jane. And she sprayed him with Mace. From the can I keep in my glove compartment. Mae's idea and purchase.

So now we knew where Herb Williston had gone for his sick leave, and it didn't take Sherlock Holmes to figure out why. Seems he wants Jane badly enough to travel three thousand miles to get her.

But Jane incapacitated him with Mace and we made our getaway from the Post Office, leaving a crowd of mostly retired folk staring at Herb.

Back at the house I got on the phone to Maude. It was 8:30 here, which made it 11:30 back East and Maude is gone around that time as often as she's there. Today I got lucky.

"Guess who showed up in California this morning," I began.

"Herb Williston."

"How did you know?"

"It's a small world, Dick. Herb made his flight reservations at Tyler Travel Agency. Mrs. Tyler was my favorite teacher at Appalachian State. She called to chat yesterday—she's been following this case, you see—and let it drop about the ticket. How aggressively did Herb Williston go after Jane Doyle?"

I turned to Jane. "How hard did Herb try to grab you?"

"He would have reached in and had me if he could of," she said with a pout.

"Quite aggressively," I relayed to Maude. "Can we have him picked up?"

"I'm working on it. The state police here say they need more evidence, documentation, eyewitnesses. But they do have docs that say Herb owes the IRS half a million dollars."

That's news. And it reminded me of what Jane had told me in the motel room just across the Colorado River. I said to Maude, "Hold it just a second." Then to Jane: "That girl you got the post card from, do you have her address in Bangkok?"

"Yoni might. But you know we ain't allowed to send out letters and stuff—"

"Maude, Yoni may have the address of the last girl they grabbed. Can you get to Yoni today and find it?"

"What evidence would it provide, this address?"

"She's in Bangkok doing drugs and prostitution. She told the kids this in a post card that got through the monitoring. And her route there was through Herb and a Mr. Chin of Boone.

"And Yoni has her address?"

"So says Jane. You'll have to find out, Maude."

"I'm not sure I can, the code of secrecy being what it is among those kids."

"Mrs. Allen, the sixth grade teacher," I said, my memory jogged. "She's been upset about the treatment her students have been receiving at Grandmother's Home. If you call her and explain the situation, I'm sure she'll help, or try to. And the kids love her." From the corner of my eye I saw Jane nod her head at this, as she sat with Mindy on her lap. "If Yoni still has that card, she'll turn it over to Mrs. Allen."

"I'll give it a shot," said Maude, "and call you back. What time's best for you?"

"Anytime. We're leaving—since Williston's still lurking about somewhere—but I'll leave the answering machine on."

I recited Kent and Anna's number and said goodbye. When I talked to Jane's mother yesterday, she didn't sound like she had her head screwed on straight, quite. I couldn't tell whether this was because she was so surprised to hear from me, or surprised that Jane was half an hour's drive up the road, or if she was sloshed on booze or faded out on drugs. And I didn't feel entirely good about taking Jane to see her. So I thought I'd give Jane some options.

"Where would you prefer to go, Jane?" I began, and ran down a set of choices. We could go up into the mountains—I pointed out the kitchen window to show her—to my friend's house, or we could call your mother, or we could call your auntie. Jane's quick response surprised me.

"Mom."

"You want to see your mom?"

"Yeah."

"But you said yesterday—"

"That was yesterday."

"How long has it been since you've seen your mom?"

"I was eight. Four years, almost five."

"That's when she abandoned you."

"She took off with some dude."

"Have you forgiven her?"

"Hell, I don't know, Dick. Do I have to go through *psychiatry* just to see my mom?"

"No, but you could see your auntie in West Hollywood, or stay with my friends up in the mountains," forgetting momentarily that the Knors would be in Hawaii by this time.

"I want to see my mom."

"Okay. Let's call her."

Among the peculiar human quirks I discovered while working at Grandmother's Home was that children, no matter how badly battered and abandoned by their mothers, would still choose to go back to Mom, in most cases. When they've had enough, they turn away from Mom forever. Jane, if her records were anywhere near accurate, had been both battered by her Mom and left in a wretched situation with a father who was a drunken Bible babbling degenerate. No matter, Jane now wanted to see Mom. Push come to shove, we agreed she'd call me here if things don't work out. We have to get her out of Williston's way. There's no way he could know her mom now lives in Oxnard.

She packed an overnight bag, which meant she'd be leaving about half her clothes here and taking half with her to Mom's, and I called the number in Oxnard. As I listened to the rings, I felt a jolt of hope that Mom would not be there. I did not have good feelings about this visit.

But finally a husky voice, sounding like it was speaking from the bottom of a barrel, said, "Hello...?"

"Hello, Mrs. Doyle? Eh, I mean Mrs. Bixbe?"

"Who wants to know?"

"Your daughter, Jane Doyle."

"Jane! Oh!" And now she was breathless. "You're the guy called me yesterday, huh. Is she there? Can I talk to her?"

I handed the phone to Jane.

"Mom? Oh, yeah, Mom, I'm in California! Sure, I'm right by the ocean. Here, I'll hold up the phone so you can hear the surf."

Actually, the surf, two and a half blocks away, was only audible now and then, when traffic was light. Jane held the phone up a moment, then said, "Hear it, Mom?

The upshot was, I made arrangements to drive Jane to her Mom's for a one-day visit. I would pick her up at sundown.

Before we set out on that brief journey, I wrote down Kent's phone numbers at home and at work, and Anna's number where she taught school in Santa Barbara. "If anything goes wrong, Jane, call this number first, this house, then try Kent at work, and then try Anna. Got that?"

"Oh, Dick, you worry too much," she said, stuffing the note in the back pocket of her jeans. "What could go wrong? I'm gonna see my Mom... after all these years. You know, I haven't seen her since I was eight years old."

"She'll tell you you've grown," I said, feeling irked.

"I done a lot more than growed."

At the address in Oxnard, I was startled by Helen Bixbe's appearance, although I tried not to show it. What had been the sort of hair she bequeathed to Jane—thick, wavy, dark chestnut—now fizzed out in a huge halo, due, I suppose, to the leftovers of a hairdo she'd had some time ago. Her brown eyes stared with a wild intensity and the corners of her lips turned down, giving her the expression of one who feels wronged. Her figure was still slim of waist and girlish, owing to a sturdy body, but the entire effect she had on me was of someone who felt mauled by life.

Mother and daughter first peered closely at each other, as though not sure the other was the real thing, then slammed into each other's arms. So far, I saw no reason to suspect it wouldn't be a lovely reunion.

While they were embracing, I walked into the house; Mom had left the door open. It was a one-story wood frame with a living room separated from the kitchen by a bar, and a single bedroom off the living room. No one else was there.

That inspection done, I walked back out to the front porch and said my goodbyes, making it clear that I'd be back for Jane before dark.

As I was going to the van, though, Jane rushed after me and grabbed my arm, clutching it tightly. "When you coming back for me, Dick?"

"I just told you. Around sundown."

"Today?"

"Of course. What's wrong, honey?

"Nothing. Just don't be late, hear?"

18

Me, when it looks like I ain't got no choice, I daydream, try to make things better than they really are.

I daydreamed that my mom lived in a real nice house right on the beach. But when Dick found the address, it was a house on a dusty dirt street, and behind the house was a big field. Strawberries. With some rainbirds shooting water out over them.

Dick parked the van in front of this house. It has a porch and some broken steps in front. We walked up to the front door with Mindy on her leash and I called, Mom! Hey, Mom!

And she come out blinking like the sunlight hurt her eyes. Her throat seemed to hurt, cause when she talked, she sounded like she had a cold. Gruff. Hi, Jane. When she smiled, I saw she'd lost a tooth right in the front, one of her Bugs Bunny uppers.

We hugged but she didn't seem real happy to see me. And to be real honest about it, I wasn't real happy to be there. Dick talked to her awhile, anxious to get gone. I hooked Mindy's leash to the porch rail and went inside the house and looked around. The back door opened and a man walked into the kitchen. He was dark and scowled at me like I was some kind of sci-fi creature.

I went back outside on the porch just as Dick was saying goodbye. I walked him out to the van. I said, Dick, when you coming back for me?

He says, Sundown.

Okay, I says, cause I'm not sure about this.

I won't leave you here overnight, I promise.

When I went back inside the house, the guy was in the living room with my Mom. She says, Jane, this is Enrique. Spells his name for me. He spreads his lips out to a smile, then it disappears like a light bulb switched off. I get the creeps just looking at him. I want out of here already!

My Mom says, Well, what shall we do?

Let's go to the beach.

Yeah, let's go for a walk on the beach.

I meant we should go to the beach and swim, play in the sand, that kind of stuff. But she only wanted to walk. She said, Oh don't bring your bathing suit, honey, it's too cold. But you can bring your puppy. We'll just walk.

We got in an old sports car with two seats and no top. Enrique had to push the car to get it started. He wasn't happy about having to do that. I'm glad I got Mindy on my lap. Mindy don't like this guy neither.

Mom parked in the driveway of some old deserted house near the beach, and we walked. And walked and walked. She said, How's your Dad? And, do you see much of your cousins? And, tell me where you're living now.

I didn't feel like telling her much of anything. Didn't seem like she really cared to know, anyhow.

We walked to a place where a river flows into the sea and we couldn't cross it without getting soaked cause it was high tide right now. We sat down on some big old boulders. Mindy was having a ball trying to climb them rocks, and that's when my Mom started crying. I put my arm around her shoulder and said, Mom, don't cry. I'll take care of you, it's gonna be okay now. You'll see.

No, no, you don't understand, she says, I *owe money*. So much money I don't think I'll *ever* get it paid.

Who you owe money to?

Some people. That's why Enrique's in the house. He come to collect. But I can't pay him, I just can't. I work a waitressing job every night but it's just not enough.

Well Mom, maybe I can get 'em paid.

She dried her eyes then and smiled at me, and says, Honey, you're so sweet. I love you dearly, you know. Even if I did have to leave your Daddy. Promise me something. Don't *ever* drink or do drugs. Will you promise me that?

Hell, I already drunk and did drugs, but I said I promise, just to make her feel good.

Then we went back to the car and got it running with a rolling start down that driveway, and drove back across this town. A lot of Mexican people here. Mindy sat up and stuck her head out the side so the air would blow in her face.

Enrique was asleep on the couch when we got back and the phone was ringing. Mom answered it and said something about making a delivery as soon as possible.

Enrique woke up while she was talking on the phone. He dumped out some coke on a mirror, chopped it up, made lines, sniffed a couple and handed the mirror to Mom. She sniffed a couple lines and put the mirror down on the coffee table and started telling Enrique where to go for this delivery.

While she was talking to him, he was looking at me. And in the middle of her talking, he lifts up the mirror and holds it out in my direction, asking if I want to do some coke.

But I ain't taking no coke from Enrique. He scares me. Just the way he looks me over. I shake my head and wander out to the kitchen to see the rainbirds in the strawberry fields out back. Then I feel eyes on me and look back and here's

Enrique, standing in the kitchen doorway, feeling his wiener and staring at my butt.

Mom yells, Enrique! Get out of here! Go make that drop!

Enrique acts like he don't hear her. Staring at me with this hang-jaw, droopy-eye look.

Mom shoves past him into the kitchen and grabs me by the hand and says, Come on, Jane, let's go for a walk out back. See the strawberry fields.

Got me out from under Enrique's look, and I was glad for that. But Mom didn't seem... well, she didn't seem all there. Stumbled a lot. Couldn't seem to keep her feet under her. I said, Mom, are you okay, is something wrong?

Wrong? What should be wrong, honey? No, nothing's wrong.

How come you're having trouble walking?

Oh, I need to take some medicine for that, she says, and that's when I smelled the booze on her breath. I says, Mom, I don't want to go back in there with Enrique.

Oh don't be silly, Jane, he's harmless. I won't let him lay a hand on you. Anyhow, he went out. Won't be back for a couple of hours. Maybe longer.

That *sounded* okay. We went back to the house and Mom made us a couple of lunchmeat sandwiches and gave me a soda. She drank a beer.

Halfway through eating that sandwich, here comes Enrique and some other old dude. This other guy is wearing a suit and tie, and he's Mexican or something Latin. He drove up in a Lincoln Town Car right after Enrique parked his topless sports junker.

They come walking in the house and out to the kitchen where I'm sitting on a stool by this counter, and this guy in the suit walks right up to me and feels my ass. I scramble away from him. Mom yells, Get your hands off my daughter, you—

Enrique cuts her off with a *whomp*, a backhand to her mouth.

I jump up and run to her, laying on the kitchen floor, crying. I say, Mom, come on, let's get the hell out of here.

She says, Oh darling, I can't, I ain't got nowhere else to go.

Yes, you do, I says, we can go where Dick's at. He'll protect you.

You don't understand, girl, she says. This is it for me.

Then, before I could argue her out of that, Enrique grabs me by the armpit and yanks me up, says, You are going to have fun now. You are going with Mr. Gonzalez here. He's going to give you candy and good things to eat.

Shoves me toward this guy in the suit, who's reaching out to take me when I twirl away, kick him in the shin and run.

I run straight out the front door, grab Mindy's leash and jump off the porch and don't stop running till I'm a few blocks away. Nobody followed that I can see. But I don't know where the hell I am. I been having to half-drag Mindy cause she can't run so fast yet. I hold her and calm her down.

Then I go on walking, Mindy on her leash, till I come to a gas station, a lot of Mexicans sitting around drinking sodas. There's a pay phone here so I put through a collect call to Dick's number at Kent's house, but a machine comes on and the operator cuts me off before I can leave a message.

Shit. What now? There's a big round clock over the door of this gas station's garage—it's almost two o'clock. I can't think of what else to do so I take off walking, heading toward highway noise. Mindy's trotting along at my feet now, okay.

I hike up an onramp says 101 North and stick out my thumb. Ain't but a couple minutes when this shinny big tractor-trailer comes hissing to a stop, and a trucker opens the door for me. Big and fat, beard, bib coveralls. Looks like a TV wrestler. I climb in with Mindy on my lap and say, Can you get me to Carpenter, just up the road?

Sure, he says, but the way he says it don't sound right. He drives this interstate awhile—six lanes going both ways—then he swings down an off ramp and parks by the beach. Cuts the engine and looks at me.

I say, Okay, thanks for the ride, I'll walk the rest of the way. And I'm opening the door to jump out when he grabs me, lifts me off my feet, tries to stuff me into this bunk he got inside this cab. I'm kicking and screaming and raising hell, and Mindy's on the floor yipping and yapping, and I can't get loose.

Says, Make it easy on yourself, bitch. He's got a hold of my hair with one hand and is unzipping his pants with the other.

Mindy's crying.

If I ever get back to Dick, I'm gonna make him give me a can of Mace all my own. This trucker's wiener stinks like skunk spray and tastes worse. When I can't get to it, he slaps me so hard it makes my ear buzz.

Afterwards, he just opens the door and shoves me out with his foot. Mindy hops out with me. We land in a rolling tumble among a lot of thrown-away cans and bottles and road junk. Then he fires up the truck engine and pulls away, sending off a spray of dirt and dust with his wheels.

All I can do is start walking. I know that if I keep the ocean on my left I'll come to Kent's house sooner or later. Come on, Mindy. I take her by the leash and we start out.

You can't walk the beach all the way, though. Got to cut inland and walk along the interstate here and there. And Mindy's real tired and hungry, worse off than me, she's so little.

It's dark by the time I see the campground up ahead, the one Dick and I couldn't get into the first night here. I know how to find Kent's house from here. It's a few blocks further up the beach and a couple blocks in. Come on, Mindy, not much further.

19

I should have figured Herb Williston would be waiting for me at Kent's house when I got back from dropping off Jane. He'd tracked down my forwarding address, so surely he could get my son's address.

He had a car I remembered seeing at the post office, a rental, white Chevy, now parked in front of Kent and Anna's house, Herb leaning against it, arms folded over his chest. Our eyes met as I turned the van into the driveway. I continued into the back yard and parked as though I hadn't recognized him.

As I was getting out of the van, here he came, walking toward me with his sergeant's grin and his right hand extended.

The word *unctuous* comes to mind. Although I once heard Maude Jennings call him a greased pig. He always seems to be sweating. His horn-rim glasses keep sliding down his pug nose. He seems to have perpetual wet patches under his armpits and keeps spreading his knees like he needs to air out his crotch. Yet even though he and his wife Emma are both grossly overweight, I've seen them both move with incredible agility, like they were taking some very funny prescription drugs. At Grandmother's Home, they were the staff's design-nated instructors in the properly legal way to restrain the children. They took great pride in their ability to pounce upon a kid—be he or she ever so large and strong—and bring down their prey with the skill of karate experts.

This physical agility, plus a certain demonic dimension they shared, made me wonder if I would crumble like a wet cookie if they ever launched a physical attack on me. I was really quicker and stronger than both of them combined, but it was that demonic dimension that gave me pause.

"Howdy, Dick," he shouted, in the tone of an old friend suddenly encountered. "I thought I'd find you in, sooner or later. I'd like to have a little chat with you, if you don't mind."

His Appalachian accent was so thick, Mae had to translate for me the first couple of weeks on that job. Both he and Emma made it a point of pride to speak "downhome Hillbilly," and pretend to believe that anyone who didn't understand their dialect had an educational shortcoming.

I ignored his extended hand and just looked at him.

"Well... what I want is for you to help me understand something."

I waited.

"I want you to help me understand how come you run off with Jane Doyle."

"Don't give me that crap. She stowed away in my van. I didn't even know she was there till my second night on the road."

His feigned cheeriness went up several octaves at that, and he couldn't resist a thigh-smacking laugh. "Hot darn, Richard, if you ain't swifter than a New York second! Hot darn!"

I remained motionless and deadpanned, standing beside my van, arms folded over my chest, waiting for this fake fit of hilarity to subside. When it did, the hint of a sneer came to his lips and he fixed me with a cold stare.

"Well, my friend, I'll come to the point. I have plans for Jane, and you is messing up them plans."

I remained non-responsive.

"Ya see, what you done, taking Jane way out here to California, ain't good, my friend. Ain't good atall. You're in a lot of trouble with the law, boy. Do you follow my drift."

It was a declaration, not a question.

"Now, ya see, the reason I come way out here after Jane is, I got a *fine adoptive family* lined up for her, people with money, can offer her great opportunities."

I was tempted to let him know what I knew about those great opportunities, but I held my tongue and just stared up and away, watching the leaves of my son's oak tree fishtail in the breeze.

"If we're too easy on 'em, Dick," he said in a singsong, "we won't be able to do a damned thing with 'em, will we. They'll overrun us like a stampede of vermin."

I stared at him hard, looking deep into his eyes, hoping I was communicating that I now knew what lurked deep in his hypocritical "Christian" soul.

He tried another ruse. "We got ya clear to rights, Dick. Kidnapping! And when Jane sings, I'll bet she'll add rape, molestation. Serious charges. Where you wanna do time, podnah? California or North Carolina?"

Again I looked off, remaining silent, waiting for his next attempt. When he realized I wasn't going to say anything, he huffed and sighed and yelled:

"Well? Why you giving me the silent treatment? Come on, let's talk this through. I need to do the right thing by Jane. We do, don't we. So where is she? Where you hiding her?"

"Don't you think we'd better call Maude Jennings about this?"

"Oh, the DHS will get the paperwork when it's ready. No need to call Maude. Where you hiding her, Dick?"

"This nice adoptive family you have lined up," I said, "could that be Mr. and Mrs. Woo Chin of Boone, North Carolina?"

"Indeed, that's the very folks."

"I hear they are wealthy, Herb, but I also hear that the three girls they adopted previously are no longer among us. What became of them?"

"What girls? Who you talking about?"

"Wendy Miller, Nancy Gardner and Pamela Striker."

"Dick," he said with a patronizing attitude, "them girls has moved on to better things. Things they got by being adopted by the Chins. Oh, don't you worry about them girls. They's fine."

"Where are they?"

"I don't know exactly *where* they is at this very moment, but rest assured they're doing fine. Point is, I need for you to tell me where Jane is so I can bring her back and get her ready to be adopted by the Chins."

"And I just finished telling you, Herb," I said, becoming testy now, "that I'm not going to turn Jane over to you until I find out what happened to those girls. I want to know exactly where they are right this very minute, so I can call them and talk to them directly."

"Richard, that ain't possible. Neither is it necessary. Look, you're out of a job now, right? No income. Are you pushing me to have you arrested for kidnapping and child rape so you can find food and shelter in a country club prison or something? I don't think they'd make you do *hard* time, since you ain't got no record or nothing, but shoot, what do I know? You want I should let you take your chances?"

I took a deep breath and ordered myself to keep calm. "Two can play that game, Herb. You owe half a million dollars to the Internal Revenue Service. So I wonder: If you don't keep up your quarterly payments, you're on *your* way to one of those places, right? Now, put me in touch with those three girls and let me speak with them directly. If they are, as you say, doing fine, I'll turn Jane over to you. She won't like it, and we'll have to do it with sensitivity for her, but it can be done." I wondered if he knew I was bluffing.

"You're trying my patience, Richard." He leaned against my van and pulled out a pack of Camels, the old fashioned non-filtered kind, lit one up and stared at the top of the house as he exhaled. I resisted the urge to pull out a cigarette of my own and just watched Herb inhale and blow smoke.

"Richard, you're right, I do have problems with the IRS, but help me understand something here. Help me understand how you hope to get away with kidnapping a little girl, taking her all the way out here to California. A girl you know as well as I do will bust your butt for molestation, give her half a chance. Help me understand why you done that."

"Are you staying somewhere in town here, Herb?"

"Stick to the point."

"If you're staying somewhere handy, I'll be delighted to visit you, when you're able to put me in touch with Wendy, Nancy and Pamela. Until then, I'll ask you to make yourself scarce. Unless you want me to pursue this business about how much money you owe the Federal Government and how it would be impossible to make payments on your salary from Grandmother's Home. And what this, your financial situation, may have to do with the three girls."

"Got nothing to do with no girls. And my finances ain't none of your business. I still got my old business running. I sold it, but I retain forty-five percent interest in it. There's paper on that. My old business makes them payments, so you forget all about my finances now and turn Jane over to me, or your ass is in lockup, Richard. You understand me?"

I walked around the van, locking all the doors. It wouldn't do to have Herb Williston sorting through its contents after I went into Kent's house.

Momentarily, I wondered if I dove for his throat, could I knock him to the ground, keep him down and strangle him. Maybe I can, given the anger I felt. It would be no contest if we were younger. For he had evolved from Appalachian poverty runt to his present condition, while I had deteriorated from my youth on athletic scholarship to my present condition. While I'd been a pretty good free safety on the football field, he'd been a green beret, undergone special forces and commando training, jumped from planes into enemy territory, learned every way to kill a man the army could teach. And much of this while I'd been doing two-martini business lunches. I decided to chill out. Physical violence wasn't going to resolve anything anyway.

"I'm going to leave you now, Williston. I'm going to walk into the house. And if you're not on your way out of here by the time I get inside, I'm going to call the police. You can tell your story to them and we'll take it from there."

If he is really as innocent as he tries to pretend, he will sic the cops on me. If he's as sinister as Jane says he is, he will avoid the police.

"Kidnapper!" he yelled at my back as I walked away. Yelled loud enough for the neighbors to hear. The right-wing conservative rumormongering tactic was one of his staples.

At the back door, I turned and evil-eyeballed him a beat. He hitched up his pants, tossed his cigarette into Kent's back yard and walked toward the street.

The back door opens into the kitchen. I had no sooner closed it and heaved a sigh of relief when I was assaulted by chirping phones. Kent and Anna have two phones downstairs and two upstairs, plus a cordless that gets carried all over the place. I picked up the one on the kitchen wall.

"Dad!" came a voice I knew but couldn't identify momentarily. "Why haven't you come by to see me?"

Hampton, the son I so rarely hear from.

"You didn't even tell me you were coming out here to California. Are you playing favorites?"

"Not at all, Hampton, how are you?"

"How am I? I'm filing for divorce—or else Charlene is. We both are, I guess. It's going to get very messy. I've got to fly down to the Caribbean later today. I own an offshore bank, you know."

"No, I didn't know that." I didn't know much more about Hampton than his current address and home phone number, that he was married to this Charlene somebody whose father established a trust fund for her. She can't touch the principle—several hundred million, I'm told—but she lives off the interest and borrows on the principle. And Hampton, who had a masters in financial management from USC, had worked tirelessly to enlarge their combined financial worth. That's all I knew of his current life. Charlene preferred her wealthy friends and showed cool disdain toward her in-laws.

"So now you know. I want to see you. I was wondering if you'd drop me at the airport this evening, pick me up when I get back. And while I'm away, you can drive my Mercedes. Deal?"

"Son, I'll be happy to drop you at the airport. That will give us time to talk. But I don't need your Mercedes. I have my van."

"That old thing? Dad, how long have you been driving that broken down contraption? Do us both a favor and drive my car while I'm gone. That way, I won't feel qualms of conscience for asking you to pick me up when I get back."

"I'm on a pretty tight schedule," I said, enjoying my sudden hold over him. "Have to be in Oxnard before seven."

"No problem! My plane leaves at five thirty. Drop me off by five and you'll have two hours to get back to Oxnard. I'll zip over there and pick you up. We can talk. This is my first divorce, Dad. I need help."

"From me? I've never been through a divorce. How can I help you?"

A long silence, then: "You're my dad. I need to see you."

"Come on over. I love you, Hampton."

After that, I felt very tired. As I lay down on the couch in Kent's living room, I thought how the main thing in this life is to carry your burden and endure. I don't know where I got that idea, but it has stuck with me as a *given.* To endure until your time comes, then to die without regrets. To surrender totally to your inevitable and, perhaps, surprising end. No fears, no regrets, none of those depressing thoughts I'd been having since Mae passed.

And that thought led to the question: What's happening with Jane? Her mother looks in poor condition to take her. And I didn't hold out much hope for her auntie, either. But she's between the devil, Williston, and the deep blue sea of going back into the system.

20

I don't know what time it is when I get to the house. I know it's real late cause the lights are out in almost all the houses on this street, and they're out in Dick's son's house.

Mindy's so tired, I been carrying her under my arm for the past couple of hours. She's asleep.

By the time I walked back the driveway to the yard and seen the van, I was so bone tired I just plopped myself down and sat with my back against the rear tire. Get out Mindy's leash and fasten it to her collar and hook her to the van. She lays down in the grass and keeps on sleeping.

I stared at the house a long time, wondering if I should knock on the back door. Probably it would be Kent who come downstairs to answer the knock. He'd let me in, I knew that. He's nice. He'd let me sleep on that mattress in the room with the other kids.

But I'd have to explain what happened, how this man tried to grab me and I ran. How this guy hit my Mom, and I got picked up by a trucker who...

I really didn't even want to see my Mom. It's just that Dick gave me them choices. I hate mountains and don't know those friends of his, and I ain't seen my Auntie Phyllis since I was six. I barely remember her and she probably forgot I exist.

But my Mom, she's another story. She couldn't forget I exist. Or could she?

Funny how when you're dog-tired your worry wheel is liable to spin overtime. Mine sure was on overtime that night. I was thinking how I had it in the back of my head that my Mom would be happy to see me and want me to come live with her. And we'd do mother-daughter things, like go food shopping and clothes shopping. She'd get me into a school somewhere and I'd make her proud by doing my homework and getting good grades. And on weekends we'd jump into her car—which I imagined was new and big and shiny, a Caddy or a Lincoln or something like that—and we'd go touring around California. We'd see all those places they show in movies, like Disneyland and Magic Mountain, the Golden Gate Bridge, that kind of stuff.

I had all that and more in the back of my head when Dick drove me to that house this morning, and now here I am, dog tired from having to run away, get raped by a goddamn goon, and walk all those miles back to this house.

I thought about the other kids back in West Wing, and wished I could call Yoni, my best friend. But you can't make calls to the kids in Grandmother's Home. Can't even write to 'em without your mail being read by the staff, and if you say something the staff don't like, the kid never gets your letter, never even knows you sent it. I know ways around that but still...

Then I thought, Lord 'a mercy, why bother anybody inside the house, I can pick the lock, and then I can make a phone call to West Wing—I got the number in my memory—and I can tell old Enema Williston to shove her head up her fat ass.

But I didn't do nothing, just sat and stared at the house and let stuff run through my mind. Pretty soon I nodded off. When I woke up of a sudden and saw where I was, I got up, found the van's back door open and crawled in, flopped down on that pile of stuff I hid under, and went straight to sleep. Didn't even look to see if Dick was sleeping in his bunk bed.

113

21

S hortly before Hampton arrived at Kent's house, around one P.M., I put through a call to Maude Jennings and learned there'd been a new development in the case.

"There's nothing I or anyone else in this department can do about Herb Williston, Dick. The law enforcement people tell me they just don't have the evidence to justify having him picked up and formally charged."

Her tone had an irksome quality, conveying her frustration.

"So what you've got to do is put Jane on an airplane and send her back to us. We'll overnight mail you a ticket, which will fly her from Los Angeles to Atlanta, and have someone meet her there. Give me an address."

"She won't go, Maude."

"You're the adult authority in her life now, Dick. Getting her back here is your responsibility. Give me your address and we'll overnight the ticket, and you *put* her on that plane."

When Maude spoke in terms of "we," I had learned, it usually indicated that she was acting on orders.

I said, "You know the situation there—how can you want me to send Jane back to that?"

"I don't."

"Your department is wasting time and money. Jane will run."

"I understand your concern, and I'm with you about the Willistons. We're not going to send her back to Grandmother's Home—rest assured of that. I don't know what we're going to

114

do. It's become an extremely complicated case. We'll put her in lockup if that's the only way."

"I can't believe you're—"

"Look, Dick, we've discussed this case endlessly, and that's the decision, to bring her back here and take it from there. There's nothing else I can do."

"Have you tracked down Mr. Chin in Boone?"

"Yes, I spoke with him personally. Said he had no idea what I was talking about when I brought up the private school in Phoenix. He said the girls he adopted all have moved away and are doing fine. And since we have no evidence to the contrary..."

"Where did they move away to? Did you locate those girls? Talk to them?"

"He said we had to get a court order, and for that we'd need somebody in authority to say there was reason to believe... and there are people in high places who don't want to open this can of worms, and anyhow beyond the age of eighteen these kids are no longer our concern. That's the bottom line."

"Those three girls aren't over eighteen."

"I know that."

"Did you talk to Yoni about those post cards?"

"Yes, but Yoni went blank on me and said she didn't know about any post cards. We've nothing to go on, Dick."

"Do you have any idea why Herb Williston would care enough to fly out here to the Coast and try to grab Jane?"

"That's another thing I just found out. Herb was *sent* to the Coast by Grandmother's Home administration. By Mr. Sinclair himself. With orders to find Jane and bring her back. That makes it very above board and legitimate."

"In other words, your department will believe those kids when they say they've been molested, but you won't believe them when they say they're being *sold* into prostitution and drug addiction by staff members of Grandmother's Home. Is that it?"

"What it comes down to is that we have absolutely no evidence that any such a thing has happened to any one of those girls."

"I don't *believe* you, Maude."

"That's understandable," she said, then let a long pause go by. Too long. I sensed someone in authority was standing over her. "What's your address out there?" she finally asked, in a flat monotone.

Almost involuntarily, my hand returned the phone to its cradle.

I slumped back into Kent and Anna's beige couch to contemplate this latest change—and the door chimes sounded.

It was Hampton, wearing a dark blue blazer and white turtleneck. Handsome as a movie star at age thirty and driving a midnight blue Mercedes that looked like it had just come off a show room floor.

We embraced and quickly set off for the drive to Los Angeles. He asked how I was and I wanted to tell him about Jane. I said, "I'm very worried about that child, someone's after her."

Either he didn't hear what I'd said or chose not to discuss it, for he responded by talking about himself and his life, so it quickly became a one-sided conversation. I learned more about his life that afternoon than I cared to know. The marriage to Charlene and how nasty it had become, the offshore bank which only he, his lawyer and now I knew of, the wheelings and dealings he'd been involved in for commercial real estate, currency trades, and blocks of stocks and bonds, much of this done from the offshore bank, and how he'd been on the boards of two S&Ls which had declared bankruptcy or been shut down by the feds.

He said at one point that he was still grieving the death of his mother, yet what he showed me was anger over this breakup with his wife. Well, Hampton had always been self-absorbed, while Kent, his younger brother, had always been outgoing, generous, a tree-hugger concerned for all humanity.

"She's suing, of course," he said as he drove, "and I anticipate a nasty court battle over the property. That's why I've got to fly down to the Caribbean. I'm going to disappear some money so she can't get her meat hooks into it. I could deposit it in my bank in LA and do a wire transfer, of course, but then there would be a *record*. It's got to disappear without a trace."

I started to argue that this was not fair to Charlene, but checked myself. Charlene had her trust fund of several hundred million dollars. Hampton's reasoning was that she didn't need any part of his "hard-earned" money. Which he would not have "earned" without his marriage to her. For what he had done was borrow using her wealth as collateral, and parlay this into his own little fortune. It really wasn't the money that bothered him, I knew. The money was only a weapon in their battle.

He also said he might decide to live in the Caribbean somewhere—he wasn't yet sure which island he preferred. And he wondered if I might like to visit him down there, once he got settled. "They have these old estates, Dad, with magnificent guest cottages. You could live out the rest of your life in *style*."

I found that idea curious, since Hampton had been fairly remote from his parents and brother for the past few years. This remoteness began when he was a student at USC and, to be candid, his mother and I had felt wronged by it. After all, we had sacrificed considerably to put him through USC. Would the divorce change his attitude? I wasn't ready to believe it would.

Finally, around five P.M., while we were having a drink in the airport lounge, I stood and said, "I've got to go now, Hampton. You have a good flight and call me when you know when your return flight will land."

"Where are you going, Dad?" He looked hurt and amazed that I had a life of my own to worry about.

"I have to pick up that girl I told you about."

"What girl?"

I gave it to him again, this time in a nutshell. "She's twelve years old and she hid herself in my van. Ran away from that agency your mother and I worked for. She's desperate to stay out of the system."

His eyes narrowed to a squint as this penetrated his mind. Inspecting his chiseled features, I thought again how surprising is the transformation that occurs as children mature into adults. And as adults collapse into old age. I momentarily found myself wondering how Hampton would age.

"Dad, how can you take care of a twelve year old girl? You're too old for that."

"Yes, I am. But at the moment I have no choice. I'll get her placed somewhere eventually. Right now, I've got to drive up to Oxnard and—"

"Charlene and I... we can't have children."

"Why not?"

"They don't know. Seems my sperm count is plenty high enough, but a woman is... well, a more mysterious organism. I've often thought that if we adopted—"

"Adopt a newborn," I tossed out quickly, anxious to get away from this subject.

"Newborns are too much trouble. But we're going for the divorce. Forget I mentioned adoption."

I tried to imagine Jane settling in with Hampton and Charlene as her adoptive parents. The image swiftly fast-forwarded to her seducing Hampton, and then of him facing child molestation charges. I looked at my watch and said, "Well. I very much enjoyed our talk, Hampton. Let's do this more often. See you when you return. And be thinking of when would be a good time to scatter your mother's ashes at sea. Bye." And walked away.

He caught up to me. "You forgot the keys to the car, Dad." He took hold of my hand and raised it, plunked the keys into my palm, then gave me a hug. "I won't be so distracted by my own problems when I get back."

He patted my shoulder. Towering over me as he does, it made me feel vulnerable, even childish. You struggle to raise 'em, they grow rich, and then... For a moment, I envied Mae and her escape.

Across from the terminal, in the gigantic parking garage, I had to walk a mile or so searching for the car. I wasn't paying attention when he parked it. Then the drive to Oxnard was straight into the setting sun, reminding me that the last time I'd had my eyes examined, the doctor had said I would eventually need an operation to get rid of a cataract, which was now developing in my right eye. Growing old isn't easy.

By the time I got to Oxnard, I was talking out loud to my memory of Mae, telling her I did not want to go on living this way, grieving for her loss, trying to care for a teenager who'd been damaged by abandonment and sexual molestation and the cost-effective short-changing of Grandmother's Home, from whence she would be launched into the world of sex for money. Until she was deemed "too old," or "over the hill," at which time she would enter a world she knew little or nothing about, at what age? Well, knowing Jane, she would probably hang on longer than most.

At the front door to the house at the edge of a strawberry field, the former Mrs. Doyle stood in the doorway, an elbow against the doorjamb, and told me, in slow, halting words, "Jane ran away. Nobody knows where she is."

"Why did she run away?" I asked, noticing Mrs. Doyle's blank, zombie stare.

"How should I know? She just ran."

Mixed with the shock at that news was a feeling of relief. Putting myself in Jane's shoes, I think I would have run away from her mother's scene too. As I drove back to Carpenteria, I thought, That does it. If I ever see her again——how will she know how to get back to Kent's house?—I'll just have to put her on that plane and ship her back to whatever fate Maude and her DHS people can provide for her.

I was at the pits of despair when I got to Kent's house. I declined dinner and put through a call to Maude's home number. "Just called to give you my address here, Maude, so you can send that airline ticket."

But Maude's climate had undergone another change. "Don't give out your address. Lay low. I can't talk now, but there's more news. I'll tell you later. Call me later." It was that cryptic, over before I could get in another word. I was wondering if Maude was playing with, as the saying goes, a full deck. No, delete that thought. Maude is bright. Something's up. I'll find out later. And I'll have to tell her Jane has again disappeared.

When I told Kent and Anna that Jane had run away from her mother's place in Oxnard, Kent said, "Well, come on, Dad. Let's drive there and find her."

How could I tell Kent that Jane, an expert at getting herself picked up by strangers, was not likely to be found as easily as a stray dog. I tried to state the situation as simply as I could.

"If she wants to come back here, she'll come. Otherwise, there's no point trying to find her. If we did happen to find her— which is doubtful—she'd either be on her way here or else she'd be into something else and refuse to come to us."

I went out to the van and lay down in the bunk, snoozing for a couple of hours. When I awoke, I wondered what I'd be doing here if I didn't have Jane to worry about. Could I justify my existence by taking care of Kent's kids?

I rose and went back into the house. Everyone else had gone to bed by this time, around eleven o'clock. I thought about calling Maude. How, I wondered, was I going to pay for all these long-distance calls when Kent got the bill? I'll worry about that later. I called Maude.

"What I have to tell you, Dick, is that the latest is Alfred Sinclair is on his way to California."

Alfred Sinclair was the administrative director of Grandmother's Home. "After he sent Herb Williston out here?" I asked, astounded.

"That's according to one story. According to another, Herb took off on his own. I don't know which is true. But another thing, Dick: there is one law enforcement personnel, whose name I cannot divulge, who has taken it upon... himself to continue the investigation. I don't know who to believe any more, and I have so much work piled up it's ridiculous. Now, can I speak to Jane?"

"She's not here."

"You said she would not overnight at her mother's. Where is she?"

"When I went by her mother's place to pick her up, I was told she'd run away."

"Well... She'll come back, she always does. Listen, if I were you, Dick, I'd make myself scarce for awhile."

"I'll do that.

"Yes, and don't forget to keep in touch. Things keep *changing*."

Indeed. For around two o'clock, I awakened at the sound of the van's back door squeaking open. Jane's slim figure slipped inside, closed the door, and flopped down on the pile of camping stuff. I heaved a sigh of relief and started to speak, to ask her where in the world she'd been. But I hesitated. She was utterly exhausted. In less than a minute I heard her whispery snores. I got down from the bunk, got out a quilt and put it over her. I'd ask her tomorrow what had happened.

22

Next morning, he woke me up with a lot of fussing. Mindy's licking my face and making me laugh, and he's fussing. Said he thought he'd lost me forever. Said, What the hell happened, Jane?

I told how some man went after me and I ran, how I walked from where my Mom lives to this house. Didn't tell him about the trucker. What for? He'd only rise up into another boil.

Jane, he says, scrunching up his face all worried like, why didn't you call? I gave you those numbers.

I tried, Dick. Nobody was here. By the time I got the answering machine, the operator cut me off.

If no one's here, call the other numbers. Someone will come.

No need to call, I say, cause I ain't leaving here no more.

Well, sweetheart, he says, Herb Williston is prowling around. It's not safe for you here. So let's grab a quick breakfast, then figure out where you can go. I'll deal with Herb Williston.

Dick, can you get me my own can of Mace?

No no, honey. What I've got to do is get you out of harm's way. Till we get to the bottom of this Williston business.

I told you what Williston's doing. Him and Mr. Chin. And some others.

What others?

I just give him a look—how can I tell him more than I done told him. I say, I'm hungry. Ain't et since lunch yesterday. I ain't saying nothing more till I get fed.

Everybody was gone from the house again today. We had the big old house to ourselves.

Dick cooked up a mess of scrambled eggs while I took a shower and put on clean clothes. I put down them eggs like I hadn't et in a couple of weeks. I didn't have no supper last night, that's for sure. Only that lunchmeat sandwich at my Mom's house. Which kind of stuck in my throat after what happened.

I could tell Dick was real nervous about Herb Williston, cause he kept walking into the front room and looking out at the street, saying, Let's not dillydally, let's get a move on. Herb is bound to come back here.

After breakfast, he says, We're down to two choices. Which will it be? Do you want to visit your auntie in West Hollywood?

I wasn't sure.

Okay, let's drive up to the mountains. We can stay there, at the house of my friends.

I say, I don't like mountains. Reminds me of Grandmother's Home. Call my auntie. West Hollywood sounds cool.

I think I ought to take you to the mountains.

I *hate* mountains. Ain't going to no mountains.

Will you promise not to run away?

I won't run less I have to.

Well, if you have to, do you promise to call all those numbers I gave you?

All I need is money for the pay phone.

Okay, let's check out your auntie. I've got to get you placed somewhere, Jane.

Dick gets out his notepaper, the one he picked up in the motel when we first made it to California, and dials. Says, Hello, Phyllis Angelica? My name is Dick Steel, and I'm wondering if you're the sister of the former Mrs. Doyle.

Then he says, I'm calling about your niece, Jane Doyle. Yeah, she's with me right now. Would you like to talk to her?

123

Puts me on, and I say, Hello, Auntie, it's me, Jane. And she says, Oh Jane, so good to hear from you. How are you? Where are you? Are you in California?

Sounds real glad, so I tell her I'm in this town called Carpenter something. And she says, Wonderful! Let's get together! So I says, Okay, and hand the phone back to Dick.

He tells her we plan to be in LA and he can bring me to her place. Today. She seems to hem and haw over that but Dick says we'll be there in an hour and a half.

I hold up Mindy and say, Ain't going there without Mindy.

He says, Uh, can Jane bring her puppy? Okay, I'll tell her. Then he hangs up.

You can't bring Mindy, he says.

Then I ain't going!

Okay, then it's the mountains.

But why can't Mindy go?

Some people just don't like dogs.

You take care of Mindy. I'll go see my auntie. I ain't going back to no damn mountains.

Then we go outside and get into a car, a big old Mercedes. Newer and spiffier than the BMW Hurt and Enema drive. I never even noticed it was here. Dick tells me it's his other son's car. I say, Well, Mercedes is expensive, Dick. Your son must be rich! When can I meet him?

He says, When this blows over. Now we have things to do.

I left my overnight bag at Mom's when I made my get-away, so Dick takes me to a store and buys me another bag, and a new blouse, panties and jeans. He don't buy me the jeans I want, the ones with the patch on 'em, says *Jordache*. Buys me ones with no name on 'em and tells me it don't take no brains to design jeans, cause they done been designed for over a hundred years. He don't understand sex appeal. Well, he's old.

Walking out that store, I says, Dick, how come you won't buy me the Jordache?

He says, Jordache! What does that name mean to you? It's just a name to triple the price. What's so important about it?

I got Jordache on my ass, I'm class. Ain't gonna track cow shit into nobody's living room. Means I'm clean and sweet and got money and so everybody should love me.

Says, Oh Jane, drop it and let's move on. Jordache isn't going to change the shape of your rear end.

No, but it's gonna make me feel a whole lot better about it.

You don't have to *buy* feeling good about your butt, Jane. You're a beautiful young woman. Thank your maker for that.

So who's my maker?

Come on, you know, you've been to church.

I hate church.

Well, he's the Great Spirit, Creator of the Universe.

Okay, Dick, you got me in over my head. I'll shut up.

Then we go to this other store, and Dick buys me a new toothbrush, some toothpaste, a comb and hairbrush and some other stuff, and a little bag to carry this stuff in. And after that, we hit the interstate again, heading for LA.

Auntie Phyllis Angelica, turns out she lives in this real fine house way up on a hill. You can stand on her back porch and see nothing but city forever. And smog. You can see the yellowish brown smoke rising up off freeways all over the place. It's like being on a mountaintop looking down, except instead of valleys and rivers with fog and mist, there's buildings and freeways with yellowish brown smog.

Auntie Phyllis says she's just got divorced and she got this house in the divorce settlement. You don't got to put two and two together to figure she got money too. This house and the clothes she's wearing says it all.

Auntie Phyllis gets us sitting around on her back porch, looking at the view, and brings out coffee for Dick and her, and a glass of orange juice for me. I wish she'd of brung me coffee too, but I don't let on.

They make small talk awhile, and Dick goes with Auntie Phyllis for a little tour of her house, then says he has to get back. While he's standing in the living room beside my auntie, he gives me this look, like a tiny nod and a little smile. I know what he means by that. While we was driving down here, he said he didn't know what to tell my auntie about my situation, so we'd just wait and see what she already believes. What she already believes is Dick is my foster daddy, I guess. Or else she just don't care who he is to me, cause she ain't asked no questions and we ain't told her nothing.

Dick's getting ready to leave and I start worrying. What the hell am I gonna do all day and night with this auntie? But Dick keeps giving me that little nod, saying it's gonna be all right.

Well, you two, he says to my auntie, have a nice visit.

Oh we will, says Auntie Phyllis. How long can she stay?

Overnight, says Dick, I'll pick her up tomorrow. I'll call before I come. She has my number—several numbers for me—if you need to get in touch.

Just when Dick's leaving, getting into that big old dark blue Mercedes, the phone rings and after Auntie Phyllis runs back inside to get it, Dick says, Now you be sure to call if anything goes wrong, you hear?

I don't know, Dick. Something don't feel right about this.

Oh, it's just that you haven't seen your mother's sister in so many years. Get acquainted. Have fun.

I feel like everybody's trying to get rid of me. Dick drives off down the hill and I go back inside the house, and Auntie Phyllis says, Guess what! Your Mom just called. With real good news.

What good news?

Some gentleman from North Carolina—you know, that place you was staying, what's the name? Grandmother's Home. He's such a nice man! He's gonna get your Mom out of debt and take you back there on an airplane.

I ain't going!

126

She looks at a little slip of paper by the telephone and says, Herb Williston's the name, and he's such a wonderful man, he's gonna help your Mom out of debt! Just for picking you up to bring you back to North Carolina. Ain't you lucky?

I ain't going, I tell her again, but she ain't listening. She picks up my overnight bag and says, Come on, honey, come see the nice new car I got.

She opens a door in her kitchen and it goes out to a garage, and here's this big old Jaguar, green and sleek and all.

I says, Auntie Phyllis, you got a nice car and I'd sure like to go for a ride in it, but I ain't going back to no Grandmother's Home with no Herb Williston. And that's final!

Oh well, she says, come on, let's go for a ride then. I'll show you some West Coast sights.

She slings my overnight bag onto the back seat and we get in. Coasting down her long hill, she says, Now why wouldn't you want to help out your poor mom, girl?

Why you-all selling me to Herb Williston?

Honey! Nobody's *selling* you. We're just saying, why not go with that nice man, honey? You'll be *well* taken care of.

He ain't no nice man. He's a lying scumbag child molesting *crazy*!

Well, that's not a healthy attitude, she says. Honey, in this world you gotta *go* along to *get* along. Now I know your mama wouldn't tell me this man's nice if he wasn't. Besides, darling, your mama needs the money he's gonna pay to get her out of debt and back on her feet. And you *do* want to help your only ever-loving *mama*, don't you?

Why is everybody always trying to get rid of me, I yell, and start to cry.

Honey, it ain't nothing like that. You hush that crying right now! You hear me? You listen up. I got the full story on you and that kidnapper who drove you to my place.

Dick ain't no kidnapper!

Your mom got told by the administrator of that home you was in that if she cooperates with the man who brung you here, Dick, she's gonna wind up in prison along with him.

Prison!?

And this other man, Mr. Williston, is here to see that your mom gets the help she needs and that you get taken back to North Carolina like you needs. Is that clear?

Auntie Phyllis, stop the car, I'm getting out.

You hush your mouth, young lady, and sit tight. I ain't stopping till we get to your mom's house.

I ain't going in there, some man tried—

Oh yes you are. You're too young to be out on your own.

My insides feel like a blender on high. I stare out the window, watching hills go by. Then we pass shopping centers and office buildings and apartment houses. Everything looks a little hazy here, like that yellowish smoke from the freeways is so thick in the air, it's like fog. Guess that's why they call it smog.

What the hell am I doing here? Why don't Dick just take me somewhere and we'll live together like father and daughter? Who needs such an auntie as this? Taking me back to my Mom's, where I damn near got snatched the day before.

My heart's pounding when we turn off the freeway and go driving back this street and that, and pretty soon we're pulling up in front of Mom's place.

And there's two cars in front. The crummy little sports car with no top and a brand new white expensive brand.

Auntie gets out of her Jaguar and yells, Yoo Hoo, Helen!

And out onto the front porch comes Mom and this guy Enrique, and some other guy, dressed real spiffy, I ain't never seen before.

I don't think twice. Grab my overnight bag, out the car and take off running. Across this dirt street Mom lives on and back between houses, then left down an alley toward the ocean. I can move a lot faster without Mindy, but I miss her.

23

Her Aunt Phyllis' address in West Los Angeles turned out to be more reassuring than her mother's in Oxnard. Phyllis Angelica's house perched upon a hillside overlooking the city of angels, the sort of place which had been built a few decades ago and added onto several times. Its current market value, I would guess, is somewhere in the neighborhood of a few million, barring a downturn, and there hasn't been a turndown in California real estate since the Great Depression. That suggested that Auntie Phyllis could do wonderful things for her niece, if she chose to.

Phyllis Angelica's appearance was not as reassuring, however. Oh, she was dressed expensively, in keeping with her piece of real estate here, but she emanated something that caused me to feel a bit insecure. Something I couldn't name or define at the time.

She had thin lips and a large gap between her upper lip and the base of her nose. She spoke like a ventriloquist, very little movement of her lips. Her eyes had a doleful expression, lids at half-mast, cow-brown pupils that seemed to be unfocused. The only resemblance to her sister, Jane's mother, was her wavy chestnut hair, which was tied loosely with a pink ribbon and hung down her back halfway to her buttocks. She obviously took good care of herself and appeared to have been treated a lot better by life than her sister. Still, there was something that made me feel uneasy and Jane wasn't entirely at ease either. But I was willing to give it a try. For one overnight.

After that we'd talk and maybe try another overnight. We'd take it one step at a time and see what sort of relationship would form between aunt and niece. I was hopeful that something good would come of it. Certainly this woman had the money to take care of Jane, if she wanted to. And once we got Herb off our backs, the legalities could be worked out through Maude.

Before I left, we had a little chat, during which I told Ms. Angelica that Jane had visited her mother yesterday, but that visit had not gone so well. I told her I hoped things would go better with her, for Jane really needed to reconnect with the family she'd been born into. Ms. Angelica said she wholeheartedly agreed.

When I got back from Los Angeles, my plan was to call either Kent or Anna and tell them I could be reached at my friend Knor's place in the mountains for the next few days. I had no desire to just hang around this house as a sitting duck for Herb Williston. He was probably tracking me and was not going away until he had what he'd come for—-or gotten himself arrested trying. And there was still the possibility that he'd try to have me arrested for kidnapping. I really didn't think he was crazy enough to try that, but I couldn't discount the possibility. Up in the Knor's place in the mountains, I'll have time to see what Maude comes up with next.

I enjoyed driving Hampton's Mercedes. A lot swifter and surer ride than my old van. So my immediate plan was to transfer what we'd need in the mountains from the van to the car and take off. If Herb tried to follow, I knew I could lose him in the mountains.

This plan was abruptly aborted, however, when I drove the Mercedes up the alley to the backyard to park it next to the van, and almost ran into the rear end of a Ford Taurus. Sinclair stood beside the Taurus, smiling broadly.

Sinclair was always smiling broadly. He stands about six feet six inches tall and resembles a bowling ball. *Round* is the word. From the seemingly basketball-sized head that sits on shoulders without benefit of an apparent neck, down to the huge belly that flares out in three directions to culminate at the top of his thighs—but even his legs are round, right down to his extralarge shoes which must be extra-wide too, for the toes aren't pointed, they're *rounded.*

When there was no reason to smile and considerable reason to be serious, this wide grin on his rotund face was disconcerting. Even more painful to contemplate were my suspicions that Maude's vacillations were due to his manipulations.

Mr. Sinclair's main responsibility at Grandmother's Home was to raise money. From the United Way and among church people, who were only too pleased to hand over thousands, thus massaging their social consciences. Since everyone of any importance in those parts of North Carolina were church people, and since they *loved* Sinclair as an orgiastic release for their guilts, there wasn't much they wouldn't do for him. He had only to ask.

"Hi, Dick!" he flashes me with his wide, toothy, public relations smile. "Bet you never expected to see me here."

I'd never known there was so much money to be made in the child-care business until the evening he and his Mrs. had Mae and me to dinner in their splendid ten-bedroom house. He couldn't have done better if he'd plundered a major corporation. I reasoned that a man who could pose as such a devout church-go'er while amassing such a fortune in the childwarehousing business could probably terminate my life without missing a line in his hymnal.

131

He was at my car window in a New York second, as Herb would call it. Leaning elbows on it. My finger was on the button to raise the window, but I resisted.

"Dick, I've got to talk to you. Have you seen Herb Williston?"

"Why do you ask?"

"I believe he's... eh, I believe he's..."

"He's what?" I'd never known Sinclair to get tongue-tied before.

"I don't know but there are some nasty rumors about selling kids to sex rings. I don't know what it's all about but we've got to find him. Where's Jane?" That was his real question.

"Not here."

Sinclair was famous for leading with a misleading statement. If he gave the impression he was aligned against Williston, that could very well mean he was trying to sucker me into a trap. The general feeling among staff at Grandmother's Home was that you could count on only one thing when dealing with Alfred Sinclair: ulterior motives. Whatever he led with was probably a smoke screen.

"She's still under our legal care, you know," he said. "Which means we've got to take her back to Grandmother's Home. You know that, I trust." A sarcastic smile spread his lips.

"Excuse me," I said, "while I park the car." I backed out of the driveway and was tempted to keep going and leave all this behind, but curiosity stopped me. Was Sinclair really looking for Williston? Or was he with him in the sex slavery business?

I wasn't about to take his word. He'd lied about the salaries he would pay Mae and me, then lied about providing us with a free apartment—he charged rent—and the use of an agency vehicle—once he knew we were there to stay awhile, he "advised" that we use our own personal vehicle. Little things but they add up.

"Well?" he said as I entered the back yard. "Where is Jane? And how can we get hold of Herb Williston? It's imperative that

I bring Jane back to North Carolina, Dick. I hope you understand that. For your *own* good as well as hers."

"Let's go inside and have a cup of coffee, Mister Sinclair."

That's what we staff called him, Mister. We called him Alfred only in derision behind his back.

"I have a hunch," I said, "that if we hang around here, Herb will show up."

"And Jane?" he asked, following me up the steps onto the back porch.

"I need guarantees that she will not be sold into prostitution. Which is what has happened to some other girls from Grandmother's Home. Wendy Miller, Nancy Gardner and Pamela Striker. Those three have been named. Might there be others? Where do you fit into that business, Sinclair?"

No doubt he heard my words as snotty, uppity, disrespectful.

He didn't reply until we were both inside and I'd ushered him into a chair at the large kitchen table. "Dick, this nasty rumor could ruin Grandmother's Home." He didn't allude to what it could do to him personally. "That's why I'm here." His grin had lost some of its toothiness.

"If the allegations turn out to be true, Herb belongs in jail, for a long, long time. So does his wife Emma. And anyone else that's mixed up in this. Including you, if—"

"Don't get crazy on me, Dick! I hate this business as much as you do, probably a lot more. I have so much more at stake. But this thing is not going to the police or a court of law. We're going to handle these allegations ourselves, my friend. Do you understand me?"

The coffee maker's automatic power cutoff had kicked in while I was away. I poured two cups, put them in the microwave to heat up. This activity gave me time to think before I said:

"You're not going to drag me into this, Sinclair. It's not my job to defend you. I'm only interested in keeping Jane out of you-all's clutches," I said, trying out an acquired Southernism.

He sounded a sinister note: "You don't have much choice, my friend. I can have you picked up in a matter of minutes for kidnapping. And that's exactly what I'll do if..."

He beamed his biggest grin and held out his round arms. Even under the dark gray suit and vest, the arms bulged. His entire presence was hammy, ridiculously grinning and cunning. He was a cunning son of a bitch who routinely cooked the books and shortchanged the kids to enrich himself.

He hadn't filled in the words after the "if." I took our two coffees out of the mike and brought them to the table. "If...?"

"Dick, what do you think will become of those children we care for at Grandmother's Home if this thing gets into the courts?"

"Maybe they'll be subjected to a lot less hypocrisy," I suggested.

"Be serious, man," he insisted, beaming even wider than before, his globular brown eyes trying to gleam above his bright white teeth.

"Tell you what," I said, lacing my coffee with half-n-half and sweetener. "You wipe that shit-eating grin off your ugly face and I'll hear you out. If I like what I hear, I'll cooperate in bringing in Herb Williston. But not Jane. She's out of the system now and wants to stay out, and I'm not turning her back in—unless or until we get to the bottom of what happened to those three other girls."

"That's kidnapping, you know." He made an obvious effort not to grin.

"So have me arrested."

"No police or courts, Dick. Don't you understand the cones-quences?"

"For you, sure. I'm not mixed up in any of that."

"Okay. First things first. Where can we find Williston?"

"Just cool your butt awhile and my guess is Williston will show up."

"Maude Jennings says that Jane stowed away in your van. Is that *really* what happened?" he asked with a conspiratorial smirk.

I ignored the implication. "Yes. I didn't know she was in the van until my second night on the road."

"Well, when you discovered she was in your van, why didn't you call us," he asked with a lift of his heavy eyebrows, "or hand her over to whatever social services were nearest?"

How could I tell Sinclair that Jane had me in a damned-if-you-do, damned-if-you-don't bind? Williston could understand this but not Sinclair. It was not a noble choice I'd made but I was stuck with it.

In response to his question, I merely shrugged and glanced at my wristwatch. Fifteen minutes to three o'clock. I wondered how Jane was getting along with her auntie in West Hollywood. I also wondered how I was going to get moved to the mountain house and pick her up tomorrow, now that Sinclair was here.

"You could have saved everyone involved a lot of trouble," he said, cunning curling the ends of his mouth, "if you'd done the right thing."

"Would handing her over to you-all to be sold into prostitution be the right thing?"

"If that is what Williston is up to," he said, now wearing his bargaining smile, "we'll certainly put a stop to it. You can count on that."

"You've never done anything but lie in the past. Anything changed?"

He held the cup of coffee close to his lips. His grin transformed to a pucker momentarily as he blew at the steaming brew. He sipped, put the cup down, looked me straight in the eye and projected sincerity. "What Williston has done has put all our lives in great danger."

"Seems to me that if you wanted to nail Williston, all you'd have to do is put out the signal back at your agency. The kids would come up with the evidence you need."

Then, as if I'd said the magic word, door chimes sounded. Guess who'd come calling.

"You know why I'm here," said Herb Williston.

"Come in, I've got a surprise for you."

His face lit up with anticipation. I'm sure he thought my surprise was a compliant Jane.

24

My legs are still sore from walking all those miles yesterday. My left heel got a blister, too, so I take off my sneakers and go barefoot.

Coming out the end of one alley, I see that topless sports car cruising the street. I duck down behind a trashcan and wait till it goes by. Damn! Close call! And I'm still a long walk from the beach.

I stick to the back alleys and keep going, but then you run out of alleys and have to walk the side of this highway, past a boat harbor and a park and some condos and whatnot, before you can make it onto the beach. If there's a shortcut, I don't know it.

Must be high noon by the time I get to the beach. Gotta keep walking with the ocean on my left. Gonna be night again by the time I get there.

If I get there. Both my feet are sore and so are my legs. Dog tired. Hungry. Then I remember how Dick told me to call, and this money he give me. Five-dollar bill. In case you get stuck, he said. Give me a call. And he stuck three phone numbers in my pocket.

I come to the place where this smallish kind of river flows into the ocean and sit down on them big rocks to rest. Take out the piece of paper with the numbers on it.

Sure does make more sense to call him than to keep on banging my sore feet against the ground. But where can I go to find a phone?

I head inland and find a road. Turn left on this road and up ahead is a boat harbor with stores and stuff around it. One of them stores says Liquor.

I'm jogging along, anxious to get to that liquor store and find a phone.

There's one outside beside the door. But now I need change, so I go inside and there's a gray-haired old dude with gold-rim glasses behind a cash register. Can I help you? Yeah, I need change to make a phone call.

Dick said call collect. Just drop a quarter in and dial O first, then this number. I try Kent's house with the old dude peering out the window at me, wondering what's going on. I give him a none of your business look.

I get through the recorded voices and finally hear Dick on the other end. Where are you?

I'm in front of some liquor store near a boat harbor.

Give me your phone number, I'll call you right back.

I read off the numbers on the pay phone, then hang up and wait. Seems like an hour before the phone rings.

Okay, says Dick, stay where you are.

I gotta stay here, Dick, I ain't got no legs left.

Okay, give me the address there.

I said, by a boat harbor.

There's more than one boat harbor in your area code, Jane. Is there anyone there you can ask? Ask 'em for the name of the street you're on. I need an address so I can find you.

I let the phone hang and run back into the liquor store. Where is this? Give me the address of this place here.

The old dude says, You're at Haley's Liquors in the Ventura Marina.

I shoot back to the phone and tell Dick. He says, Stay right there and don't move. Don't go anywhere. You hear me, Jane?

Only reason I might have to move, I tell him, is if my Mom and her boyfriend drive by and spot me. Or my goddamn son of a bitching auntie does.

I can hear him breathing at the other end awhile, then he says, Okay, keep out of sight as best you can. You know my son's car, don't you?

Blue Mercedes.

Right. Keep an eye out for it, that's what I'll be driving.

Hurry, Dick. I'm so damn dog-tired I feel like I'm dying.

Just one question, Jane. How did you get from L.A. to Ventura?

My auntie come up with this bullshit, how Herb Williston's gonna get my Mom out of debt if I go back to North Carolina with him.

Wait a minute. Run that by me one more time.

See, my auntie took me in her car back to my Mom's house, cause she said my Mom said that Herb Williston... Oh, shit, Dick, can you just come here real fast and pick me up? I'll tell you all about it then. They're trying to sell me to pay off my Mom, is what it comes down to.

Hang on, Jane. I'll be there in about half an hour.

25

I got a perverse kick out of foxing Herb, for it quickly became evident, when he found Sinclair in the kitchen, that his quest had now become much more urgent. I momentarily regretted that the can of Mace was in the van and not hooked to my belt.

While Herb stood there gaping at Sinclair, I said, "You take your coffee straight, right?"

As I read their body language at this point, they were not on friendly terms. Sinclair's perpetual smile had taken on hints of the sinister, and Williston extended his handshake while keeping his body as far away from Sinclair as possible.

Even so, it was as though we had moved our regular monthly staff meeting from the old stone buildings of Grandmother's Home to Kent's kitchen. Their muttered half-hearted hellos over the distant, cool handshake was followed by Williston pulling up a chair at the end of the table to Sinclair's right.

I poured another cup of coffee, heated it in the microwave and put it in front of Williston. No one said anything for quite a while.

Finally, Sinclair grinned his widest at Williston and said, "Been hearing some strange rumors about you, Herb. Care to fill me in?"

"Why, Mr. Sinclair, I'm just doing the job you hired me to do. Which, if I had the cooperation of Dick here, would be a whole lot easier to get done."

Sinclair pondered that a few beats, then showed his magnificent teeth again and said, "Rumor has it that you have no intention of bringing Jane back to North Carolina, Herb. Help me understand how such a rumor could get started."

They talked like they were reading a script. I wasn't buying it.

"Well, Mr. Sinclair, you know how rumors fly about on campus. Why in the world would I not bring Jane back?"

"Rumor has it you might sell her."

Herb rocked back in a hearty laugh and slapped the table with the palm of his right hand. "Darn! If that don't beat all! Sell Jane? Who in the world would *buy* Jane?"

Sinclair shot me a look, his perpetual grin frozen in place.

"Perhaps you could tell us that, Herb."

"Why," I asked, "did you try to grab Jane yesterday while I was in the Post Office? She had to spray you with Mace to stay out of your clutches."

"Dick, you must be imagining things. I have no idea what in the world you're talking about."

"Talking about three girls who were signed over to the care of one Mr. and Mrs. Chin in Boone. From there they seem to have been sent to a boarding school in Phoenix, which may or may not exist. And from there, they are said to have been sent to such exotic places as Tokyo, Hong Kong and Bangkok."

Sinclair's frozen smile looked a little strained, I noticed. Williston's lantern jaw had been lifted a notch and thrust out more Mussolini-like than before. The two of them were eying each other now. Was each waiting for the other to speak to this point? Were they really at odds? Or in cahoots and trying to throw me off?

Just then the four phones chirped. I left the pair of them suspended in their standoff and picked up the kitchen phone.

It was a collect call from Jane. Without giving away who I was talking to, I quickly told her to give me the number she was calling from and I'd get right back to her. I wrote it down on the same scrap of paper I'd been carrying around since the motel in Blythe, amazed to find that her area code was 805 rather than 213 in LA.

"Gentlemen, I must leave you to make an important business appointment. Help yourselves to more coffee." They did not appear pleased to be left together. "I'm going upstairs to change clothes. Be back in a minute."

Upstairs in the master bedroom, I sat in an easy chair and dialed the number she'd given me. She picked up on the first ring.

I had to get her to give me her location, which meant she had to find this out. This took a couple of minutes. I worried that either Williston or Sinclair might listen in on the downstairs extension. If they did, I'd know it by the change in the connection sound. I heard none.

Jane said she was in front of Haley's Liquor Store at the Ventura Marina. I wasn't sure what part of the Marina this was, but I would find her, even if it meant driving from one end of the marina to the other. Before we disconnected, I quipped, "You seem to have a proclivity for liquor stores."

"What's a proclivity?"

"Look it up."

"I don't got no dictionary here."

I tried to find out how she'd gotten from LA to Ventura but her explanation was confused and confusing. I'd find out later. I changed my shirt.

When I got back to the kitchen, I tried to read Sinclair's and Williston's feelings. They seemed more at ease with each other now, or was that my imagination? They were now less tense, less formal with each other, as though they now shared a secret. Or maybe had forgotten the act they were putting on for my benefit.

"Gentlemen," I announced, "I must terminate this gathering. Urgent family business. One of my grandchildren needs my attention. Where are you staying?"

Sinclair pulled from his jacket pocket a card from a motel in Carpenteria, The Great Western, only a few blocks away. "Room two ten," he said.

Williston was not as forthcoming. "I'll be in touch," he said, heading for the door. "No need to see me out. I know the way."

Herb wouldn't find me in this house again, for I'd be in the mountain house from now on.

Sinclair, after we'd heard the front door close, winked and said, "You're going to pick up Jane, aren't you. Did she run again? That girl! Always running, then calling to be rescued."

"I'm picking up my grandkids at their school."

"Sure," he drawled. "Don't worry, I won't try to follow you. I have other resources."

I shook my head and said nothing. I opened the back door and waited for him to take the hint. He stood, smoothed out some wrinkles in his splendid attire, grinned and said, "Dick, don't get yourself in over your head. You know what the law says. Do the right thing."

"Keep in touch," I said snidely.

He walked out, hesitated on the back porch as though he wanted to say one more parting word, then thought better of it and walked to his rented Ford Taurus. As he turned the key to start the engine, he shot me one last public relations grin. I closed the door.

Then I grabbed my white hooded jacket, locked up the house and went out to the Mercedes. Grandmother's Home supervisors were known to use bugging devices to get an inside line on staff members. Sinclair had not had a chance to monkey with the Mercedes, but what about Williston? I hoped he'd not come prepared to do that, or had not had time to do it before I was behind the wheel.

143

I guessed one or both would try to follow me, and the rear-view mirror soon framed Williston's white Chevy a block or so behind.

I drove to the nearest onramp going north toward Santa Barbara, then floored the accelerator and averaged around 90 miles an hour, weaving in and out of traffic averaging around 70. The white Chevy faded. I'd pushed the needle up over 110 before I made it to the next off ramp, got off there and drove under the freeway, and got back on headed south.

The white Chevy was nowhere to be seen.

I had no trouble finding Haley's Liquor Store. Jane came popping out of it, carrying her sneakers in one hand and feeding herself a sandwich with the other, her dark curly hair in disarray, a worried frown creasing her forehead.

"Gawd, Dick! Am I glad to see you! Where's Mindy?"

"She's fine, with Kent and Anna. Now tell me. What in the world happened this time?"

"First you gotta promise me."

"Promise you what?"

"That you're gonna quit trying to get rid of me. I can't take this no more. My Mom don't want me and neither does my auntie. You gotta let me stay with you, Dick. Promise!"

My heart went out to her, yet how in the world could I take care of her? I was in no shape to take care of myself. I would have to find some solution to her plight, though, for otherwise I couldn't live with myself. "Okay, what we've got to do first is get you out of harm's way."

"Yeah," she brightened. "How we gonna do that?"

"Let's drive up to the mountains and see what we find there."

"Mountains! Gee-zuz, Dick! Do you have to take me back up into *mountains?*"

"Either that or turn you over to—take your choice—your mom, your auntie, Sinclair, or Williston. Which will it be?"

When I got no reply, I glanced over and saw a tear running down her dusty cheek.

"Don't worry, sweetheart. I won't turn you over to any of them."

"If you adopt me, Dick, I swear—I promise—I'll go to school and get all A's. I'll do anything you want. Just adopt me or foster me or whatever, and I'll be so good you'll love me forever and ever. I swear on a stack of Bibles a mile high!"

The tearful pleading of a girl on the cusp of womanhood. I needed to get the latest from Maude as soon as possible.

I gritted my teeth and drove for the mountains. After awhile, Jane forgot her grief, switched on the radio and tuned in some country music. I gritted my teeth some more and wondered why I was doing this. Where would it all lead?

"Now tell me," I said, "what's all this about your auntie taking you to your mom's, so your mom could turn you over to Williston—*for money?* Did I hear you right on the phone?"

"You heard. That's about the size of it. My auntie says my mom could get herself out of debt from the money Williston would give her for handing me over so he could take me back to North Carolina—but there ain't no way I'm gonna let 'em do that."

I wondered how deep in debt her mom was. And how much Williston had promised to pay. And what motivated her auntie to go along with such a scheme.

Jane could be shockingly candid about some things and just as shockingly misleading about other things. Her story left me with questions but the larger, more important questions concerned Williston and Sinclair.

I kept an eye on the rearview mirror as we turned off 101 and headed up San Marcos Pass. I pulled off the road and waited a couple of minutes to make sure neither was following. Jane sat with her jaw clenched, staring straight ahead, saying nothing.

26

Gee-zuz-fucking-christ-all-son-of-a-bitch-mighty! Dick took me up in the mountains!

All my life somebody been taking me away from where I want to be and setting me down where *they* think I *should* be. Telling me it's for my own good.

People I love. My Dad. My Mom. My social worker.

Dick.

At least I got Mindy. She's looking for me to take care of her. I see it in her eyes.

Well, okay, I know I'm not a full grownup. I *feel* grown up, but then Dick told me the other day that he *feels* young. He ain't young. And I ain't all the way growed up. I can understand that.

What I *don't* understand is why I ain't got the right to live my own life my own way. People all the time telling me I'm wrong and trying to get rid of me. Or trying to drop me off the planet.

It's like I'm living in a closet blindfolded with people beating on me with clubs. I don't know why I'm in this closet, why I'm getting beat, or who's beating me. All I know is I hurt.

It's like in Washington D.C. they decided that anyone whose mom or dad couldn't take care of them because they couldn't make enough money, then those kids had to go into the system. I heard it on the radio news. And in the system, you're told that you are a pile of shit—otherwise why would you be there—so being a piece of shit, you got to raise your self-esteem. When I was younger, the word esteem sounded to me like steam. I had to raise my steam. My self steam. So I steamed out every which way I could think of. Got me in a lot *more* trouble. *More* people telling me I should raise my self-esteem. Put me in the mountains, where there's no way to raise nothing.

If I only had *one* somebody in this life. One somebody who really loved me. Didn't want to get rid of me. Just took me for the acting-out slut I am and loved me anyhow. If I only had that one person... I wouldn't care, I'd go with it. I'd get a suntan of the soul from it.

I thought, back when I first run to Dick's van, that he could be that someone. Him and Mae—us kids called them Mr. and Mrs. Sweet and Sour. They was the mostest sweetest grown-ups I'd ever known. They never tried to dump their own emotional garbage on us. They always tried to find out how we really felt.

So when Mrs. Sweet died so sudden, it went right down into my gut. That's when I started laying plans to hide out in Dick's van and go with him, where ever he gonna go. California? I found out he was going there from rumors and then from listening to him talk to himself. Or maybe he was talking to Mae, his wife. Whatever. I said to myself, if Mr. Sour is going to California, then I'm going with him.

Guess if you was a social worker or such, you could say I had a crush on Dick. Gray haired old pot belly and all. Okay. But he was *from* California, going back to California, and I was only this poor old broken down girl who wanted to have a grown up person to talk to, to take care of me. If he was broke, I could go out and bring home some money, no problem.

So we get out here in California and what happens. He tries to get rid of me. He sends me to my Mom, she can't take care of me—she's too wigged out on booze and drugs to take care of herself. I almost get grabbed by some weird dude there, then I get raped by a trucker looks like a TV wrestler.

So then Dick sends me to my Auntie, who is rich rich rich, but she only wants to take me back to my Mom's, to get my Mom out of debt. Am I only something to sell?

If anybody's gonna sell me, it oughta be me.

Old Hurt and Enema always banging it into my head that they hate my pussy and my ass, my... feelings. Calling me Miss America, like they think that I think I'm better than everybody else. I don't think better or worse. I only want to feel okay. Right now, right here.

Funny thing is, this house Dick brings me to, it makes me feel okay, even though it is in the mountains. I don't know why. Makes me feel like I own what's inside my own skin. Don't *need* nothing else. I'm an inside out Teenaged Ninja Turtle. I carry my house around inside myself. I karate kick from my mind and will power. I can fight back and win sitting still. That's how I'm feeling when Dick takes me into this mountain house. Next to a rush of water, makes me feel... just so. Not good, not bad, just so.

And I ask myself, What's the name of the game? What you supposed to do here in this life, girl? And staring out at the flowing water, the answer comes to me. Get rich rich rich. Then nobody can second-guess you, nobody gonna tell you what they think you *should* do. They only gonna suck up to you cause you rich.

And I ask myself, How am I supposed to get rich? Gone downhill since I was born. How am I gonna turn my trip around and go uphill to rich? Ain't no big mystery. Sell what I got that people want. What they want off me is sex. Be a hooker, like I been before. Prostitute.

Staring out at the river, looking flashy white in what's left of the sunlight, rushing along, going where it's going, not worried about a thing, I say to myself, so if I'm gonna sell sex thrills to strangers—which is what prostitutes do, right—then who's gonna protect me from the crazies? Cause I seen more than my share of them already. And there ain't no answer to that... except Dick.

I know, I know. Dick's got a big problem with prostitution. Maybe he thinks I just ought to get pregnant and collect welfare, I don't know. But I ain't got no big problem with making money on my ass. Ain't like I'd have to go to school to learn how.

My only problem with prostitution is the crazies you meet. If I had somebody to protect me from them, we could both get rich rich rich. And why can't that somebody be Dick? He needs money. I seen him sweating them prices on the road.

27

I was surprised when Jane said she felt safe in this mountain stronghold. The house is just off Paradise Road, a winding blacktop that runs from San Marcos Highway to the foothills of U. S. Forest Service land, a wilderness that extends many miles to the north and east. Once you turn off San Marcos onto Paradise, there is a limit to how far you can drive into the wilderness. The blacktop turns into a network of unpaved roads that lead only to campgrounds. Beyond those campgrounds is nothing but fire roads and wilderness, and the fire roads are usually blocked to the public and next to impossible for cars anyway. Strangers easily become lost here. This gave me the feeling that I now had Williston and Sinclair at bay, bamboozled, and soon to be gone.

Strange how you can know without acknowledging it that a loved one is dying. In your heart you can *feel* the signs accumulating like the subtle warnings of an approaching storm. So that by the time the storm arrives, you're a little better prepared for it—you've stowed the sails, battened down the hatches, tightened the lines. Not that preparation eases the fright of the storm.

As Mae's death approached, she'd found reason to separate meaningless knickknacks from heirlooms. Last time I stopped by the house, I'd noticed Winnie's knickknack collection. First thing I noticed as we entered the house now was the knickknacks were gone. That triggered the thought, somewhere in the back of my mind, that Winnie was ill, and that was the real reason the Knors were not at home right now.

Jane may have sensed something ominous, too, for she became subdued and contemplative. She sat on the sun porch overlooking the Santa Ynez River, which each May, in cycles of seven years, is either swollen or a trickle. This fine spring it rose and rushed but did not threaten to overflow. She stared at this loud-singing rush of white-capped water. Dressed in the new blouse and jeans I'd bought her this morning, she looked like a normal girl in her early teens contemplating the powers of nature. But knowing Jane as I do, I was not surprised when she turned around to face my direction and say:

"Dick, tell me something. What's so wrong about them three girls making money over in Asia?"

I ignored her question, inspected the Knor's bookshelves for something interesting to read. They were book collectors who had snapped up many first editions over the years, and these were all neatly packaged in clear plastic wrap to preserve their jackets. Jane came into the living room and I sat down on the couch in front of the fireplace. It was going to be a chilly night; there was a stack of firewood outside.

"Well," I began, oppressed by this subject, "to begin with, they *sold* those three girls into prostitution and drug addiction. Do you think one human being has the right to do that to another?"

Her brow furrowed as she said, "Everybody I know's addicted to cars. To get from one place to another. And prostitution, ain't that what they do with ball players? The player has an agent and the agent makes a deal with a team, and the player gets *sold*."

"Good observation, Jane, but it's not the same thing. Ball players work hard to get good enough to earn big money playing professionally. Little girls get sold because they have no one to protect them from being exploited sexually until they're no longer appealing, then they are discarded like yesterday's garbage."

"Okay, tell me something else. Suppose a young girl *wants* to make money in sex. Can't she do it and then get out, without being... discarded like yesterday's garbage?"

"If she's that one in a thousand. And takes good care of herself, has high self-esteem, plenty of self-discipline. Maybe, yes. But the chances—" I was about to say the chances are slim to zero when she interrupted.

"Okay, suppose she has a good agent. He could help her get into prostitution and make a lot of money and then get out without becoming yesterday's garbage, right?"

"Are you suggesting I ought to turn you over to Williston and let him agent you?"

"No, Dick," she sing-songed sarcastically. "I'm not suggesting anything. I'm just asking. What if *you* would be my agent. I could make a ton of money selling it, you know. I already proved that, right? I mean, there have been times when I run from Grandmother's Home that I peddled my ass and made out real cool. If I had somebody to protect me from the fiends and monsters, I could do a whole lot better. Then neither you or me would have to worry about money."

"What makes you think I worry about money?" I said to gain time.

"Don't fool with me. I'm asking a serious question here."

"You want to know if prostitution is a good way for a beautiful young woman like you to make a lot of money and then retire to a life of luxury. Is that your question?"

"Close enough."

"The answer is no no no, a thousand times no."

"How come?"

"Now there's a worthy question. How come. Well, a lot of people in this culture—and I'm not saying this is the same all around the world—a lot of people believe that sex is evil.

Number one. Number two, they believe that beautiful young ladies who sell sex are evil. Number three, they believe that because those lovely young ladies who sell sex are evil, it's okay to brutalize them. Usually after first enjoying their sexual favors. Do you understand what I'm saying?"

"I think so. Like the truck driver who picked me up hitch hiking and raped me. Is that what you mean?"

"What truck driver was that?"

She huffed with exasperation. "I didn't get his name, Dick. I'm just saying yeah, I get what you're talking about. People who go to church think sex is evil, so they beat up sexy girls."

"Not everyone who goes to church is that way. It gets complicated. A lot of people who go to church support congressmen who sell their lawmaking powers for the money they need to continue getting elected. They peddle their asses to wealthy special interests, as they're called. They're probably the worst whores God ever made because they do more people more harm than any other kind of whore. That doesn't make any kind of prostitution right."

"Congress—ain't that another name for fucking?"

"Let's stick to one thing at a time."

"Do them congressmen wind up dumpster diving for dinner?"

"No. They wind up... rich. But they don't have anything to do with sex, they're just thieves. Anyhow, someday people will realize they've been ripped off and consign them to the garbage heap... these things happen in historical cycles, they happen in slow motion. What else would you like to know?"

"Hurt and Enema—you know, Herb and Emma? Why do they hate the kids in West Wing so much?"

"What makes you think they do?" It was a stalling question.

"What you said about people who think sex is evil. Good church go'ers."

"Some church go'ers, not all," I corrected.

"Whatever. Herb molested me, you know. Lots of times. And Emma, one time she got me alone and beat the piss out of me without putting a mark on my body. For *nothing!*"

We were getting into treacherous legal waters. But could I believe Jane, notorious teller of tall tales? I'd conducted group sessions in which she described being molested in stories that came off like the Marquis de Sade had scripted them. Like the time she told the group about this dude who had showered dollar bills down on her bare ass, as he held her captive. And when Mae asked what had happened to all that money the group cracked up laughing, falling down and rolling on the floor. So much for Jane's tall tales.

Even so, I'd long suspected that Herb Williston had done something to her, or she'd seduced him, and that's why he kept up his steady verbal humiliation of her. I said, "What did Herb do to you?"

"Well, you walked in on him one night. Remember?"

"No. What night are you talking about?"

"The night you and Mrs. Sweet come on duty cause Emma was gone."

I had to think a moment. Yes, I did remember. One night I'd walked into West Wing expecting to relieve Herb of duty just after the kids had gone to bed. Emma had come down with some kind of illness. Not finding Herb downstairs, I went upstairs and knocked on their bedroom door. No answer. I thought maybe he'd left the kids alone, knowing I'd show up—which is against regulations, of course, but then I also knew the Willistons had somehow acquired the right to break regulations if they chose.

I then walked down the hall, checking on the kids in each room, to make sure everyone was okay. When I came to the last room on the left, Jane's room—the only kid there without a roommate—I had heard something strange. Hard breathing.

I went in. It was utterly dark and I was coming in from a brightly lit hallway and Jane's bed was off in a dark corner. Suddenly Herb's voice boomed: "Dick! You're early! Come on in, I was just helping Jane understand something here."

As my eyes adjusted to the darkness, I saw Jane sitting on edge of her bed with Williston standing over her, and heard her whimpering.

"Miz Amurrica here," he said, half turned away from me, "got some strange strange strange notions in her empty young head. Don't cha, Jane? She thinks I want her vagina. She thinks I find her ass *purty.* She thinks she's an irresistible sex attraction. Don't cha, Jane?"

Jane only whimpered—now playing to me, I suspected.

That tableau did seem strange and had aroused my suspicions—at the time; later, I doubted my initial impression. Jane was a round-the-clock problem. Now I was ready to rethink that moment.

"Remember?" Jane prodded.

"I remember walking into your room one night and something... something was going on. But I never knew what."

"And you never bothered asking me, neither, did you. Well, I'll tell you what. Herb was making me suck his wiener. That's what."

"Making you?"

"Yeah, making me. Okay, he was giving me a *choice.* I could keep on crying and he'd have to restrain me, or else I could unzip his damn fly and fish out his wiener and take it in the mouth."

"You realize that you're charging Herb Williston with a serious crime, don't you."

"Well hot-fucking-damn, of course I do!"

"How many times did he do that to you?"

"I didn't keep count, Dick."

"Why didn't you ever report him?"

"Are you out of your mind? Do you know what happened to the last kid that tried to send old Hurt and Enema up the river?"

"No."

"You don't want to know."

"Maybe not. Look, Jane. It's late. Let's get a good night's sleep and pick this up tomorrow. If you bring changes against Herb out here in California, you'll be taken seriously, I assure you."

"Hey, I *know* I'll be taken seriously—not only in California but back in North Carolina too. My problem is, how do I keep from getting killed by fucking Hurt and Enema? Dick, you don't realize them sons of bitches is killers!"

I sighed. "I know I walked in on something happening that one night, Jane. And I was suspicious, but I really had nothing to go on. But aren't you... going over the line into your imagination? Killers?"

I was trying to get her to tell me more, but it didn't work.

"No, I ain't making that up. But... let's drop the subject. I'm tired. Been through a lot lately. Anyhow, if you don't want to help me make some money selling it... Where do I sleep in this place?"

"There are four bedrooms."

"They got a kid's bedroom?"

"That one"—I pointed to one that faced north—"is where their grandchildren sleep when they're here."

"Okay," she said, yawning, rising from her chair at the kitchen table, shuffling over the Persian rug covering the Knor's living room, going into the room. "Night," she said, closing the door. It was still light outside.

In Grandmother's Home, the children were not allowed to close the doors to their rooms. I realized that this was, for Jane, another luxury of freedom.

But her freedom from the system had become my bondage. I felt overwhelmed, like a drowning man calling for help—if only

I could make myself heard, if there were only someone to hear me.

Maude Jennings.

If I called now, I'd probably catch Maude between office and home. I'd wait till later.

The Knors, although they drank very little, kept a fully stocked bar. I hadn't had a drink in a long time. The bar functioned as liquor cabinet and a separation between living room area and kitchen. I got up and walked around this partition and inspected its contents. I'd venture there are commercial bars with less variety.

After looking over the offerings, I selected Benedictine and Brandy. It was made by monks in the Alps. I liked the idea of that. I poured myself about four fingers in a short cocktail glass.

It was now beginning to get nighttime cold. I set the glass down on the table in front of the fireplace and went outside to bring in an armful of split logs, arrange them on the grate in the fireplace, open the flu, turn on the gas, light it, watch the logs catch and then turn off the gas. Then I sat back on the couch facing the fireplace and stared, watching flames lick through dry oak and perform their elemental dance.

I didn't have to look for a pen and notepad. They were sitting on the coffee table in front of me, as though the Knors had anticipated I'd need them. I sipped the B&B and began my list of questions for Maude Jennings.

Number one: Why had Alfred Sinclair decided to follow Herb Williston to the West Coast? If Sinclair sent Williston in the first place, had something gone wrong?

Number two: What was the latest on the sellers of girl children into Asian prostitution rings? Had anyone come up with any hard evidence yet?

Number three: Had anyone there tried to locate those girls in Asia? Had anyone tried to find out anything about that supposed school in Phoenix? Anything about Woo Chin's role in this?

I held my head a moment and took another sip of the sweet brandy. A deeper sip. More like a gulp.

Number four: Did anyone back there in the highlands of North Carolina still believe that I had kidnapped Jane? And if so—or even if not so—how could I return her to her native environment in a way that would be safe, for both her and me? Who was going to take responsibility for seeing that Jane, a very intelligent and potentially wonderful woman, would be *placed,* once and for all, with a family or an agency or whatever, who would see to it that she grew up to fulfill her potential?

And while you people back there are floundering around in your mess of investigations and canceled investigations, I'm here with this kid, trying to protect her and keep my sanity. And it's beginning to look like I'm not going to be able to protect her indefinitely. Unless I get some backup.

By the time eleven o'clock came—two A.M. back in North Carolina—I had finished two glasses of B&B and was feeling the additional effects of the recent series of stresses I'd been subjected to. I decided to make the call now and to hell with what time it is back there. Well, it wouldn't be the first time her duties as social worker had awakened her in the wee hours. This was a real emergency and I needed information. Needed to tell her what was happening here, too.

I dialed. She picked up on the third ring, sounding wide-awake. "Hate to call you at this hour, Maude, but we've got to talk. Things are happening here. Sinclair is here, for one."

"Dick, I can't talk right now. Can I call you back?"

"I'm at a new number. Let me give it to you." I recited the numbers, then: "When can you call back? Can you tell me what's going on there? How come you're up at this hour?"

"I'll call you there as soon as I can. Bye."

After I hung up and had another B&B, I came to the conclusion that I might get more and better answers to my questions from Mae's shade. Which got me back into the mode of talking to myself. I said, "Okay, Mae. You've been watching all this from wherever you are. Tell me. Come on, tell me something. Give me your fix on this."

I knew I was getting crazy drunk but just didn't care.

28

I tried to pour out my heart to Dick but he wouldn't hear me and then I couldn't sleep. I went in this one bedroom, supposed to be the kids' room, and there wasn't nothing in there except two bunk beds, the kind they got back at Grandmother's Home. Stacked on top of one another. Somebody's gotta get the top and somebody's gotta get the bottom. Whichever one you wind up with you feel short-changed. Like my life. If I prosty I'm damned, and if I don't I'm damned because they put me back in the system.

This room has a sliding glass door, opens out onto a porch. I can't decide which bunk to sleep in so I put on my jacket and go out on that porch and sit, listen to the bugs buzz and the water flow and the wind play with the leaves in trees. It feels good outside. Feels good to be able to close my bedroom door, too. But I'm so much *alone.* Just me and Mindy against the world.

That's the problem, being so much alone. If only I had somebody to talk to who understood. When Mae was alive, she understood, and maybe that's why I thought Dick would. But he don't. I tried to tell him I could do things, I could make us enough money to not worry for the rest of our lives. But he just sat there doing his Mr. Sour number and never even heard what I was trying to say.

Felt at the end of my rope. Dick don't want me, won't listen to me. Won't let me do nothing to help myself and him too.

Mom don't want me except to sell, pay her bills. Auntie don't want me except to turn over to my Mom. Daddy don't want me cause I cost more than he can pay.

Only motherfucking person in this whole wide world wants me is Hurt and Enema, and I'd as much as kill Herb as look at him, and anyhow he just wants to peddle my ass to Asia. And her, Enema, I'd like to put her into hell and watch her burn up inch by inch.

Got to feeling so sorry for myself and so pissed off, sitting out there on that porch, I decided I might as well torch this house and see who picks me up then. Decided to go back out to the living room and find me some matches.

Not that I was *really* gonna torch the house, it's just that if I had matches in my hand I'd feel like I could. If I really wanted to.

What I found instead was Dick, laying half on a couch, half on the floor. Had one arm and one leg up on the couch, other arm and leg dangling down to the floor, asleep. With a glass of some kind of booze sitting on the table. Guess he drank himself to dreamland, like my daddy. I sniffed it. Took a little sip. Wasn't half bad. Sweet. Mr. Sour likes sweet.

I woke him up. Reminded me of times when I was just a young 'un, waking up my Dad when he got drunk. Got him on his feet and says, What bedroom you want to sleep in?

He says, That one. And points. I point him toward that bedroom. He goes in pretty much on his own legs, though. He ain't all that drunk.

I'd really like to talk some more, but he ain't up for it.

Walk back into the living room and see that glass he was drinking from. It's still half full. Take another sip. It's really sweet. Fire's in the fireplace. Warm. Nice. And over to the right of the fireplace there's a TV.

I tuned in a movie and stayed up till close to dawn watching it, and sipping that sweet booze Dick was drinking. Comes out of a funny looking squat kind of bottle.

Watching that movie and sipping this sweet booze, I remember how I caused my Daddy to get religion. It was just after my Mom left and I was only eight and some dude on a motorcycle kept buzzing me from the street. He'd ride by and look up—I was out sitting on the balcony—and he'd smile. We still had the apartment then. My Daddy was working late, and I got scared this dude was gonna come after me, and I'd heard he was one crazy, mean mother. I didn't like him.

So instead of sleeping in my own bed that night I crawled into Dad's bed. When Daddy come home, he crawled in beside me. Drunk as a skunk, again. Probably didn't even know who it was in bed with him. It hurt and I knew it wasn't right, then it felt warm and wet, and later it felt sticky. I just didn't want him kicking me out.

Next morning when he seen it was me in bed with him, he got himself into such a state he left the house and was gone a long time. I *was* gonna go to school but when he left, I decided to stay home and wait for him.

Come back around noon carrying a Bible and talking Bible talk. Set me down and read me from the Bible. Shook his finger at me sometimes. Acted real crazy.

A little while later this preacher come by, and he did more Bible reading and finger shaking, and this went on till dinnertime, when they quit and we all ate a big meal and felt good. Which is when I first learned that I could get a grownup man to have sex on me and drive 'em nuts. I know a lot more about it now, naturally.

Once, before the system scooped me up, my Daddy took me to a revival meeting and I got saved. That preacher took hold of my head and dunked me underwater, then pulled me up and said, Now you and Christ are *one*. The spirit of Christ is *within* you.

Next couple of days, I walked around like that was so. But that ain't how other people saw me. Even the preacher, he acted like the spirit of Christ was in outer space somewhere, not inside me.

I cussed them all out, my Daddy, the preacher, till one day in science class, while I was looking at a picture in my book of an atom and molecules, the teacher put up a picture of the solar system, and *they looked the same*!

That old preacher never saw them two pictures side by side. Neither did my Daddy. If they did, they wouldn't be looking *up there* for the spirit of Christ. They'd close their eyes and imagine their own atoms and molecules, and how they are the same *in here* as *up there*. Don't know where that thought come from. Maybe I heard it and forgot I heard it.

I get sleepy and go back to the bedroom, pull out my favorite shortie, slip out of my clothes and put it on, go back to that lower bunk and sleep like I'm a zombie till I hear something.

There's a lot of birds outside making a racket, and there's a telephone beeping somewhere in the house, and then there's an answering machine, and after that I hear this rumble. Can't figure out what it is, at first. It vibrates.

Get out of bed and open the door, look out, and then I can hear that it's Dick. He's talking. He's just woke up and his voice is rumbly, like he's got a cold or something. So he's talking rumble rumble rumble.

I don't know who he's talking to, but I hear him mention my name. What gives him and whoever he's talking to the right to talk about me like I'm some kind of *thing* with no mind or feelings?

29

I was awakened out of a dream of Mae by a persistent chirping which, mixed with the chirping of birds just outside my window, had me wondering what strange new bird had invaded this area. Took me awhile to come awake and realize where I was, and that this other chirping was coming from a telephone on the table next to the bed. I looked at it, then the chirping quit and from outside the guest room, in the hallway, I heard the Knor's answering machine. It was an old fashioned machine; you heard the outgoing message, the beep, and then the incoming message.

"I'm calling," came a female voice I didn't recognize immediately, "for Dick Steel. Unless I'm mistaken he told me he was at this number last night. Are you there, Dick?"

Maude Jennings. At six in the morning my time, nine hers. I picked up the bedside phone and said, "Yes, Maude."

"Dick! You certainly do move around a lot."

"So do some people from North Carolina, like Williston and Sinclair."

"That's what I want to talk to you about."

"I'm listening."

"If you're confused about who are the evil do'ers in this thing, join the crowd."

"What crowd?"

"The law enforcement people here in North Carolina. They dropped their investigation into allegations that someone, or some group, was selling kids into prostitution."

"You told me that."

"And I believe I also told you that this one person from law enforcement had taken it upon herself to pursue that investigation. Did I not?"

"You did, except you said it was a him, not a her. And you said you were going to send a ticket to fly Jane back there, and then you said you weren't."

"Right."

"So, are you more confused than me? Or have you picked up new information?"

"Last night, this lady came by my house. We were up most of the night. Can you hear me okay? I don't want to yell this out to the whole office here."

"You're coming in loud and clear. Who is this lady and what did she have to say?"

"Well..."

I am not a patient person by nature and was becoming agitated by Maude's hesitations.

"The lady's name is Sandra something. Her last name escapes me at the moment. I'll think of it. I'm groggy, need to get this coffee down. She's from Philadelphia and has been working for the state's special investigations division. She's the one I told you about. Pursuing the investigation on her own."

"Good. What did she have for you?"

"A lot of questions. We wound up driving to the office and getting out some files. Nothing definite, but she's pretty sure our Mr. Chin is mixed up in something and she's flying out to Los Angeles."

"Why? Why is she flying here?"

"Telephone records. She's gotten hold of his telephone records."

"I haven't heard from this Mr. Chin. Should I expect a call from him?"

"No, but you should expect a call from Sandra. She's flying out there today. She's using sick-leave days to do this. Will you cooperate with her?"

"If she's not here to grab Jane, I'll be happy to cooperate. How can I be of help to her investigation?"

"No, she's not going to pick up Jane. I told her Jane is in good hands with you. Maybe you could meet Sandra at the airport in L.A."

"Give me the vitals."

"Her name is Sandra Mulholland."

"Famous name in California."

"And she'll be arriving this evening at six thirty on Continental. Can I call her and say you'll meet her?"

"What's she look like? How will we connect?"

"I showed her a picture of you. As for what she looks like, well, she's of the black persuasion, I guess you'd say."

"No, *you'd* say that, not me. I would say she's an African American. Is that what you mean?"

"Okay, African American. Except last night, after we both got relaxed, she told me she's also Irish, Cherokee and some other ethnic mixes. English, German, Dutch, the list goes on. Anyhow, she's good looking, about twenty-eight years old. She'll be wearing a burgundy suit and carrying a black briefcase."

I didn't recall coming to bed last night, and now I saw that I'd left the guest room door open. Jane was up and about. Wearing her shortie nightshirt, a see-through mini-skirt sort of outfit, and finding some reason to parade back and forth in front of my opened door. Eavesdropping.

"Jane," I said, "no need to eavesdrop. I'll tell you all about it. Would you like to speak with your social worker, Maude Jennings?"

"Hell no!" she said in a whimpering voice.

"Maude? I'll meet this Sandra Mulholland at six thirty, and I'll do what I can to help. She sounds like an unlikely candidate to be employed by the North Carolina special investigations division."

"She's doing this on her own, Dick, taking sick leave days."

"Oh. How do you feel about her?"

"How do I *feel?*"

"Yeah. Give me the benefit of your womanly intuition."

"Funny you should ask," she said, then said nothing for about five seconds. "She was in the system as a kid. But she was adopted when she was about Jane's age and is making a success of her life. Went to college, graduated with a masters in criminology. But... I don't know how to say this."

"But?"

"You asked me about my woman's intuition. It is picking up something here that doesn't add up with what she's doing and saying. I don't know."

"In other words, you're not sure you trust her. Is that it?"

"Yes, but maybe that's just because she's so damned beautiful. Wait till you see her. Actually, I trust her more than I trust a lot of other people. Sinclair especially, and his church people, and those law enforcement people who called off the investigation."

"Okay, thanks for that fix on her. I'll have my antenna up."

There followed about ten seconds of heavy breathing before Maude said, "What doesn't quite add up is all the energy she's putting into this particular case. There's plenty of others she could focus on. Why this one?"

"Do you get the impression that there is something strangely *charismatic* about Jane Doyle?"

"I don't know about charismatic, but there sure is something strange going on."

"Yeah, there sure is."

Seconds after I'd uttered the word charismatic, Jane again appeared in the doorway to the guest room, posing in her see-through shortie nightgown. Leaning against the doorframe with one foot up, leg blocking the doorway. Chest out, emphasizing her budding breasts, her back arched to show off her buttocks. Head up and staring off into space, as though entranced. It was what Yoni called her Pretty Baby pose, referring to a movie called *Pretty Baby*, starring Brooke Shields as a child prostitute.

I said goodbye to Maude, then slid down in bed again. I sleep in the nude. It's an old habit. Then I said, "Jane, why are you standing there like that?"

"Just curious."

"Curious about what?"

"What you and Maude Jennings was talking about."

"I'll be happy to tell you all about it. But first, let's get dressed and have breakfast. Shooo!"

She collapsed in a fit of giggles that verged on the hysterical, then disappeared. I got up, closed the door, and went into the adjoining bathroom for a shower. As I soaped up, I made a note to put through a call to the Knors and ask if they'd mind my inviting this African Irish Cherokee lady here. That would give me a chance to inspect her close up, and maybe use her to get Jane out of her vamping mode.

30

Turns out Dick was talking on the phone to my social worker. He says there's somebody else coming out here this evening and we're gonna meet her at the airport.

What's this somebody else coming here to do?

To find out what became of those three girls.

I say, Well shit, Dick, he don't gotta come way out here for that. Why don't he just ask the kids?

It's a she. Maybe she did ask the kids. Maybe they didn't feel safe telling her.

Yeah, you got a point. But if you promise to look out for me, I'll tell her.

What will you tell her?

First you gotta promise you'll look out for me and quit trying to get rid of me.

Okay, he says, I promise.

No, you can't just say it. You gotta give me something that means it.

Like what?

Let me think. Oh, I got it. The ashes of your wife, Mae.

He slaps his forehead with his hand and falls back and says, I can't do that!

Okay, I can't tell you what happened to them girls.

But, he says, what would you do with my wife's ashes?

I'd hold 'em hostage. You said you was gonna scatter 'em on the ocean, right? So I'd hold 'em till you get around to that. If

I have them ashes, you won't be so damn quick to push me off on somebody else. I won't be so likely to wind up lost somewhere, tramping around strange streets and alleys and beaches, trying to get away from people want to grab my ass, trying to get back to you!

He thinks awhile, then he says, Okay, Jane. And he goes and gets this big jug, looks like a fancy flower vase with a stopper in the top. Sets it down in front of me. Says, Okay, you guard Mae's ashes until we're ready for the ceremony.

I say, Okay. What do you want to know?

Says, Are those three girls really in Asia? And if so, how did they get there? And what are they doing there? And who is involved? We've got to be really clear about this, Jane.

Well we got that card from Peaches, Pamela, from Bangcock, so she's got to be *there.* Or how else could she send that card?

Okay, he says, so far so good. How did they get there?

See, there's this dude named Johnny Hooper, lives in Memphis. That's in West Tennessee. He knows Mr. Chin in Boone, and *he* is buddy-buddy with Mr. Sinclair and Hurt and Enema. Got it?

Got it. But how do you know this? Did you ever *meet* this Johnny Hooper? Or are you just making all this up?

I met Johnny. I *seen* him a couple of times before this, when he come for them other girls. He come to town and looked me up at school, is how I met him. Said he was my uncle from Memphis. That's what he told 'em in the school office, see. Just wanted to talk to me a few minutes during recess. They let me out to see him, and we took a little walk about. I give him some good good head and he told me if I ever want to run and can get all the way to Memphis, here's his address and phone number. And if I can't get to Memphis, give him a call, he'll come pick me up, see that I make tons of money.

Dick gets me to dig out my address book and check out this Johnny Hooper. I say, See, he's how them girls get overseas, way out of the system.

What are you saying? That Johnny Hooper is... that school in Phoenix?

You got it!

Dick goes right to the phone with this and puts through a call to Johnny Hooper's number. He's about to blow it. So I say, Dick, he ain't gonna tell *you* nothing. Hand that phone to me.

He does, and I hear Johnny's voice on the other end saying, Hello?

Johnny Hooper? This is Jane Doyle. Remember me?

Grandmother's Home, yeah. You're the cutest thing I ever seen, Jane. Where you calling from?

California.

How'd you get way out there?

It's a long story, Johnny. Reason I'm calling, I'd like to know how to get in touch with Wendy and Nancy and Pamela. You got phone numbers for them?

Jane, they're way across the ocean. Wendy and Nancy's in Hong Kong and Pamela's in Bangkok.

Bangkok sounds like a great place to be, I joke with him. Can you give me Pamela's number there?

No, can't do that, Jane. But I can ask her to call *you.* Next time she calls here, I'll give her your number and tell her you want to talk to her. Okay?

Okay. Wait a second. I got to find out the number here.

I find out from Dick, and relay this to Johnny Hooper, and then he says, Listen, Jane, do you want to make some real good money?

You bet your ass I do, Johnny.

Everybody knows Johnny's a pimp. But he's good people. Don't hurt nobody. If a girl don't like staying with him, she's free to hit the dusty road.

He says, Fly into Memphis. I'll meet you.

Maybe I'll do that, I says, but first I got some stuff to take care of here in California.

You out of the system?

Sure am, baby.

Great! How'd you swing that?

It's a long story. I'll tell you when I see you. Right now I gotta hang up and... take care of business. I'm starving.

Okay. But listen. Keep in touch. And whichever one of them girls calls me next, I'll tell her your number there.

Thanks, Johnny.

Dick's been sitting beside me all the time, listening with his head next to mine. He says, You amaze me, Jane.

Been trying to tell you. You ought to listen to me more, Dick.

You're right. I'll try to remember that.

Good. Now, what's for breakfast? I'm starving.

He says, One more call. I don't want to raid the refrigerator here until I've talked to the Knors.

Then he turns on the answering machine and runs through some messages, most of them from some man trying to reach Dick. Says, Dick, are you there yet? Okay, when you get to the house, Dick, here's our number in Hawaii. Area code, and gives the ten numbers twice, just to be sure.

So Dick dials and talks to this man, Dr. Malcolm Knor, spelled with a K.

Hey, Doc, how's the weather over there? And, I have someone with me here, hope you don't mind. A kid from the agency Mae and I used to work for. Adopt her? Not likely, doc. And looks at me with a shitty grin.

On and on. Tells this doc that he's got someone else might like to stay here too. Tells him she's an investigator from North Carolina looking into a possible child prostitution ring. Makes it sound like we're doing a TV series or something.

After that, we go to the refrigerator and I volunteer to cook bacon and eggs. Which we don't got, so we have to hop in the car and drive to some old country store and buy. Dick grumbles at the price while we're buying half a pound of bacon and half a dozen eggs.

Back out in the car, I say, How come you're always grumbling about prices but you won't let me sell some ass so neither one of us has to worry about money?

We're back to that, are we.

Yeah, Mr. Sour, we're back to that. How come?

I thought I explained that last night.

Well, you talked a lot but you didn't say nothing, really!

I said you might make a lot of money as a child prostitute but you'd wind up in the human garbage heap.

Bull! We could save some money and buy a business. Come on, Dick! I'm serious!

So am I, Jane. Let's see what those other girls have to say about it. If they call you. Do you know how old they'd be now?

Let's see. Pamela's a year older than me, so she's thirteen going on fourteen. Wendy, she's about the same, I think, and Nancy Gardner, she's the oldest. I guess she's around fifteen, maybe sixteen. They was gone before you and Mae come on, right?

No, Pamela was there for a month or so, before she was adopted by that Chinese couple in Boone.

Yeah. Woo-woo Chin! They's rich rich rich, and it ain't from that dumb old Chinese restaurant they own, neither.

What do you know about them, Jane?

Not a whole lot. Pamela called me at school before she took off for Arizona. That's where Johnny Hooper takes 'em. And then he sends 'em overseas somewhere.

Very interesting, he says.

Drive faster, I'm hungry.

31

A s Mae used to say, "The kids at Grandmother's Home know a lot more than the grownups give them credit for." Well, I guess that's true of kids most everywhere. Except the kids in the system have their minds on areas of life most kids know little or nothing about.

By eight o'clock that morning, I had some valuable bits of information for the arriving Sandra Mulholland. All from Jane, or through her connections. I felt like a fool for not having gotten these specifics sooner. Better late than never, of course, but I vowed I would trust Jane more in the future.

Once she knew what I wanted to know, though, she demanded a "hostage," to make sure I didn't drop her off again. I wasn't about to do that anyway, but I let her "hold" what she demanded: the urn containing Mae's ashes.

It was something we shared, Jane and I, for the kids had adored Mae. Mrs. Sweet, they'd called her. They'd called me Mr. Sour. I can understand that. I don't present the world with the happiest of visages.

Well, the urn was unbreakable and solidly sealed, so I saw no reason not to let her carry it. I put it on the mahogany cocktail table in front of her, as she sat on the couch facing the fireplace. That satisfied her. She talked.

She knew how those three girls had gotten from Grandmother's Home to the Orient, or knew enough about this route that she could probably manage to get herself there, if she really wanted to. Through someone named Johnny Hooper in Memphis, Tennessee.

Together we put through a call to this person. Jane did the talking. I wrote a few notes about his role in what was coming into focus as a pipeline of teenaged girls to Asia. Where Jane, now and then, thought she would like to go, especially if I dropped her off again.

Now she was awaiting calls from one or all of those girls, who checked in with this Johnny Hooper, according to him. He's a pimp, Jane explained, but "a nice person."

Nice person, indeed! But I suppose if you're coming from where Jane is coming from, Johnny Hooper is a gem. He'll transport you out of the system into what seems like freedom.

I was anxious to meet that incoming plane now. After a pretty good breakfast of bacon and eggs, fixed by Jane, I called Kent to see if there was any news on his end. He'd had two gentlemen knock on his front door the evening before, wondering where Jane and I were. He told them he had no idea. I wasn't surprised when he described them: "Some big guy must weigh around two eighty, maybe three hundred, and another guy with a beer belly and a Jay Leno jaw. Are they from that agency, Dad?"

"Yes, the big guy runs the place, and the other one is Herb Williston, half of the couple your mother and I were partnered with there."

"They didn't smell good to me."

"How do you mean?"

"They kind of reeked of fear. I can practically smell it when I meet someone who is feeling a lot of fear, and they both are."

"They have plenty to fear, Kent. I'm learning things from Jane. They're mixed up in a plot to sell kids into prostitution."

"You're kidding!"

"I wish I were."

"Are you safe up there, Dad? I can drive up with my forty-five. You need protection?"

"No, don't drive up here, Kent. I suspect they may be keeping an eye on you, hoping you'll lead them to Jane and me."

"Good point," he said matter-of-factly. "But Dad, how did you drive up there without them tracking you?"

"Timing. And I made sure they weren't following me."

"I'd like to make sure they can't do you any harm."

"I'm no good to them dead, my boy. It's Jane they want."

"She's gorgeous," he said with such a sense of awe it momentarily bothered me.

"There are lots of gorgeous young girls who have been abused or neglected—abandoned, is the word I prefer. Those two gentlemen don't need to fly across the country to find one. They've got kids like Jane back there by the dozens."

"So why are they here?"

"That's what I'm trying to get to find out. Seems the law may be onto them. Or maybe it's more sinister than that."

"Take care, Dad. And keep in touch. I have your number there, I'll check in with you now and then."

"I'll be driving down to LA this evening to pick up someone from the North Carolina special investigations something or other. I'll leave the machine on, with Doc Knor's outgoing message."

"What time do you expect to get back?"

"Let's see. Her plane is supposed to arrive at six thirty. Evening traffic. Nine o'clock."

"Call me when you get back. Or I'll call you there around nine to make sure you're okay."

"Thanks, son."

We were now in the second week of May, so schools would soon be letting out for summer. Even if I could get Jane placed here in California—which I suppose would be possible, but probably would take a lot of red tape time—summer would be upon us. And I have to get to the bottom of this child prostitution business before I even try to get her placed. It wouldn't do for a courtroom trial to drag her out of school just when she was adjusting. She'd had that happen too many times before.

She seemed content this day to dance about the living room as she watched MTV. The kids at Grandmother's Home were not allowed to watch that channel, so of course it becomes the first one they tune in when they get the chance.

I tried to think what I would do if I were Herb Williston or Alfred Sinclair, and needed to find Jane. How would I find out where Dick Steel and Jane Doyle were hiding? Well, I'd keep an eye on Kent and Anna, figuring they would be in touch with Dick. And knowing how much bugging equipment Sinclair employs routinely at his agency, he and Herb may already have Kent's phone wired.

At the agency, the calls from parents to the kids—which were allowed only on Saturdays—were recorded and listened to later at staff meetings. Both incoming and outgoing mail was routinely read by the staff, many of whom referred to the kids as "losers" and found their plight deeply amusing. Amazing how the USA has changed. The America I grew up in would have seen this invasion of privacy as Nazism. Even children had a right to their own private thoughts back in my childhood.

About the only folks who did not admire Sinclair back there were teachers and administrators of the public school where the kids were dutifully bussed each day. When Sinclair ordered the faculty to report any instances of "his" kids having contact of any kind with people outside the school, the faculty balked. Said no. Even tried to initiate legal action against Grandmother's Home for child abuse and violation of human rights. Probably would have succeeded if Sinclair didn't have such fine contacts with church people, one of whom "explained" things to the teachers: Grandmother's Home children composed much of their school population, and without the federal money for those kids, the local school would be in big trouble. Federal money quieted the furor.

I reasoned that even though Williston and Sinclair had not yet found us, chances are they would, given enough time. Which meant that Jane and I, and soon Sandra Mulholland too, should be planning our next move.

All this was in the back of my mind when I stood with Jane in the Continental Airlines waiting area, watching people walk out of the tunnel connecting them to incoming planes, and head for the luggage pickup. I had no trouble spotting Sandra: cinnamon skin, eyes like two dark blue gems that glow rather then reflect. My first impression: here's a young woman who should be making a fortune as a model. Why is she in law enforcement?

She recognized Jane and me in the crowd, and waved, smiled, lit up the room with her strong, even, bright white teeth. If Mae were alive, she'd be muttering at me and pinching my behind right now, play-acting a fit of jealousy.

Sandra first bestowed her glowing joy on Jane, saying, "I'll bet you're Jane Doyle. So pleased to meet you. You're lovely! And I'm told you're also very bright. How are you, Jane?"

"Fine," said Jane, suddenly shy.

"And Dick Steel." She extended a surprisingly firm hand. "I hope it's no trouble for you to come here and meet me like this. I told Maude I could just catch a car rental, then get a motel somewhere. But you know Maude."

"He's Mr. Sour," Jane put in as we walked the long corridor toward the luggage pickup. "That's what us kids call him."

The tough bimbo who'd been contemplating a life of prostitution a few hours ago had metamorphosed into a little girl with adoring eyes for Sandra.

Soon Jane and Sandra were holding hands like old pals. Sandra titled her head or bent down whenever Jane said something, showing that she was anxious to hear. Jane was talking nonstop as we waited for and then collected two suitcases and walked to the car.

I insisted on carrying Sandra's larger bag, she carried the smaller one she checked through. I slowed down at the crosswalk, an opportunity to admire them as they walked together, holding hands, chattering away like they'd known each other all their lives.

At one point, as we were searching for the car, Sandra turned around and said to me, "You've got my clothes. I've got my gun." She patted the case she carried and smiled. I thought perhaps I hadn't heard her right. I watched her more carefully. She walked with a cat-like grace that suggested potency held in check, readiness, strength.

Soon we were encapsulated in Hampton's showroom-new Mercedes, rushing through the night lights like exotic fish in a phosphorescent sea. During the drive, I learned that Sandra's motives sprang from a life much like Jane's, except that she'd been lucky enough to be adopted at age twelve by a couple who understood the effects on children of early abandonment, and were patient with Sandra. She told Jane about this as we drove.

Jane, who usually listens to adults with averted eyes, heeded Sandra with rapt attention. I felt a rush of joy, realizing that Sandra was probably the first and only woman Jane had ever met who came from a group home and made a success of herself. Most kids from group homes, even the ones who eventually got adopted, struggle through life, if they manage to avoid prison. Most people from normal homes have no awareness of this syndrome.

When we were back at the house, after getting Sandra settled in another of the four bedrooms, I said to Jane, "Sweetheart, maybe you'd like to tell Sandra what you know about those three girls."

"What I know?"

"Yes. How they got from North Carolina to wherever they are in Asia."

"Oh. Sure."

As she did, Sandra beamed as though Jane were telling her a delightful little tale of wonder. Then she opened her briefcase, took out a notebook, and jotted down the particulars, especially Johnny Hooper's address and phone number, which Jane was happy to make sure she got correctly.

Then Sandra came up with a book from her briefcase, a novel written for teenagers. "Here," she said, handing it to Jane, who inspected it carefully, as though it were something of extreme value. "Maude says you're a very good reader, so I think you're grownup enough to really enjoy this."

Jane beamed like a normal little girl, then lowered her face to the book and was soon lost in it. And becoming drowsy.

Sandra shot me a wink. But before I could react, the phone shattered our togetherness.

It was Kent, assuring me he had taken the precaution of putting this call through from a pay phone. He said that as far as he could tell no one was keeping an eye on him, but he was taking precautions anyhow. I said I would like to drive down later this night and get some things out of my van. He then told me he had a friend who worked the desk in the motel where Sinclair was staying, who was keeping an eye on this masterful public relations man's comings and goings. He would check with this friend, and if Sinclair ventured out, he'd call back in a few minutes.

When I'd finished speaking with him, Jane was in her room, reading, her door open, and Sandra had disappeared into hers. I knocked on her door and it almost drew me with it when it whizzed open.

"I'd like to drive into town and pick up some things," I said. "Now that you're here to keep tabs on Jane."

"No problem. That novel I gave her will do a fine job of baby-sitting. Anyhow, I can't see her trudging down that road we drove in on, can you?"

I smiled at the thought. "Terrific having you here," I said.

"Thanks. I'd be livelier company but it's one o'clock by my biological clock and I'm pooped."

I was able to drive away under the sound of the rushing waters of the swollen Santa Ynez River. Jane would never know I'm gone. I drove down the mountain to Carpenteria, collected from the van the belongings I needed, had a nice visit with Kent and Anna, and got back before midnight.

Jane's bedroom light was out, the door still open. So was the sliding glass door to the porch overlooking the river. The soothing sound of its springtime rush had transported her to sleep.

32

Dick told me after breakfast that we have to drive down to LA this evening to pick up somebody.

I want to know who, where from?

He says it's a lady investigator from North Carolina. I say, You son of a bitch, you turning me back into the system? He says, No no, nothing like that. It's a lady investigator, wants to find out more about Wiliston. Oh, okay. I can tell her a lot about that guy.

So don't get worried, he says.

I say, I ain't going back to that auntie.

Oh no, he says, don't worry. Nobody's trying to send you there.

I ain't going back to North Carolina neither. What I really ought to do is run from you, Dick, and find Herb so he can get me over to Asia too. That's what I'm beginning to think.

He says, Before you do that, hear what those other girls have to say about it.

I'll do that.

Besides, he says, you're the keeper of Mae's ashes, remember?

Then he goes into his room and lays down to take a nap. I get to thinking, and I get a wild hair up my butt. I go out in the kitchen and get on the phone there, where Dick can't hear me.

His room's down the hall and around a corner from the kitchen. And I put through a collect call to Maude Jennings in her office.

She's there. Says, Jane Doyle? Is that really you? How are you, child?

I say, I'm fine, no thanks to you. And I ain't gonna tell you where I am, cause you'll only call the cops on me.

Oh, Jane, she says real sticky sweet. I won't do that.

Hey, lady, I just got one thing to tell you. Your brains are shit and your ass is a toxic waste dump. You ain't gonna get me back in the system no matter what you do.

Then I hang up. There's such a thing as tracing a call, and I ain't staying on long enough for her to do that... in case Dick didn't already give her this number.

I decide to go out for a walk along the river. It's called a river but it looks more like what we call a crick back in North Carolina. Rushing white water. Dick says it'll be down to a trickle come summer.

I walk along the river bank awhile, don't see nobody else. There's a park, picnic tables, benches, cookout things. No people.

When I get back to the house, Dick's up and looking crazy. Where have you been? he says, all puffed up.

Just out walking. Nothing to worry about.

He wipes sweat from his forehead and says, I got to get you placed. And soon.

Oh no! Placed is what they call it when they put you in the system. I got Mae's ashes, remember?

Sweetheart, he says, I don't mean sending you back to Grandmother's Home.

Well you ain't putting me back in no system no kind of way. It's full of shit, Dick.

Well, he says, cool down. You just gave me a scare. Don't wander off on me again. And don't worry, there's no plan to send you back to North Carolina.

I got Mae's ashes—and I hold up the jug to remind him. So it's a Mexican standoff. You try to send me back and I'll lose these ashes.

Around suppertime, we get in the Mercedes and head for the freeway to L.A. He stops at the country store and buys me a sandwich to hold me, then I nod off and sleep.

When I wake up, I find I'm in the biggest, spookiest parking lot I ever seen. It's indoor and outdoor and all over the place, and all around it is this airport, LAX it's called. We walk into the Continental Airlines waiting room and sit. I bum a couple of bucks from Dick and buy some candy.

I don't know who this lady is, coming from North Carolina. But I know one thing. I'm gonna let her know early on there's no way I'm going back. Dick says that ain't the plan but I know plans can change.

That's what I was thinking when her plane come in and pretty soon, here she is. Looks like she stepped out of a soap opera! She's black, redbone black, as Yoni calls it. She's kind of copper colored with long dark curly hair that shakes when she walks. And I can see by the way Dick's looking at her that he's gone on her. I can understand that. This gal got a smile could take out a regiment.

I get along with her real good, once she knows I ain't going back to no North Carolina with nobody. She tells me she's here on an investigation, and asks do I know anything about how them girls got from Grandmother's Home to Asia. I sure do know. Simple. Hurt and Enema fix 'em up with Mr. Chin as their adoptive parent, and he sends 'em on. I even tell her it's Johnny Hooper gets 'em on the plane out of this country.

Her eyes get big when she hears all this, and she pats me on the back and tells me I been more help than anyone else, and she wants me to work with her on this thing. I say, Sure thing, Sandra. Her name, Sandra. I like her a lot. She's real people.

After we drive back to the house in the mountains, she says, I brought you something. And pulls a book out of her bag. I start to groan, cause I don't think of a book as a present. But the way she hands me this book, I get the feeling it's special.

And since I'm getting tired anyway, I take it into my bedroom, get on my shortie and start to read it. It's about this girl who gets put into the system. Her mom and dad die in a car crash, and she ain't got nobody, nobody wants her. So she winds up at a place like Grandmother's Home, only it's called Serenity Farm. Nobody likes her at first. She's ugly and feels rotten about herself and everything.

I get so caught up reading, I'm still awake when I hear the front door open and close. I go out the sliding glass door and here's somebody backing the Mercedes out and driving away! Run inside and put my ear to Sandra's bedroom door. She's in there. Got to be Dick driving away.

That got me up in a boil of worry. Why don't he tell me where he's going?

Then, just when I'm heading back to my room, walking past the table with the phone on it, the thing goes off and I grab it without thinking. My hand's so close when it goes off, it's just natural to pick it up.

And what do you know? It's Pamela, calling me from Asia. She says, Jane? Is that you, girl?

Sure is, baby! I'm in California!

Yeah? How'd you get away from Hurt and Enema, girl?

I tell her all about it, and then she tells me what she's been doing. Says she's been turning tricks for big bucks, sometimes a thousand a pop. I say, Good God, girl! You must be rich rich rich. Not exactly, she says, cause she has a management keeps her money for her, gives her an allowance, but keeps her turning about ten tricks a day.

I say, Girl I remember the time me and you run and we put our butts our on the corner for a couple days and we turned more than ten a day.

I know, she says, but it weren't for this kind of money.

No-oh-oh! I say, Pamela, serious now, how can I get in on this?

You don't want in on this, not if you know what's good for you. That money ain't mine, and I got such a habit! That's the one thing they give you plenty of here, dope. At first it was a blast but now I can't turn it loose. I have no idea how I'm ever gonna get out of here. I'm *stuck*, girl! I ain't never gonna get back home. You heard of youth in Asia? When you tell 'em, let me die? That's what you do if you let 'em send you here. Youth in Asia. It's a dead end, sister.

Can't be worse than being in the system, I say.

I didn't think so at first, but now that I been here a while, yeah, it's worse. You ain't stuck in the system forever, you know. Here...

And her voice chokes up and she bawls! Says, Don't let them send you here, Jane! Stay away from Hurt and Enema and Mr. Chin and Johnny Hooper. They sell your ass and keep you hooked on dope, and pretty soon you need more and more and more, and there ain't no way back, girl. No way out. Hear me?

I hear you, Pamela. But maybe I can figure a way to get you back here with me in California. Mr. Sour. You remember him? Mr. and Mrs. Sweet and Sour? Well, she died and I'm with him here in California.

Good for you, girl. You stay right there and thank your lucky stars. You got it right. Gotta run now. Another john coming up here. Bye.

After she hangs up, I sit there with the phone in my hand a long time, thinking, yeah, maybe I do got it right. At last!

33

I called Malcolm Knor the next day and explained the situation. I wanted to stay in touch to put his mind at ease about us using his house, and I wanted his fix on this thing, the picture that was beginning to emerge about selling those kids. What I'd learned from Jane, and then from Sandra, had my mind spinning.

Malcolm Knor, besides being a highly educated economic historian, was a broadly experienced man and he had never, in the past, failed to show me another perspective on a problem. I like to kid that he has an uncanny knack of fitting human irrationality into logical syllogisms. I hoped he wouldn't let me down this time.

"Dick," he said, when I'd finished describing what I knew or thought I knew about the selling of kids, "let me share a personal observation with you."

"Please do." We'd done this sort of thing quite a lot, and I could see in my mind's eye his brow knitting, his eyes narrowing to slits.

"There are a huge number of abandoned children among us in this world now."

"That's my impression too, but who's been keeping track?"

"My next point. Nobody's been keeping track. We don't have statistics. Numbers. Not reliable, commonly agreed upon numbers. But you and I—I believe you'll agree—came of age in a *much different social environment.* Agreed?"

We'd often sat up late in friendly disagreements. "Agreed," I was pleased to say.

"Children were either assets or had the potential to return more than their cost to the family coffers. That is in stark contrast to today, when children are either—and this is my point—either big expenses or opportunities for profit."

"I know of scant few who are considered profitable, professsor."

"Let me expand on this. Your Jane here was apparently far too expensive for her birth parents. They were, and are, I gather, poverty-stricken. So she was put into the system, as it's called, where she became an opportunity for profit."

"At Grandmother's Home," I interjected, "she paid out about ten percent profit on the money collected by the agency per child. They come out ahead by about ten percent per child."

"But as a sexual commodity her profit potential would increase dramatically."

"No doubt about that, sad to say."

"Compare! How much money went into her sustenance at that agency you and Mae worked for? I hate the name of it."

"I don't have firm numbers. They *claim* it costs two thousand dollars per child per month. But they include maintenance costs and everything else you can think of in that figure and they do cook the books big time. I would guesstimate about one thousand dollars a month. Eight hundred of that comes usually from their home Department of Human Services office. Church and United Way contribute another thousand a month for each child. That's according to a public relations pamphlet they put out, that figure. Two thousand dollars. Ten percent of that is two hundred. Times twelve kids a cottage, seven cottages. Sixteen thousand eight hundred a month. Roughly. Maybe more, maybe less."

"Okay, and how much can a girl generate as a sexual engine of income? Per month."

"The girl who says Jane called her last night, according to Jane she said each trick pays a thousand dollars, and she turns ten tricks a day. I don't know, that sounds impossible to me, but let's say she makes half that, twenty-five thousand a week. A hundred thousand a month. Whew! Can that be possible?"

"Let's suppose her gross profit potential as a teenaged sex commodity is something like that. Could be more, could be less. Neither of us knows."

"If her North Carolina promoters were collecting only ten percent... that would be ten thousand a month." My mind staggered. Sinclair and Williston. "God," I exclaimed, "no telling how much they're making on those three girls."

"Do you think those numbers are close to real?"

"I suspect they are."

"Then it's understandable why those two gentlemen you mentioned are determined to recapture your young lady. She's worth a fortune to them, if this is what's really happening."

"If they could make just ten percent of Jane's monthly gross as a budding teenaged hooker in, say, Tokyo, they'd do quite well for themselves, no doubt about it. What if they split fifty-fifty? I think Sinclair would take more like ninety-ten, but for the sake of this 'what if,' let's say they split. Let's say they'd split half of what each girl makes per month. Times twelve months, that's a lot more than they could make any other way."

"They now have three girls. That we know of. Jane would make a fourth. Now we're talking pretty good untaxed income here."

"I'm made dizzy by all this, Malcolm. Of course we haven't even wondered what Mr. Chin might take. But our figures may be conservative, and they may have sent other girls there, girls we haven't heard of."

"Perhaps you and your investigator there can check it out."

"Perhaps. The girl who called here didn't leave her number. I guess she was calling from Bangkok. What's the going price for a roll in the hay with American teenaged prostitutes in Bangkok?"

"I don't have any idea, but from what I know of the Japanese gentlemen on the island of Hawaii, they'll pay a handsome sum for the delights of a tender young sprout. It does not seem to be part of their culture to care if she's under a legal age here in the States. Maybe you could check what Jane would fetch in a Las Vegas situation and double it. Maybe even triple it."

"Always count on your mercurial mind to shed new light on things, professor. How's Winnie?"

He hesitated and I heard him sigh. "Winnie's been having problems. That's one of the reasons we're here just now. We heard that there are Hawaiian healing methods that have gotten remarkable results. We have her in a combination of acupuncture and special massage. Seems to be getting results. She's certainly doing better than she was back there. We'll see."

"What's the problem?"

"Oh, neurological complications from an ongoing diabetic condition is the word from doctors. She keeps the diabetes under control with the usual medications, but this neurological thing—well, she tried some prescription drugs but they didn't work. So we thought we'd give these alternative methods over here a try."

"Give her my best, and let me know when you'd like to come home. I've got a house full. Jane, myself and now Sandra Mulholland, the investigator from North Carolina. I'll have the house cleaned before you get back."

"Don't worry about cleaning. Make yourselves at home. We plan to be here awhile. It's good to have people in that house, and we know you'll take care of it."

"Yes, well, Jane has a puppy."

"Our dog Champ is in a kennel just now. I don't mind puppies. As long as your Jane will wipe up after it."

"She's pretty good about that."

We said our goodbyes then and I went in search of Sandra to talk over this business of the profitability of child prostitutes, but she was nowhere to be found.

Neither was Jane or Mindy. I stepped out on the porch and looked north along the river. In the distance, they appeared as two brightly-dressed figures and something small bobbing around their feet. Jane and Sandra seemed to be in a deep discussion, for their heads alternately tilted toward each other.

I fixed myself a cup of coffee and took it out to the porch to sip and admire the scenery. The house was built in the middle sixties by a contractor who'd built lots of tract homes in this area. One porch is off the dining area. Another porch is off Jane's bedroom, and a third off the master bedroom. This one was enclosed and looked from the outside like a greenhouse. We called it the summer porch because the bugs couldn't get at you here, and the bugs became thick during the summer.

Mae and I had loved this house. We'd been happy here. Both boys were away at college, coming home for holidays. We'd bought the place free and clear and anticipated no overwhelming bills, only property taxes. And so it came as both an irony and a shock when Mae's health had taken a sudden turn for the worse, and the medical bills began arriving, and our financial situation quickly deteriorated. The Knors understood our predicament; they came to dinner often here. When push came to shove, they'd made us a generous offer, so we didn't even have to put the place up for sale. We just cleaned out our stuff, and set off for North Carolina as the Knors were moving in. Seems like only yesterday.

After the two ladies returned, Sandra fixed herself a cup of coffee too and joined me on the porch while Jane fed Mindy. I told her what Malcolm had suggested and asked if she knew of any way we could check these figures. She was way ahead of me.

"I have been in contact with the Memphis police. They said they would pick up this Johnny Hooper on suspicion of child prostitution and question him. I should be hearing something soon."

"Maybe they won't get anything out of him."

"Maybe. Or maybe they'll persuade him to turn state's witness to save his own butt."

"If that happens," I speculated, "Sinclair and Williston's level of anxiety would be raised considerably."

"Yes. And there was one hint dropped back in North Carolina which keeps haunting me."

"What's that?"

"That Sinclair and Williston had been paid upfront money, a down payment if you will. By whoever oversees this operation. Which might be our Mr. Chin of Boone."

"That down payment, I gather, would be for Jane."

"That's the assumption."

"And if they don't deliver the goods, they're in trouble."

"With people who would rather see them dead than alive to turn state's witnesses."

"If these speculations are on track, they desperately need to get Jane on her way overseas."

"Mind you, these speculations are not hard information. I'm not at liberty to reveal the source, yet, but I consider it a reliable one."

"Then we've got to assume Sinclair and Williston are desperate."

"Yes," she said quietly, calmly. "I suspect they got into this for the big money and are now scared and confused."

We were quiet for a time. The river rushed on in a steady monotone, a seemingly never-ending command: *Hush.* Now and then the wind argued by fluttering leaves in the surrounding oak trees, a sound that seemed to say, *Never.*

"I've heard several different versions," she said, "of how you and Jane came to be together."

"Together," I repeated, giving the word a twist of sarcasm. Rather than argue that point, I said, "Mind telling me those several versions? And which one you believe?"

"Not at all. The first version I heard was that you had kidnapped her. But as I learned more about both of you from Maude Jennings, I discarded that one. Then I was told you had probably enticed her. That both you and your departed wife, bless her soul, had found Jane *special.* And that Jane helped ease the pain of your loss and loneliness."

I grunted and said, "I guess that one takes the curse off the kidnapping version. But I want you to know I'm not enchanted by the company of teenage girls. I much prefer grownups."

"And when I talked to the other residents of West Wing, I came away with the impression that your wife, Mrs. Sweet, might have wanted to adopt Jane."

"Mae and I did talk about adopting Jane, but that was when we were new there. We soon realized that was a hair-brained idea, thinking adopting any of those kids would be easy. Jane especially."

She shot me a sidelong glance. "It was while going over her record with Maude, her social worker, that I got the powerful impression—and mind you, this is only an impression—that it was Jane who adopted you. One might even say enticed or kidnapped you. I prefer adopted."

"You may also have gotten the impression going over her record that Jane has developed a neat way of putting male adults in a double bind. She told me that if I turned her in, she'd accuse me of molestation, even rape. I reasoned that Herb and Emma Williston would have loved to back up that accusation, along with making a kidnapping charge stick. But then Jane put a move on me when I was least expecting it. I realize she desperately needs someone to care for her, and sex is her primary coping mechanism. The world has taught her it's her best way to get what she wants."

"Dick," said Sandra with a pleasant grin, "I want you to know I believe you would never hurt Jane."

"Thanks, that takes some pressure off."

"I also want you to know that your version is pretty much what Jane told me, just now when we took our walk. That she ran away by hiding out in your van. And that she has... well, she wants to live with you."

Hearing Jane's flip-flops slapping the hardwood floor just inside, I hurried to cap this conversation. "I want to keep her out of the hands of Sinclair and company, but I do not want to adopt her—or be adopted by her. I'm way too old to tackle the job of raising such a problem child. But I do want to place her with people who are up to this task. When this is over, if I can find such people.

34

I was reading the book Sandra give me when my mind starts wandering. I get to thinking how I'm okay right now, but what's gonna be happening tomorrow? Next week? Next year?

I don't like to wander that way. What can you do about tomorrow or next week? I like to stick to right now. But, you know, when your mind wanders, it takes you with it.

So I come in from the porch off my bedroom and I turn on the TV, pick up MTV, some rock group I never seen before. But that's okay, I like MTV to bring my mind back. Dancing does that.

There's a big mirror at the end of this room away from the kitchen, and I'm watching myself dancing in that mirror. I ain't bad looking in jeans. One foster daddy told me I got a classical figure. I can't even remember his name no more. There's been so many.

I'm dancing to the music and Sandra comes along and says, Hey Jane, what's there to do around here? You been outside along the river?

Sure. I hit the off button and say, Let's take a walk along the river. There's a path there, and we can take Mindy. She likes it out there by the river.

I put the leash on Mindy—not that she's big enough yet to run very far, but you never know. I tell Sandra how they call this thing a river but back home in North Carolina, it ain't nothing but a crick or runoff, all loud and fast and going to a *real* river somewhere. It's got whole tree branches and parts of cars, Lord knows what all floating down it.

Then Sandra pulls me up short by asking if Dick really kidnapped me.

I laugh and say, Hell no! That must be some story they cooked up back at Grandmother's Home, or else my social worker put it in their heads.

How did you two come to be together then, she says.

So I tell her. I run by hiding out in Dick's van. I knew he was going to California—heard it on the grapevine—and I needed to run. Hurt and Enema kept saying they was gonna get me adopted by the Chins, real soon. In other words, they was fixing to sell my ass to Asia. So I hid out in Dick's van the night before he left. That's how we come to be together here.

What happened, she says, when he got picked up in New Mexico.

Oh, I could see that coming. I knew soon as I seen them two cops walk in this place where we was gonna eat, knew those mothers was there to grab me and put me back in the system. Knew who put 'em up to it, too. Maude Jennings. My social worker. So I quick ducked into the ladies room and went out the window. Figured if I was wrong, I could just walk in the front door again and no big deal. But I wasn't wrong. Went and hid under that building, a restaurant and store and whatnot. Stayed there a long time. Knew them cops was gonna either hold Dick for kidnapping or come back here after me. And if they come back after me, they was gonna bring Dick with 'em, cause how else would they know which girl was me?

Makes sense, she says. So what happened?

I was watching from under that building all day. It had a crawl space about one and a half foot high. Lotta pipes and wires and some trash blowing around. Clump clump clump, people walking around on the wooden floors above my head.

Long about dark, I come out of there and snuck into Dick's van—he's always leaving doors unlocked and this time he left the back door of his van unlocked, see. About an hour later, I hear him outside calling for me. I didn't holler back cause I thought them cops might be with him. Anyhow, pretty soon he got behind the wheel and we drove on.

So you were on your way to California again. What did you think you were going to do when you got here?

Figured I was gonna get Dick to take me, keep me, help me out. He's a lonely broke old man and I can be good company for him, and I could make us some get-ahead money too. We could make a life.

Oh! Then would you like to *stay* with Dick?

Yeah. For now.

How do you mean, for now? How long?

I don't know, long as it works out, I guess.

He's taken care of you so far, hasn't he?

Well, he tried to dump me off—to my mom and then to my auntie. But now I got his wife's ashes. Hostage. That's how I know he ain't gonna make no sudden moves on me no more. His wife's ashes. He tries anything I'll hide her ashes and her ghost'll give him hell.

So, she says, raising her arms to the sky, sounds to me like you want to stay with Dick forever and ever.

No no no! I ain't done growing up yet. Just till I finish growing up, that's all.

Got it! she says, and gives me a big hug, lets me know she means it. Such a big hug it makes Mindy jealous and she starts yipping around, so we both pick her up and hug her, let her know we ain't gonna turn her out.

I like Sandra. She understands. Last night she told me she was like me when she was my age, and now look at her. At first, I thought that was half bullshit. You know, a lot of grown-ups say, Oh I know just what you're going through, I went through the same thing. But not Sandra. She's for real.

197

35

The next morning when I stumbled out to the kitchen for a wake up coffee, Sandra was sitting on the couch hunched over the mahogany table that separates couch from fireplace, the phone held to her ear by her left shoulder, as she worked a ballpoint on a notepad at whizzing speed. At the top of the lined page she had written, "Johnny Hooper," in large letters. Below that, her notes read: "Admits dealing with two men—sent girls to Phoenix. Drove girls to L.A.—put on plane to Hong Kong. Quick money—in cash."

As I read, Sandra's large, almond shaped eyes turned their dark blue lights on me with a look. She had finished jotting notes for the moment and was listening, saying an occasional, "Uh huh," and tightening her lips, shooting me that look.

Surmising that Johnny Hooper had been picked up by police, questioned and had revealed information—true or false—I continued into the kitchen, where Sandra had made a pot of coffee, helped myself to a cup and carried it back to the living room. She'd hung up the phone and was studying her notes.

"There's more," she said before I asked. "Hooper told the Memphis police he dealt with two men. Says he never knew where they were from. Or why they picked him. Said they approached him several years ago and asked if he'd like to make some quick money. What did he have to do? Just meet a girl when she landed at the Phoenix Airport, drive her to the LA Airport, and put her on another plane. Nothing else."

"And the two men?"

"That's the kicker. Said he never heard of Mr. and Mrs. Chin. He named a Mr. Jones and a Mr. Johnson. The names they gave him. He was to call Mr. Jones after he'd put the girl on the plan to Hong Kong. An eight hundred number. Mr. Jones would then overnight mail him the money. Five thousand dollars a girl. Cash."

"Jones and Johnson?" I asked with a smirk.

"Hooper said he realized the names were phony."

"Jane told me Hooper came to her school posing as her uncle. That suggests he knows Sinclair and Williston. Told Jane if she ever wanted to run and make a lot of money, gave her his number and address in Memphis. And yesterday he became Jane's connection to Pamela. He forwarded Jane's number to Pamela, who called here."

"That's the good news," said Sandra. "The bad news is, Hooper is out on the street again. They're expecting him to contact Sinclair and Williston. They have him wired."

"Which means," I said, "that he's probably contacted Williston and Sinclair, and told them about being questioned. And given them Jane's latest phone number here at this house. They probably used the number to find out exactly where we are."

"And so we have two very frightened and desperate 'gentlemen' on our hands."

"That's my guess." I shuddered at the thought of those two just outside, watching this house. "Let's move on. No point staying here as sitting ducks."

"Let me show you something," she said, and got up, walked to her room and came back holding one of those guns with a clip of bullets that curve out the bottom of the thing. An automatic assault gun of some kind.

"It's an Uzi," she informed me, flopping back down on the couch with the thing aimed at the empty fireplace. "And I'm quite proficient with it."

"How did you get that thing on the airplane?"

"It has its own traveling case and papers. It gets special handling when I travel."

"If we stay here, you might not get a chance to use it. They'll probably surprise us. They have no reasons left to beat around the bush."

"I have a surprise for you," she said, laying the gun on the couch beside her. "A few Santa Barbara City PD guys have agreed to make a little extra cash by keeping a round-the-clock vigil at the highway end of Paradise Road. I talked to your son Kent, too. He learned from his friend at the Great Western Motel in Carpenteria that Mr. Williston has moved into the motel where Sinclair is staying."

"You've been busy," I said.

"Their two rental cars are under surveillance by Carpenteria PD. If they leave the motel, we'll be called here. If they turn off San Marcos Highway onto Paradise Road, we'll get another call."

"So you're saying they can't surprise us."

"I don't think so, but they are desperate and frightened. They feel the noose tightening. Let's try to think along with them. Knowing these types, they probably have the lives of those girls insured. They may also have taken out a policy on Jane, or shifted her Grandmother's Home policy to themselves, or some paper shuffling like that."

"You're saying the girls are the evidence and they might want to get rid of the evidence, plus collect on insurance policies. Is that it?"

"That's one possible scenario."

The palms of my hands were sweating and I'd only had a few sips of coffee. I heaved a sigh and wondered how, at age sixty-three, I could find myself in such a mess. After living most of my life with no more danger than driving drunk once, years ago.

She continued: "But here's another. Maybe they'll need to get Jane alive. Maybe they've already been paid some upfront money for her—perhaps by Mr. Chin, or through him—and need to deliver her, or else. And, chances are they are dealing with people who would kill them as quick as look at them. Especially if they find out the noose is tightening, that they might dime them to save their own asses."

"You're making a lot of chances-are assumptions," I said, wiping my palms on my blue jeans. "Why don't we move to someplace safer and continue this."

"Safer? What do you suggest?"

I knew this was a hair-brained idea the moment it was out of my mouth. I was remembering a motel up the coast in San Simeon near the Hearst Castle. Mae and I used to weekend there years ago. It's called The Pines and is a sprawling place surrounded by mammoth pine trees that whisper in the wind and create a feeling of tranquility. But that's not what we needed. What we needed was safety, protection. People with their eyes out for Williston and Sinclair. People with expertise in the business of interdicting scum like them.

We'd been speaking in hushed tones. When Jane came padding out, we tacitly agreed to table the matter for now. "What's for breakfast?" Jane said, rubbing her eyes with the heels of her hands.

"Let's take a look," said Sandra, standing and waving a hand behind her curvaceous posterior. Indicating the gun, I realized. She wanted me to put it back in her room while she distracted Jane in the kitchen.

While they opened and inspected the refrigerator and cupboards, I picked the thing up and, holding it close to my body, smuggled it to the room Sandra occupied. The blue-black steel felt cold and smelled of oil. It was lighter in weight than I expected. I shoved the thing under her bed, glad to be rid of it.

In the kitchen I sat at the table and stared out at the river's white-capped brown water rushing down the mountain toward the sea. It was not quite seven-thirty. I thought of calling Kent, but didn't. He would call me from a safer phone when he got to work. Then the phone chirped.

Sandra shot me another one of her looks as I was walking back to the living room, where the phone rested on the mahogany table.

"Hello, Mr. Steel? This is Phyllis Angelica, Jane's aunt. We met the other day when you drove Jane down to my house."

"Yes, of course. And then you drove Jane up to Oxnard to her mother's place."

"Oh, I was such a fool! I'm so sorry! That's why I'm calling."

"How did you get this number?"

"Oh. Jane's social worker back in North Carolina. Maude something or other. I must have called twenty people before I got this number from that nice lady."

That tipped me off that she was lying. "My my," I said sarcastically, "that's something Maude's never done before." Under the circumstances, Maude would never give away my phone number.

"Well, I want to make it up to Jane. I feel so lousy about what happened. I never *realized.*"

"Don't worry about it. There's nothing to make up."

"But there is! Is Jane there? Can I speak to her, please?"

"She's not here, and I don't think it's a good idea for you to speak to her again. We're beyond that now."

"Beyond that! What do you mean?"

"Look, Mrs. Angelica, I have things to do, I'm going to hang up now and—"

"Wait! Hold it! Please, Mr. Steel. See, I've been thinking. I should have taken that girl to Disneyland or something. She needs things like that. And that's why I'm calling, I'd like to—"

"Why did you drive Jane to Oxnard?"

"Her mother, Helen, my sister. Jane said she wanted to see her mother and her mother—"

"Wanted to sell Jane?"

"No, for heaven's sake no! I just thought it would be good for Jane."

Her lying was stark naked. I had told her when I brought Jane to visit her that Jane had spent the previous day with her mother. "Well, I have your number. I'll call if there's a chance Jane can go with you to Disneyland," I said just to end this.

After a breakfast of pancakes and sausage, cooked by Jane assisted by Sandra, and which Jane then wolfed down like someone determined to put on weight, Sandra and I were alone in the living room. Jane was on the porch with her book.

Sandra lifted her eyebrows, inquiring about the call.

"Jane's aunt," I said. "Wants to see her again. Take her to Disneyland, she says."

"Smells like she's been contacted."

"That's my guess. Williston or Sinclair. Said she got this number from Maude but I know Maude would never give anyone this number."

I called Maude while Sandra cleaned off the table and washed the dishes by hand. Phyllis Angelica had called her, Maude said, and she chatted about adopting Jane.

"Did you give her this phone number?" I asked.

"Certainly not!" said Maude, bristling with indignation.

I suspected Johnny Hooper had called his so-called Mr. Jones and Mr. Johnson, and they had put Mrs. Angelica up to her call to here.

"It's a setup for sure, and I don't feel safe here," I said to Sandra, sounding to myself more like ten years old than sixty-three.

"Compared to where?" asked Sandra.

"I don't know where."

"Then let's wait 'em out here. We have eyes and ears out there, watching the motel and watching the only entrance into this area. If those two in the motel make a move, we'll know about it."

"What if," I said, "I approach them, find out what's on their minds."

"Dick, this is a police matter, we're trained to deal with such people. Let Williston and Sinclair make the next move. They're desperate."

"I suspect they also know they're being watched by the local police."

"Probably," she said.

"And there are others involved in this ring. I'm just not comfortable waiting for them to make the next move. I'd like to go there, talk to them, feel them out. Your people are watching them and monitoring their calls, right?"

"Yes but—"

"So if I go into their room and don't come out..."

"Well, come to think of it, it might work for you to approach them. They might tell you things they won't tell anyone else."

"Incidentally, how did you manage that, the local police connection?" With daylight coming in the windows behind me, I watched her copper-toned face carefully as her expression turned momentarily wistful.

"An old friend. Moved out here a couple of years ago, joined the local force. We had a brief affair back in Pennsylvania."

"Are the local cops being paid for this?"

"By the State of North Carolina. I was told to get them to send a bill. I was also told I'd better not come back empty handed."

"So, instead of waiting for them to make the next move, suppose I go to the Great Western in Carpenteria and chat with Williston and Sinclair."

"Let's consider the scenario. You go there and talk to them. If they don't hold you, what information do you think you might get from them?"

We were interrupted by the phone's chirping, Hampton calling from his island home somewhere in the Caribbean. "Dad? Kent tells me you're in the Knors' mountain home. Is that where I'm reaching you?"

"Yes it is. Do you have an arrival time?"

"Tomorrow afternoon at four fifteen, American Airlines. Is that okay with you?"

"I'll be there."

"Kent also says things are getting, well, complicated about that girl."

"Complicated would be one way of putting it."

"I'd like to meet her. Maybe we can help each other."

"That would be nice," I said, surprised by Hampton's mention of helping. The thought made me forget he is in an income bracket where overseas phone calls are a tax write-off. I cut the call short, asking for his number there in case I had a sudden change of plans.

I turned to Sandra and said, "I really have a very strong urge to go to Carpenteria and visit Sinclair and Williston. Auntie Phyllis must be in contact with them. Which means they know we're here. If they also know that Hooper has talked, they'll be ready to bring this thing to a head, don't you think?"

"I think it's reasonable to assume that Sinclair and Williston now know the noose is tightening. They're liable to grab you as a hostage."

"Well, if the noose is that tight, why don't the police move in and arrest them?"

"We need to get a few more pieces of the puzzle. And we'd like to get those girls back from Asia, unharmed. So we have to be careful how we lower the boom."

"Sinclair and Williston, last time I saw them, they acted like they weren't on friendly terms. I think they were trying to mislead me, or they wouldn't be at the same motel now. Anyhow, since they can't make a move without your people spotting them, the only way they can get to Jane is through me."

"What the heck, okay, if you don't come out, we'll have an excuse to go in."

"Oh, I'll come out. Sinclair and Williston aren't into hostage taking. They're deal makers."

"When do you want to do this?"

"Tomorrow around noon, on my way to pick up Hampton."

We spent the rest of that day going over Sandra's notes. She'd devoted one newly purchased notebook to this project, and it was already half filled. She'd interviewed the oldest kids in West Wing, Emma Williston, some other staff members, Mr. and Mrs. Chin of Boone, and some others. She had copies of Chin's telephone bills going back two years, and had highlighted the calls made to Johnny Hooper's number, to Sinclair, Williston, and to Grandmother's Home.

One page had become her directory of names and numbers, and another page had a list of what we now knew. That Johnny Hooper met those girls in Phoenix and drove them to LA where he put them on planes bound for Hong Kong. That each of those girls had first been adopted by the Chins, and that these adoptions had been set up by Alfred Sinclair and the Willistons.

She also had found out that Williston owed the Internal Revenue Service close to half a million dollars and was making monthly payments on this debt, payments which his Grandmother's Home salary would never enable him to afford $5,000 every three months, $20,000 a year.

"Williston told me," I said, "that he still retains an interest in a business he sold."

"Not so," she said. Flipping to the pertinent page in her notebook, she added, "He bought that business five years ago, when he took his Army retirement. A picture framing business. It cost him his entire savings. He did very well for a while, then the IRS hit him for nonpayment on proven income. That's when he sold, took the job at Grandmother's Home and missed two or three quarterly payments to the IRS that first year. After that, those five thousand dollar payments four times a year were made like clockwork."

"And Sinclair? What have you found out about his financial affairs?"

"He's much better at covering his tracks. But we're working on it."

"We?"

"My boss and I. We're *officially* off the case, but."

"So all you need now to nab them is to make sure those girls can get back here safe and sound."

"That's about the size of it. And you know, after thinking it over, I do like your idea to visit those perpetrators. No use prolonging the agony."

36

Next day around noon, Dick takes off. Says he's driving down to see somebody, then he's going to the airport to pick up his son, the one owns the Mercedes. So I says to Sandra, Hey, let's take a walk somewhere.

She says, Oh! I should have asked Dick to bring back some food. We don't have anything here for dinner. Okay, let's walk to that country store and get hamburger meat, buns and some charcoal. We can have a cookout on the porch off your bedroom.

It's a beautiful spring day. Bright sun, not a cloud in the sky. We're walking along the road and a couple of guys in a red Dodge pickup cruise by slow, then stop just ahead of us. They're both turned around looking back at us.

I laugh and say, Well lookee here, they want to talk to us. But Sandra ain't buying this.

We're not interested, boys, she tells 'em. And the way she says *boys* lets 'em know what she thinks of 'em.

They drive up the road a ways, then turn around and cruise back by us. Sandra keeps her eyes straight ahead. I do the same.

She says, I hope you're not ready to jump into any red pickup comes down the road, girl. You won't last long that way.

Me? No! I'm not going nowhere with the likes of them.

Now you're showing some smarts, girl.

Takes half an hour to walk to this store. It's like a Seven Eleven, except it's got more stuff in it. You can buy hats, kites, jackets and stuff, besides food.

I walk around inside with Sandra looking for hamburger meat and buns. Then I get tired of waiting on her to make up her mind. I got some bucks in my jeans so I buy a Mars bar, and tell her I'll see her outside.

They got a long porch outside this store. Bench along the wall. I sit down to eat my Mars bar, looking out over a long valley up here in the mountains. Lots of cars and pickups pulling up, people going into the store, going out, driving away.

So I hardly notice it when this red Dodge pickup parks at the foot of the stairs to this porch. Same pickup cruised us on the road. Same two guys, redneck hoods, you know. Scraggly kind of glassy-eyed doper dudes. I'm munching on my Mars bar when one of 'em gets out and walks up the steps real slow, kind of watching me out the corner of his eye.

These guys sure ain't nobody to get mixed up with, unless I was running and needed a place to sleep. So I look away, trying to put 'em out of sight and out of mind. Blue jeans, cowboy boots, tank top. I don't let on I notice even when one don't go into the store but heads down the porch.

Walks real slow down toward me, I keep staring away, munching my Mars bar, and all of a sudden, this motherfucker grabs me. So fast it takes the breath out of me. Clamps a hand over my mouth, scoops me off that bench and carries me tucked under his arm. I'm kicking like hell and trying to scream, spitting out my last bite of Mars bar.

Shoves me into the passenger side of the pickup, on the filthy floor, his buddy takes hold of me, claps a set of handcuffs on my wrists with one hand while holding my mouth with the other. I kick and try to bite. Get some of his hand but not enough to do much harm. He's too strong for me. Gets my hands cuffed behind my back. Then he takes a damn old

209

sweaty bandana from around his neck and ties this around my face so it gags me. Wet with his stinking sweat in my mouth, chasing what's left of Mars bar taste.

Next thing I know we're moving. I'm on the floor between this guys knees, got his big old hairy legs over my shoulders and squeezing my head. Got handcuffs on, his sweaty old bandana between my teeth, feeling this pickup bumping along, then speeding up and making a big turn—onto the highway, I guess. Cause then we're going uphill a long way and I can see mountain tops out the window.

Guy that got me between his knees, he's wearing cowboy boots and a pair of shorts, no shirt. Got one of those baseball hats on, says CAT on the front. Got fat, hairy legs sticking out of them shorts, squashing down on my shoulders and squeezing my head.

Damn! Seems like I can't go nowhere alone, some gross son of a bitch grabs me! And this time, it's two of 'em. Why? Why do these crazy bastards pick on me?

Going up the highway, old hairy legs lets up on the squeezing and the one who's driving, he says, Now sweetheart, you don't know who we are but we know who you are. You're Jane Doyle, and some people from North Carolina want to see you. That's where we're gonna take you, to them.

Oh shit! Fucking Hurt and Enema gonna make a *real* mess of my life now.

I thought at first maybe they was going to take me all the way across the country this way to get me back to Grandmother's Home. But then they turned off the highway and we were going up some bumpy dirt road, felt like the truck was bouncing over boulders. It like to break my backbone. When it stops, they both push their squeaky old doors open and get out, and the guy in the shorts hauls me out by my handcuffed arms. Hurts me when he shoves his hands under my armpits and yanks.

Here's some old cabin up on top of a hill, looks like a hillbilly hideout. Nothing else around but trees and vacant fields. Got no idea where I'm at. Shorts shoves me along in front of him, up two old steps to a stoop and through the door of this cabin.

Potbelly stove, a couple of stacked bunk beds, a couch, some wooden chairs and a table, all on bare wood floors. Reminds me of the kind of place you find poor white trash living way up in the mountains of North Carolina. Rotten old wood and bare windows. Sits me down on a chair and says, Rest your buns, cutie. And don't even think of running cause there ain't no place to run to now.

Then the guy who drove picks up a phone, dials, waits a while and says, Mr. Sinclair? We got her. No problem. We'll deliver around midnight. See you then. Bye.

So! Goddamn Sin-switch is in on this! Son of a bitch had these fiends grab me. Him and Hurt and Enema.

Shorts turns on a TV set in the corner. I can't see it cause the potbelly stove is blocking my view. He leans back in his chair, lights up a joint and smokes. The driver walks by and takes a couple tokes. Shorts holds it out my way but I shake my head. Which ain't a real smart thing to do. At least they'd of had to take the gag out for me to toke, and then maybe I could have worked something out with 'em.

Pretty soon they got their heads together, talking, slipping me a glance now and then. Then Driver walks over to me, grabs me under the arm and hauls me up, turns me around, unties the gag and takes it out of my mouth. Says, Honey, you is one good-looking little bitch. And plants a gross and disgusting kiss on my lips.

That knocks me back onto the chair and almost makes me puke. Next time I look up, Driver's got his fly unzipped and is fishing out his weener. I try to look away and pretend I don't know what he's got in mind. It's swelling up right under my nose so big and wide and fat, ain't no way I *can* take it in the mouth, even if I wanted to. He puts one of his big dirty paws under my chin and tries to pry my mouth open with the other and shove his thing in—which he finally starts to do, but I can't open wide enough not to bite. Yells, Ouch! You bitch!

Then he shoves me over behind the couch, unbuckles my belt and pulls my jeans down around my ankles. Tugs down my panties and I know what's coming. Puts his filthy paw on my back and bends me over the back of the couch.

I get my mind on blank whiteout and try to coast with it so it don't hurt too much when he jams that big fat ugly dick of his at me. Seems any time I go somewhere, some ghoul rapes me. Ain't nothing I can do about it now, except blank out on it. I only know if I blank out good enough, there won't be no *me* here. I won't feel what's happening, like it's happening to somebody else.

Never did blank out far enough so I couldn't feel it. Hurt like hell! I was dry as a bone and scared, and could feel my bottom ripping cause I ain't big enough for this gross son of a bitch.

After he's done, the other one stands up like he's gonna take his turn on me, but he says, Oh shit, look what you did! You got her bleeding. What a mess!

And he sits back down and watches TV.

I slumped to the floor and just lay there crying. They both just sit watching TV, paying me no mind. Never even said nothing to me. Just snacked on crackers and cheese, and toked joints and got out a mirror and coke and did lines.

Around sundown, Hairy Legs with the shorts on walks over to me, yanks me up onto my knees, and drops his shorts, pokes his thing at my mouth. He's normal size but he tries to ram it down my throat. I'm crying and he's shoving, and the only thing that saves me is he gets off quick.

After that—me laying on the floor, my whole bottom feeling cut to shreds, my mouth numb, handcuffs cutting my wrists—

old Hairy Legs carries the mirror over to me and says, Try some of this, Honey, it'll cheer you up.

I shake my head. So torn up I can't even talk.

I ever get loose from this tie-down, I can maybe find a way to kill these motherfuckers. That's what I set my head on: getting loose and finding some way to kill these bastards.

After awhile, I was so damn numb I couldn't even cry no more. Made me think of one girl back in West Wing, Susan. She purposely eats and drinks everything she can get her hands on so she stays big and fat and ugly. Even wears men's clothes. Her daddy started raping her when she was eight years old. He was the county sheriff.

Well, I guess if it was your daddy done you like this, at eight years old, your brains would get twisted too. Me, I got to keep my head straight. I ever get the chance, I swear I'm gonna kill both these scumbags.

37

The next day around nine o'clock I called the motel and asked for Mr. Sinclair and was put through to his room, number 210.

"I'd like to visit you there, in your motel," I told him.

"Anytime. When would be best for you?" Sinclair's voice had something of your professional announcer's resonance to it, another fund raising asset of his.

"Today, around noon."

"Good. Herb's staying here, too, you know. Next door, room 211. Shall I ask him to come?"

"Please. And this time, let's cut through the game playing and get right to the real stuff."

"I'm very much in favor of that," he said in a near singsong that dripped confidence. He had to know the noose was tightening but he could still act convincingly confident.

Around eleven o'clock, I said goodbye to Sandra and Jane. They talked about going swimming in the river. Since neither had a bathing suit, and the river water was high, swift and still winter cold, this was idle talk, but Jane had at last found a role model—that was the reality of their busy chatter.

As I drove down the mountain into Santa Barbara, then took Route 101 south toward Carpenteria, I tried to summarize what I thought of as the theme songs of Sinclair, Williston and myself. I tried to imagine what we'd say to each other if we were each to be completely open and honest.

What I'd say was pretty simple. *Jane Doyle stowed away in my van. Maybe I should have turned her back into the system. But I didn't. Instead, I have become rather fond of that girl. She's far more wounded than I am. It helps me heal myself to care for her. If I can heal the harm that's been done to her, I can heal myself. So I'm here to see that you two white slavers get put away for the rest of your lives.*

Sinclair's would say: *I'm a winner, always have been a winner, a champion football lineman, straight A student, a take-charge guy who loves a challenge. And I don't intend to allow you or anyone else to turn me into a loser, so let's make a deal.*

Williston's would run something like this: *I served my country as a master sergeant for twenty years, then went into business for myself, made a ton money, got the IRS after me. Now those sons of bitches have me making such steep quarterly payments it would destroy me, if I wasn't a man of resources. But I am. I found a way to pay back that half million they say I owe. I'm going to do that and then some, and nobody's going to stop me, including a sorry old bleeding heart liberal like you, Dick.*

As I pulled into the Great Western's parking lot, I noticed another car behind me. The driver, a young man in a blue sports shirt, smiled and waved. He was apparently another of Sandra's resources, there to keep an eye on things. He stationed himself near the parking lot entrance, and the last I saw of him as I turned to mount the stairs to the second floor, he was drinking from a can of cola.

I wasn't exactly full of fear when I knocked on Sinclair's motel room door, but I wasn't exactly calm either. I had an edge of adrenalin and was focused on what I had to do here. The first thing I had to determine was how honest and upfront they were going to be.

Sinclair opened the door with a phone cradled between his ear and shoulder, and waved me toward a chair. A moment later, Williston walked in without knocking. He shook my hand and grinned coyly, his large jawbone angled in a scoffing pose.

As he was pulling up a chair, I said, "Have you two gentlemen heard from your partner Johnny Hooper?"

Williston's eyebrows went up. "Who's he?" he asked, ham-acting so much surprise it was clear he was lying.

"I'm just trying to find out how honest you're ready to be."

"Oh!" That seemed to cause him to shift the gears of his act. "Okay, yes. We have heard from one Mr. Hooper, as a matter of fact."

Sinclair was off the phone now and pulling up a third chair to our standard motel room round table near the door. "Yes, indeed," he said, smiling his usual. "Seems you've been a busy beaver, Dick."

"And it looks like you two are in deep, deep trouble with the law," I said.

"Not to worry," grinned Sinclair. "We're very good at the game of CYA. Cover *your* ass, Dick. You're the one who's going to get hung out to dry: kidnapping and statutory rape." He winked, then added, "Unless you decide to cooperate."

I presented them a furrowed brow of worry. I gathered they knew nothing about Sandra Mulholland's work. Otherwise, I don't think they'd act *this* confident. I also strongly suspected they'd planned some kind of contingency in case Johnny Hooper ever discussed their affairs with the police. What could that contingency be?

"Tell you what," said Williston, after some seconds had ticked off and I'd shown no urge to reply to Sinclair. "You're out of a job now, Dick. Is that right? Or do you have something lined up that we don't know about."

"I'm out of a job, widowed, alone and grieving. No prospects. Tell me what."

"Okay, what we'd like to suggest is that you come in with us, work with us. I know you to be a diligent childcare worker, you and Mae both, when you were with the agency. And now I want you to know that what we're doing benefits the kids involved and makes money. Good money."

"How does it benefit the kids?"

"They acquire an education!" said Sinclair, in a tone that told me I must be feeble minded for not realizing this. "And a second language, and make money doing so."

"That's not how I heard it," I said.

"How'd you hear it? And who from?" said Williston, suddenly without his Appalachian accent. This meant he was seriously concerned, allowing his fear to come through. I hoped he'd be even more fearful when he heard this:

"The suspicion in North Carolina is that you two are mixed up in a racket to sell teenaged girls into prostitution."

That brought big guffaws of laughter exploding from both. Williston slapped his thighs and Sinclair tossed back his head and roared at the ceiling. I was astounded at this laughter but kept a straight face.

Sinclair recovered first. He went from raucous laughter to intense seriousness amazingly fast. He leaned his elbows on the table and looked me hard in the eye and said:

"Dick, you know these girls who are sexually abused and abandoned grow up to be prostitutes no matter what."

"Not necessarily. I've heard they do, but I don't believe it has to turn out that way."

"Well, it *is* true, nine and a half times out of ten. It's a fact of life, man. Herb and I," he said, spreading his arms wide, "see to it that they're protected."

"Protected," I repeated, looking thoughtful. I waited for more.

"Yes! And educated. They'll come back to the States speaking Japanese or Chinese or some other Asian language, and then they'll be able to support themselves as translators."

I furrowed my brow again and nodded my head, and pretended I thought he had a good point here, as I digested this:

the girls were protected while they did what they would do in any case, and learned a foreign language in the meantime.

"How much money is involved? What would I have to do?"

"Thousands in cash each month, untaxed."

"And all I'd have to do is take girls from Phoenix to the airport in L.A.," I said, answering my second question myself and letting them know I'd found out what Hooper had been doing.

They exchanged a look. "How did you find out about Johnny Hooper?" asked Williston.

"Jane." I smiled.

They exchanged another look.

"Tell me something," I said. "Why didn't you gentlemen offer me this opportunity before, when you first found me out here?"

Sinclair rubbed his bulging right cheek with the palm of his hand a moment. "To be perfectly frank about it, Dick, Herb and I had a little falling out over this business, Jane's running off with you. We had a disagreement over how to handle it. But we've patched things up now and—"

"What was your disagreement?" I interrupted.

"Well," he said, turning his eyes to the ceiling, "Herb felt the best way to proceed would be to just grab Jane and forget about you. I felt, on the other hand, that since you now *have* Jane, it would be far better to..." he beamed at me, "*negotiate.*"

"I appreciate your candor," I said. "And your concern for the well being of everyone involved."

"Fine. Where was I? Oh. So now Herb and I have decided to offer you a much more lucrative arrangement than the one we had with Johnny Hooper. Our people will send a girl to Phoenix. You'll meet her at the Phoenix Airport and drive her to LAX. She'll be under a different name. We'll provide you with a passport for her. Then you'll do something Hooper never did—you'll fly to Hong Kong with her and be met by our people there, and you'll return with a bank check. You'll overnight mail that check to me, and I'll return your portion. You'll fly to Hong Kong about a dozen times a year, on an irregular basis, on the pretext of having business there—we'll provide legitimate exporters for you to visit—and bring back both information and money. We'll want to know the girls are safe and healthy, and that no one on that end is trying to cheat us. In exchange for this service, we'll see to it that you have a decent income. There, that's as clear as I can make it. What do you say?"

"How decent will this income be?"

"How about fifteen thou a month? Plus expenses, of course."

"I'll think about it."

"While you're thinking about it," said Williston, "we'd appreci-ate it if you'd turn Jane over to us."

"I'll think about that, too," I said. "One question: Why are the girls separated in those three cities, Hong Kong, Tokyo, and Bangkok?"

"They are residents of Hong Kong," said Sinclair, "and visit other cities all over the Pacific Rim. You see? They're well cared for, they're protected, and they travel. Is that so bad?"

Then he stood, checked his wristwatch and said something about an important appointment. Williston said, "Come on, Dick, let's you and me go downstairs and have some lunch. Talk this over some more."

"Thanks, Herb, but I've got another appointment."

"We're anxious to know if you're with us," he said. "Or not."

I thought for a moment, then told a bald-faced lie. "I'm with you. Why should I argue? I'm old and worn out, and I need the income. It's just that I want to think this thing through. Maybe I can come up with a way to make it more... profitable. For all concerned."

He patted me on the back as I opened the door to leave. "Okay, *podnah*," he said, extending his Appalachian accent into the Louisiana Delta, "glad you're aboard. Always figured you for *good people*."

"Thanks," I replied, hoping my hatred for him did not come through. "I'll be in touch."

38

Sometime after dark, they take the handcuffs off. Tell me to go in the bathroom and wash my ass off.

I can hardly walk and there's blood dripping down my leg. I stagger in there carrying my jeans and panties, close the door, and look at my face in the mirror. One sad looking girl in there. Eyes bloated from crying, cheeks puffy, lips swollen and sore, everything sore. Something really wrong with them dudes. I wet a washcloth and wash the blood off my bottom. Driver tore me up pretty good down there.

There's a shower in here, some towels. I turn it on, slip out of my blouse, let the water warm up and get in. I scrub hard, trying to get all the sickness out of my skin. They say the skin is porous, that you can take stuff in through your skin, right into your body and blood. I scrub hard so I can get all their goddamn sickness the hell off my skin. Could have been worse, I guess. I've heard of girls being killed by weirdos like them two. At least I'm still alive.

But what for?

While I'm drying off, I see a lady's purse hanging from the door handle. Black leather. Looks pretty classy. I look inside it. No ID, no money, no credit cards. Not much of anything—until I turn it over and dump everything out on the top of the toilet seat and see all this junk but *feel* something else hiding in one of those inner zipper pockets inside this black leather purse.

I unzip and finger around and what do you know. I find this do-dad, you push a button and this *blade* pops out. About six inches long. The case says, Sterling Silver Letter Opener. Real sharp, double edged. This thing's a *shiv*! You know, like a switchblade, but saying it's silver and for opening letters. For sure it's something I can use, I get the chance.

I stick it in my jeans pocket and put everything else back in this black leather purse, hang it up again.

When I come out of the bathroom, they're staring glassy-eyed at the TV. I could just walk up behind one of 'em and pull out this sterling silver letter opener, push the blade out and stick it up by his neck and slice his jugular. Trouble is, I couldn't get both of 'em. The other one would nail me before I got to him.

I look outside through the door, and I can see that running here would be a big, big problem. Nothing but fields and woods. No other houses, no people, nothing.

From behind me, I hear Driver say, Don't even think of running, Jane. I turn around and he's holding this handgun up pointed at the ceiling. And he's so ripped on grass and cocaine, he probably don't know which end is which.

I ain't going nowhere, I tell 'em. But can I have something to eat? I'm starving hungry.

Help yourself, says Driver.

Their kitchen looks like nothing clean been here for weeks. Dishes piled in the sink, pots and pans stacked on the stove, waiting for somebody to wash 'em. In the refrigerator, I find some cheese, individual slices, and there's bread on the counter. Make myself a sandwich and drink a glass of milk, around behind this wall that separates the kitchen from the living room. I'm feeling like dog shit on a clean floor, but I'm still hungry.

After a couple of cheese sandwiches and a couple glasses of milk, I feel a little better... except for being sore all over, inside and out.

Wander back into the living room and sit down on that wooden chair, and just stare at the TV. A basketball game. They're both all wrapped up in this game, and again I think how I could just wander out the door and be gone before the stupid Driver could raise his gun and shoot. They're both totally wasted.

They only keep a couple of lights on, and they're dim. After awhile I feel sleepy. I'd like to go lay down somewhere, but don't want to lay down anywhere near these monster fiends.

Still, I got to lay down or I'll fall off this chair. So finally I go over and lay down on the lower bunk bed and crash. I don't know if they're gonna hurt me no more or not, but I just got to crash.

39

I did think about their proposition, all the way to the nearest payphone where I put through a call to the Knor's house. But the machine answered. I said, "Sandra? If you're there, please pick up. It's me, Dick. Sandra?" I left no message; I'd call again from Los Angeles. What had me worried at this point was Johnny Hooper. It occurred to me that his life was in danger, and that Sinclair and Williston were resourceful criminals. They had to know that Hooper's best shot now was to turn state's witness, which means they have to find a way to terminate him. Now that they thought they'd hired me to replace him.

I was a little irked with Sandra. How could she get those incoming calls telling her Sinclair and Williston were approaching if she put the answering machine on and left the house? Suppose that pair, knowing I was going to be away from the house for several hours now, decided to drive up there and grab Jane? Sandra is armed and able, but even she could be taken by surprise.

I called again from the Los Angeles Airport. "I have a lot of news," she said in a somber voice, "all bad. Jane is gone and Johnny Hooper is dead."

I gasped. "I'm not surprised about Hooper but what happened to Jane?"

"Well, we decided to walk to the country store to buy some things for dinner. She went outside the store with a candy bar while I stood in line at the cash register, and when I came out she was gone. I'm reasonably sure she didn't run. She must have been snatched."

"Sinclair and Williston?"

"I don't think so. My people had them under surveillance all day. They never budged from their motel. But this changes the plan a bit. We have Santa Barbara County Sheriff's Department on standby ready to pick them up as soon as we know Jane's whereabouts. We'll worry about the other three girls later."

"Did she... just wander off? What happened?"

"I think somebody grabbed her. A red pickup truck with two seedy looking characters harassed us when we were walking to the store. I didn't think much about it then, but looking back on it, maybe they grabbed Jane. Or enticed her or whatever."

"And Johnny Hooper, what happened to our star witness?"

"Drug overdose. That's the official report. Six o'clock this morning, Memphis time. Less than twelve hours after he'd been released by the police there. Seems he had enough cocaine in his bloodstream to kick him into the next world. There will be an autopsy, of course, but so far no *official* reason to suspect foul play. He was a known user. I feel *sick* about Jane's disappearance."

"Well," I said, "Sinclair and Williston are up to their ears now. We've got our case."

"We can't collar them until Jane shows up."

"They offered to cut me in for a piece of the action." I shared the salient details of my visit to the motel room, how they revealed the workings of their operation.

"Truly? They *said* that?"

"Yes, they told me how the operation works, offered me a job."

"What did you tell them?"

"I said I'd do it. They offered fifteen thousand a month plus expenses. I hope I didn't incriminate myself."

"Of course not, Dick. I can vouch for your motives, and even testify that we agreed on this together, which is just about what we did, you know."

"I'm in over my head, Sandra, and finding out about Hooper has me worried."

"Let me do the worrying. Meet your son and have a good visit with him."

"Well, if anything breaks—especially if those two leave that motel—call and have me paged here in the terminal."

I'd anticipated spending more time with Sinclair and Williston, and now had an hour and a half to wait for Hampton's plane. I called Sandra twice during that stretch, but she had no news. She was very upset.

"I feel like a failure! How could I have let Jane out of my sight long enough for this to happen? I know she didn't just wander off. And the more I think about it, the more I feel those two in the red pickup truck got her. How could I allow that to happen?"

"Jane Doyle has been running away since she was eight years old. No one has ever been able to figure out why. Don't blame yourself, she does strange things all the time. If she ran, she'll come back. She's never failed to come back before. Maybe she hitch hiked into town and will show up at Kent's. Have you called there?"

"Yes, several times. They're looking for her. Sheriff's people are combing this area for that red pickup truck too. And Kent's friend is keeping his eyes and ears on Sinclair and Williston, along with law enforcement."

"Yes, I saw your lookout in the motel parking lot. Sit tight. Jane runs and returns, that's her pattern. She'll show up."

If she's still alive, I thought but didn't say. If Sinclair and Williston were behind that overdose that killed Hooper, maybe they could engineer a way to do likewise to Jane. It certainly didn't make sense that she would run from Sandra, her latest and greatest heroine.

40

Don't know how long I slept before Driver woke me. Come on, Jane, time to go, he says.

Now it's cold. I'm shivering. They don't notice. They shove me out the door and lead me to the pickup. Hairy Legs sits me on his lap but don't put the cuffs and gag on. I'm thankful for that.

Can't see anything but what's up ahead in the pickup's headlights, and that ain't nothing but dirt road and trees. Big ruts in this muddy road. Puddles the size of ponds.

I remember this fancy letter opener I got in my jeans and put my hand in my pocket to feel it. I space out on holding this blade and thinking how I could ram it into first one heart then the other, real quick.

But I ain't crazy. I know I can't do it quick enough to kill 'em both while we're driving.

We drive down the mountain, same road I come up with Dick. Got cliffs up one side, steep drop-off on the other, lots of tight curves. I think about grabbing the wheel and throwing us all over the edge. Only think about it.

Pretty soon we're on the freeway and I'm feeling slightly better. On the freeway, I know my way around. I can get somewhere from here. Still, I bide my time.

Turn off the freeway and head into the town where Dick's son lives. Must be Sin-switch is here somewhere, and they're taking me to him. Or Hurt Williston, or maybe both. I overheard Dick and Sandra saying they was both out here on the Coast. Well, I have a hunch I'm gonna get a chance to stab *one* of these bastards in the heart before this is all over. At least one, though I'd like to nail 'em all.

Then all of a sudden, Driver pulls up in front of a store and parks, and Hairy Legs gets out and goes inside, says he's gonna pick up a six pack.

Driver leans back and closes his eyes, resting his drug-blitzed brain a spell. Now's my chance. I slip that shiv letter opener out of my jeans, get a good grip on it, then quick as I can, I throw a roundhouse and stab it hard as I can right into his chest, just left of center. He jumps and yells and I'm gone before he knows what hit him.

Out the passenger side of the pickup and around back of that store so fast, his drugged brain can't figure what's happening. Last I seen, he was holding his chest and looking down at it, trying to figure what happened. That's just before I rounded the corner into pitch-black dark and stumbled, hit some garbage cans, got up and kept running.

Up a hill behind this store, there's some houses. I run for them. Got some streetlights in front of them houses, then it's dark behind that. Except for house lights. I go between a couple houses, down a driveway toward a garage.

In the dark beside the garage, I stop and look back. Hairy Legs is walking around the store, looking for me. Carrying his dumb six-pack. Can't see me up here cause I'm in the dark.

Driver comes walking around the other side of the store, holding his chest where I nailed him. Don't know how deep in I went but the bastard is still walking, so I guess I didn't get his heart.

They both walk around to the back and then I can barely make 'em out in the dark back of the store. There's a door back there, and they open it and it's lit inside. While they're standing

227

in the doorway, that's when I see Driver kind of slump down. First he bends over, leaning against the doorjamb, then his knees give out and he's on the ground in the doorway. Hairy Legs starts to lift him, gets his hands under Driver's arms and pulls, then looks like he changes his mind. Driver's down for the count and Hairy Legs ain't sure what to do.

Somebody from the store comes. I know he's from the store cause he's wearing an apron like they do in supermarkets. He talks to Hairy Legs awhile, then runs back around to the front.

I sit down with my back against the garage door and rest. I got no idea where I'm at. I *think* it must be the town where Dick's son lives. From here, I can see the freeway beyond the store, and beyond that, more town. I decide to rest here till them two dudes decide what to do.

I was almost asleep when I heard sirens. And here come a paramedic van, pulling up behind the store. Two guys hop out, grab a stretcher and load old Driver onto this, stick him in the back of the van and drive off with lights flashing and siren wailing. I hope the bastard's dead and in hell. Only wish I could of got Hairy Legs too.

Then I see the red Dodge pickup drive away. It goes slow to an onramp, then up onto the freeway and disappears.

I get up and stretch. And this is when I notice I'm wearing only one sandal. Must have lost the other running up this hill. Walk back the way I come, looking for it. Find it on the edge of a ditch. Reminds me of my whole life, on the edge of getting washed away to nowhere.

After I find the sandal and put it on, I cut to my left and walk down a dark alley a couple of blocks, going behind stores and stuff. That way, I won't have to come out anywhere near that store.

I figure I'll walk till I find a way across the freeway, and take a guess that Dick's son's house is over there somewhere. All I got to do is find the ocean, and I can locate myself and make it to Dick's son's house.

It gets cold in California at night. I get the shivers and speed up my walking. Only way to keep warm is walk awhile, jog awhile.

I find a road goes under the freeway and follow it. Comes out at a park, high over the beach. There's a path going down onto the beach. Now, which way should I go?

41

Hampton stepped off the plane looking like he owned the airline, tan and fit and prosperous. I felt like a homeless wretch, and I was irritated. Maybe it was the prosperity he exuded that raised my dander. That on top of my worry over Jane, for the more I thought about it, the more I feared that Sinclair and Williston were somehow behind her disappearance.

On the drive back, Hampton and I talked, as usual, about him. Since he wasn't going to return to his "mini estate" in Thousand Oaks, he said, he might as well join the party at the Knor's house in the mountains.

I balked at first, a reaction to prosperous men anywhere near Jane Doyle's grasp. Then the reality of her being missing brought me back to the moment. I decided to listen to Hampton rather than try to explain the situation.

He'd almost put me to sleep with his self-absorbed ramblings, when he suddenly jumped out of his Yuppie mode and said, "I wish I had kids. How I envy you and mother. The biological clock strikes the final hour. If you don't have kids, you've got no one to leave things to. No love conduit to take with you after you're gone. Oh, I'm not making sense. This kid who stowed away in your van, Dad. What's she like?"

It nudged me to ponder Jane's strange charisma. Nothing short of amazing, the number of people who were either after her cute buns or working to protect her from those who were after her. I wondered if another twelve-year-old girl, out here on the loose, could stir half as much activity. I'd watched a heart-breaking number of girls like Jane "graduate" into wretched lives. Kids whose sense of self worth could not be salvaged. And a few of them from prosperous parents. But since Jane had "adopted" me, as Sandra put it, a seed of hope had grown in me—the notion that she could be salvaged... if I played my cards right. That she could grow up to know the love of a faithful husband and her own children. Provided, of course, that she turn up again.

The Great Creator of us all had endowed her with every physical, mental and soulful means to attract the God-given procreative urges of males. But maybe her maker had not figured on Jane's getting into so much trouble so early in her life, because of how hormone-raising, death-defying beautiful she was. Is. In a time that demanded she be educated, hold down a respectable job, fit herself into a society that appeared to be disintegrating.

I had never before known Hampton to look beyond his next year's net worth, and listen so attentively. He suddenly wanted to know all about my life, and all about Jane. I roused myself to explain, to summarize what had happened in the past couple of weeks. Still, accustomed to giving him quick summaries he hardly listened to, I said, "My life has come to this: I'm wi-dowed, jobless and sinking financially. Jane's life: she's strong, beautiful and *wounded*. She has the kind of wounds that may never heal."

"What kinds of wounds?" Hampton asked, staring at me as he drove 80 miles an hour on 101. "Why can't they be healed?" The very idea seemed to violate his notion of positive thinking. An attitude, I realized regretfully, I had taught him, without adding some obvious caveats.

"Ever since she can remember," I said, "the people she's loved and depended upon, her mother and father to begin with, have betrayed her and left her. In fact this whole damned society has abused and abandoned her except when to do otherwise makes somebody a money profit. That's what experience has taught her, that she can expect nothing else. So she's something like a trapped and frightened animal, ready to perpetuate the violence she's known, or make money the best way she knows how, in order to survive."

Hampton was sobered by that thought. He said nothing for a while, then suggested we stop at a restaurant in Thousand Oaks for dinner. Well, he didn't so much suggest as turn off the interstate and park. It turned out to be a subdued, red-plush leather kind of place, conducive to quiet conversation.

He hardly looked at the menu. With his cobalt blue eyes hard on mine, he asked, "Do any of those kids ever heal? Is she a hopeless case?"

"Oh, some heal. A few do enough to function in life. It's something like baseball: If you hit three out of seven times at bat, you go to the hall of fame. For those kids, the hall of fame is a sane and sensible life. Remember, Hampton, I grew up in an orphanage. I managed to raise a family. Some of those kids acquire great insight into their problems and are able to help other kids like themselves. Sandra, for example. She's the best medicine Jane's ever had."

"Well, why don't *you* adopt her? She stowed away in your van and she's still with you."

"She's missing at the moment," I reminded him.

"But you said her pattern is to run away and come back. Let's assume she'll come back. Why don't you just do whatever is necessary to adopt her? Isn't that possible?"

I heaved a sigh and felt dejected. I didn't want to even try to explain the fix Jane was in, given the desperation of Sinclair and Williston. Adopt Jane? Might I? "It's possible, but... I can't see it working out. I'm old and broke, without the needed resources. She's set in her behavior pattern. She believes her only opportunity in life is to become a hooker. She can't see herself doing anything else. Well, maybe that's changed a bit, since she's been with Sandra. I don't know."

"Dad, you're not too old. Why, you look wonderful! Ten years younger than your age." I suspected he was pleading with his own biological clock.

"I'm also jobless, I don't have the money." I'd never before talked like this with Hampton.

"No money? How come?" He looked shocked.

"Hampton, where have you been for the past five years? Don't you know your mother suffered a series of illnesses that wiped us out financially and finally ended her life?"

"Wiped you out financially?" He wrinkled his brow, looked incredulous.

"That's why we sold our two houses and then took the jobs at that agency in North Carolina. We had huge medical bills to pay after Blue Cross paid their eighty percent. The house in town paid off that first round. Then she needed more medical attention. I'm left to pay those off. With no job, ruined credit, the whole catastrophe."

"Dad, why didn't you tell me all this before? I can pay those bills. And I need the deductions. How much money do you have left? What's your net worth right now?"

"Net worth? Let's see. That's how much money you have after you deduct what you owe from what you own, right? Okay. I have less than one hundred dollars in my pocket and something like three hundred in the bank back in North Carolina. I owe something over a hundred thousand to the great American illness industry. I won't know exactly till all the medical bills are in."

"Wait a minute!" Hampton interrupted. "How can you owe health providers a hundred thousand? You have health insurance, don't you? Isn't that part of your retirement package?"

"Roughly one hundred thousand is what's left after the insurance paid, and after what we paid by selling two properties and cashing in our nest egg."

"That's incredible! Don't you get Medicare?"

"Not till I'm sixty-five."

"I never realized Mom's illness caused such a... catastrophe." His eyes glazed over.

"So I guess my net worth is approximately minus roughly a hundred thousand. My plan is to find a job, any job, avoid bill chasers as best I can and just scrape by till I'm ready to present my carcass to the maggots."

"Please don't talk that way, Dad. You're the only family I have. Now that Mom is gone."

If Mae had ever told me that Hampton was not really mine, not of my gene pool, I would have believed her. Instead, she had insisted over the years that Hampton was like me, took after me—a selfish macho male intent only on his own grati-fications, she liked to joke. Well, I had to admit that in my salad days, I did use the trappings of affluence to prop up my ego.

"What about your brother Kent? He's family."

He looked away. After a long pause he said, "Kent doesn't like me. And he makes no secret of it. Maybe I hurt his feelings somehow, I don't know. Maybe he resents Charlene. Or maybe he's jealous of this fortune I put together."

I felt a tiger's instinct on top of a kill. "Let me ask you, Hampton, what's *your* net worth?"

"Well," he smiled, "I'm so used to lying about it, it's difficult to get honest, even with my father." He stared down at the table. "One set of books for the government, another set for creditors. Nobody asks anybody what their net worth is, Dad."

"You just asked me."

"So I did. Okay, I'll guesstimate. My offshore bank has a bit over ten million, earning good interest daily. I own commercial real estate worth another four million and appreciating. I also have another ten million that I've borrowed and invested, for a net income of about half a million a year. The difference between what the borrowed money costs and what it makes. I'm not 'filthy' rich. Yet. But I've covered contingencies."

"And your wife—I understand she has a trust fund."

"Yes."

"And in California, each of you owns half of the other's property. Looks like you'll wind up with another fortune after the divorce settlement."

He ignored that, changed the subject. "Well, you and mother are the beneficiaries of one insurance policy I have. Now I'm going to name you alone in both, since mother is gone."

I wondered what kind of insurance policy that was but said: "You're determined to get this divorce, are you?"

"I don't see how it can be avoided. Charlene and I married images, fantasies. After the honeymoon we gradually got acquainted and found out who we really are, and the marriage... I don't know. We just don't get along. She says I married her for her money but without my management she'd have blown it away by now, or half of it. She's *obsessed* with money."

"I see *you* as obsessed with money, Hampton. Aren't you projecting this onto Charlene? Wasn't it her father's fortune that enabled you to create your own? I don't know if you married her for her money or not, but you might as well have."

He stared hard at me, remaining silent. Then, "I fell in love with a girl who happened to be incredibly rich. Her father helped me get started. You were a big success in life, Dad, and I wanted to be like you. Is that bad?"

"Where'd you get the idea I was a big success? I was middle management."

"You always had plenty, and you and Mom were happy."

"I made a pretty good income, I guess, enough to send you guys to higher educations. And I was happy with Mae. She taught me how to be part of a family. I wasn't happy working for the company, though. Maybe that's why I didn't object when they suggested an early retirement. No sooner did I retire and your mother... well, her heart had been vulnerable for some time. Now the nest egg's gone, the pension's gone, the two houses are gone, I don't get social security for another couple of years, and I'm flat broke."

"I didn't realize," he said, eyes narrowing as he took this in.

"You were busy with your own life."

"I need to take a new direction in my life."

"How come you and Charlene never had children? That's what marriages are for, to bring children into the world and raise them."

"At first she said she wanted kids. She made appointments with doctors to find out why she wasn't getting pregnant. She ovulates regularly. I have a high sperm count. No medical reason why she can't get pregnant."

"What's the non-medical reason?"

"Can you see Charlene being a mother?"

"I don't know the woman. Can count on one hand the times I've seen her, and we never had much to say to each other. She's a stranger to me, Hampton."

"She *hates* kids. Kent and Anna visited us once, and Charlene was so afraid their little ones would damage her precious high-priced antique furniture, she kept them all outside by the pool the whole time they were there. Well, here comes our dinners. Let's eat."

Before we resumed our drive to the Knor's house, I put through a call to Sandra. "Still no sign of Jane," she said, "but Kent's friend Jim, on the desk at the motel, recorded a call to Sinclair. A male voice said they'd bring a 'her' by around midnight. We're waiting, ready to grab 'em then."

"Guess that explains what happened to Jane. Why don't we plan to meet in Carpenteria? Hampton would like to overnight at the Knor's, he tells me. Let's meet in Carpenteria so we can be there when this 'her' gets delivered."

"Dick, I don't have any wheels here."

"Oh, that's right. Forgive me. The memory goes first, they say."

"I tried to rent a car but they tell me they don't deliver up here in the mountains. My friend—the one I told you about from Pennsylvania—he's in town looking for that red Dodge pickup. I'm stuck here."

I was seized by another rush of fright. If Sinclair and Williston had managed to have Hooper snuffed, halfway across the country, they could far more easily have someone with sinister intent show up at the Knor's house. "Sandra, listen. Please call someone in local law enforcement."

"Don't worry about me, I can take care of myself. Besides, Jane's puppy is a natural born guard dog. It started yapping half an hour ago when a car stuck its nose into the end of this driveway to turn around."

Famous last words, I thought. "Okay, Sandra. Hampton and I will drive up there. I'll bring the van so we'll have two vehicles. No hint where Jane might be?"

"Not a one. I need to get my butt down there to that motel in Carpenteria. I'm sure she's the 'her' to be delivered."

When we got to Kent's house, I was amazed to see Hampton wrap his arms around his younger brother and give him a hug. Kent wasn't expecting this abrupt end to the cool distance of the past few years. He patted Hampton's back a couple of times, peered at him quizzically, then turned to me. "Here," he said, handing me his forty-five, handle first.

"No, no, I don't need that."

"All right, then, I'm going with you, Dad," said Kent. "You need a body guard."

"You stay here, Son. Your wife and kids need you. Keep in touch with your friend at the motel. Call the Knor's house if you learn anything."

I walked through the house and out the back door to my van.

Hampton followed me up the pass in his Mercedes. It was the post-cocktail end of rush hour, a bad time to drive the treacherous curves of San Marcos Pass Highway. He wanted to go a lot faster than me, and kept tailgating. I felt jumpy, irritable, vulnerable and disoriented. What was I doing here, anyway? We had all forgotten about Mae's ashes. Everyone was now focused on this child I'd brought out here into... this mess.

The cliff rising to the right beside the tight turns of this highway seemed extra ominous, and I had the strange fear that if I didn't drive with great care I'd sideswipe that cliff. Or that Jane's body would suddenly appear hurtling through the air and land on the road just ahead of my van. I went through a series of wide-awake nightmares, the worst being that I had killed her by not turning her back into the system.

Some stress lifted when we arrived at the Knor's and I heard Mindy yapping from her tether on the front porch. I turned off the engine and stepped out. The headlights of Hampton's car momentarily blinded me. When I turned away from them—my eyes no longer adjusted from bright light to pitch dark as quickly as they used to—I thought I saw something move at the far end of the porch off Jane's room. I ducked behind the van and looked again.

A figure rose up holding a gun. It took me a moment to realize it was Sandra and her Uzi.

42

I took time out to rest, then decide to walk to my right. All I could see to the left down the beach was high cliff on one side, water on the other. No town, no campground. So I figured Kent's house had to be the other way.

Took off my sandals so I could walk faster and jog easier in the sand. Went to the hard sand, near the water.

Got to thinking what a sorry stupid bitch I am. My Mom wants to sell me, my daddy don't want me, my Auntie wants to help my Mom sell me. Fucking Dick says he can't afford me but he won't let me make money for us. What the hell am I doing, stomping up this damn beach again, heading for Dick's son's house? Kent and Anna already got three kids of their own, they don't want me. They'll just call Dick to come get me and this whole round of crap will start all over. He'll try to get rid of me and I'll have to run, and some weirdos will pick me up and rape me again. Or maybe try to turn me in. Shit, I can't see no way out and I just can't take no more of this. Third time I pounded my sore feet up this beach, trying to find... what? And each time, I'm a sorrier pity party than before.

Thought about my Mom and what a sorry bitch she turned out to be, and about my Auntie trying to take me to my Mom so they could make money by turning me back over to Williston. If your own kin will do that, what can you expect from strangers?

Then I thought about Dick and how he's been sort of sweet. Not all the time, but some. I wish Mrs. Sweet was still alive, cause I know she'd understand better than old Mr. Sour ever could. Most staff don't believe nothing you say if it ain't in your documents but Mrs. Sweet was different, she'd listen.

Then I thought about Sandra and how nice she is. She grew up in the system too, so she knows all about it. How rotten it can be, and how bad you can get fucked over. And I thought about Dick's son, Kent, and his wife, Anna, and their kids, and how nice they all are.

Old Hurt and Enema always saying, Jane, you ain't ready to make it in no family, foster or adopted. Told me that so many times I come to believe it. Old Hurt and Enema just got their own agenda, and I know what that is. That's what happened to Pamela and Nancy and Wendy.

But where they at now can't be no worse than this. At least I'd see Pamela and make some money, instead of being raped till I bleed. I could feel a whole lot better doing that. Dick says I'd end up like yesterday's garbage. Humph! I already *feel* like last year's garbage.

When I see the campground up ahead, on this little rise, I know I been going in the right direction. Kent's house ain't far from here.

But why the hell am I going there? What are they gonna do with me? Call Dick to come and he'll start trying to get rid of me again.

I can't go on. I turn numb and just sit down.

Wind's blowing and it's cold, but I don't feel nothing no more. Sit and look at the ocean, the starry night. All you can see is a gleam when a wave comes up, then crash, and it spills onto the beach.

Numb as I feel, it won't even bother me to walk into them waves. I remember a silly thing my mom used to say when I was little, teasing me when I felt down. "Nobody loves me, everybody hates me, I'm gonna eat some worms." That used to make me smile, even laugh away my blues. But it don't help now.

I get up and walk. Don't stop till I get knocked off my feet by a wave. Now I'm under and it's soon gonna be over. I think of when I was little and used to climb up on my Daddy's lap and he'd put his arms around me and I'd feel so warm and safe and good. I think of how my Mom used to scoop me up and used to hug me to her bosoms and say, Don't cry, baby. Everything's gonna be all right. And I think of how I went to a family reunion back when I was six, and I met all them cousins and aunties and uncles I can't remember all the names of, but I still remember how we cousins all kinda looked a little like each other, and that was fun. And then I blanked out.

43

"I figured it was you, Dick," said Sandra, stepping forward with her gun at port arms, "but I'm not in a mood to take chances."

I introduced her to Hampton and she led us inside, where she was keeping the lights low.

"New development," she said, leaning her gun against the back of the couch and sitting down. "A hospital, Cottage Hospital by name, called the police when they got an emergency case that aroused suspicions. Some guy who'd been stabbed. Behind a liquor store in Summerland. Turns our he's on parole, did time for a murder that had all the earmarks of a hired job."

"Well, any sign of Jane?"

"No. Does she have the phone number here?"

"No, but she should have in her pocket a little slip of paper with Kent's and other phone numbers on it."

"It's past midnight, so apparently something has gone wrong. They were supposed to deliver Jane at midnight."

"Well, I'm very tired. Maybe you and Hampton would like to go down the mountain to Carpenteria and see what's going on with Sinclair and Williston. I'll stay here in case Jane finds her way back."

Hampton was looking Sandra over. Sandra was pretending not to notice. "Suits me," she said, now glancing over at Hampton. "Shall we take your car?"

Before Hampton could reply, the phone chirped. Sandra picked up and as she listened her eyes widened. "We'll be there as soon as we can make it," she said. Then to me: "How long does it take to drive to Cottage Hospital? They've just admitted a young girl, fits Jane's description. Five feet four inches, long dark curly hair. Somebody fished her out of the surf near a campground in Carpenteria. He wrapped her in a blanket and drove her to the hospital."

We hurried into Hampton's car, Sandra carrying her gun and taking the back seat. Hampton raced down the mountain a lot faster than I had ever driven this treacherous road.

Jane lay on an emergency room bed, wrapped in blankets. She was shivering and whimpering, weeping silently with her eyes closed. Her hair was still damp and the blankets didn't quite cover her feet. I tugged one end down over the feet, then bent close to her and said, "Jane?"

Her eyes opened wide, frightened. Her chin trembled as she tried to speak. She reached a hand out and caught my forearm in an uncertain grip. "Dick! I'm such a goddamn fuck up, I couldn't even drown myself. Some man pulled me out and brung me here."

"My God! You tried to drown yourself? How do you feel now?"

"Like a pile of dog shit on the living room rug. And I'm freezin. Can't seem to get warm."

Out of the corner of my eye I noticed Sandra had gone to a wall phone and was dialing.

"What happened to you? Suicide is definitely not your style, girl."

"I got grabbed by two goons. I don't want to talk about it."

I decided to be blunt. "But why did you try to kill yourself?"

She was just as blunt. "Cause nobody wants me. You keep dropping me off, trying to get rid of me, and nobody wants me."

I fell back a step to let the shock of that sink in. Just then, Sandra came back to Jane's bedside and said, "They're picking up Mr. Sinclair and Mr. Williston now, at the motel." Then she nodded her head toward a room off the one we were in. A policeman was standing in the doorway. I hadn't noticed him before.

As I introduced Hampton to Jane, Sandra disappeared with the policeman.

"How are you, Jane?" Hampton said, bending low.

"Been better."

Hampton stood with his hands behind his back, gazing down at Jane, who kept her eyes averted. I could tell that she wanted to look him over too, but would wait until she could do so without him watching her. She'd stopped shivering.

"Well," said Sandra, returning a second time to our little grouping around Jane's bed, "they're going to arrest the guy who came in with the knife wound. After they take him to surgery. If he lives. I just got a glimpse of him."

"Letter opener," said Jane.

"Letter opener?" inquired Sandra.

"Yeah. It ain't no knife wound. I stuck him in the heart with a sharp old fancy sliver letter opener."

She rolled onto her left side and we could see her arms working under the blankets. Then she raised one hand up, holding a black oblong object that had a silver button. She pressed this button and a knife blade popped out of the black sheath. It looked sharp as a razor, double-edged, a needle-sharp point. Lethal. Her fingers looked rubbed raw and dirty.

"He's the one in the—" said Sandra.

"Yeah!" said Jane. "The red Dodge pickup."

"I thought I recognized that face." Sandra paced back and forth by Jane's feet. I could see this was making Jane nervous. Finally she blurted her fears:

"I ain't going back. I'm out of the system, and I ain't going back. If that's what you-all got in mind, please get out of here and leave me alone!"

"Not what we have in mind," said Sandra. "Have you ever testified in court?"

"Sure. Why?"

"Because the police will definitely need your testimony to put all those scumbags away."

"He raped me, him and the other guy." Sandra had been talking about Sinclair, Williston, et al.

"Oh no!" said Sandra, expressing the shock of everyone within hearing of Jane's words. My first impression was that we'd have to get conclusive proof of this rape before it would be believed in a court, given Jane's past record.

"Oh my dear! You must have been through a horror," said Sandra. Then, to a doctor who was bending over another patient not far away, Sandra shouted, "We need medical tests here for rape. Semen samples, the works!"

"The one guy tore me up bad," said Jane, sitting up now, warming under Sandra's concern. "I'll tell the police all about it." Then to me: "And none of it will be lies, or even exaggerations. Another thing, Dick. If only you'd just take care of me, none of this would happen. No more running. No more sexual acting out. Won't do nothing but work on my problems. I swear to God on a stack of Bibles sky high."

"It's a deal," I said.

"Are you serious?" she asked with her teary eyes squinting.

"I am." Truly. I knew at that moment that I had no choice. I'd find a way. Fate had created a strange bond between us.

"No more trying to get rid of me?"

"No more! Never. I love you."

"But..." she hesitated then lay back down and softly, sorrowfully added, "You're just saying that. You can't *afford* me."

"Yes he can," said Hampton, his voice husky with emotion. I flinched at his next words: "Dad has just received a windfall." Then, realizing Jane had no idea what a windfall was, he added: "A lot of money. More than enough to keep the two of you for a lifetime."

Jane contemplated Hampton a moment, then asked me, "Is he for real?"

"I, eh, I..." I turned to Hampton. "What are you saying?"

Hampton put his arms around my shoulders and bumped his head against mine. "Like you used to say, Dad, Go with what you know. Nobody can know the future. All we can know is right now. Isn't that what you used to say?"

"Yes, but..." I wanted to indicate that no one, male or female, rich or poor, could provide *all* Jane's needs.

Hampton released me, stood back, exchanged a look with Sandra, then smiled at me and said, "I'll be there to help."

"It's going to take more than just *your* help."

"We'll find the help we need."

As I saw Jane gazing up at Hampton with a quizzical look, I thought, Son, you have a lot to learn about damaged children. But then I thought, so do I. As do so many of those psychiatrists and psychologists and social workers, child care workers and such, all those people who try to help, without much to show for their efforts. How do you fit damaged children into a damaging society?

But it was beginning to look like Sandra would be part of our lives long after this night was a memory. And if anyone knew the route to a healthy, happy life for Jane, Sandra did. That's what Maude Jennings didn't understand—and why Sandra knew she had to pursue this case. I looked at Sandra and she winked.

"Okay, Hampton," I said, "but remember, this is as big a commitment as a marriage. No, it's bigger!"

He studied his folded hands a few moments, then gave me a knowing look and said, "I'm going to find a way to heal that wound, too."

"You-all," said Jane, now smiling like a cat that has swallowed a canary, "forget one thing. I have Mrs. Sweet's ashes. In my possession. Ain't that so, Dick?"

I stroked my chin and said, "Yes, held hostage." The urn was where she'd left it, on the coffee table in the Knor's house.

"Okay," said Jane, "just give me the word and we'll do that ceremony. Scatter Mrs. Sweet's ashes on this ocean called Pacific, which—shut up, Dick, I know this—means peaceful, out of the system. But right now them ashes is *mine*. You-all can't do that ceremony without me. That's the deal, ain't it, Dick?"

I nodded, wiping a tear from my eye. "What an indomitable spirit you are, Jane."

"What's indomitable mean?" she asked suspiciously.

"Means no one can ever conquer you. You're determined to be free."

"Yeah, that's what I been trying to tell you, Dick. I'm glad you finally got it. Now don't you forget it."

"I won't, I swear on a stack of Bibles sky high."

She grinned. "Maybe we can forget the Bibles now that we're so far away from North Carolina. I trust your word."

"And I trust yours."

"Finally."

After the emergency room doctor took Jane away for tests to prove or disprove her charge of rape, we three went to the county jail to check on Sinclair and Williston. We found them sitting on a bench just inside the door, dressed in suits and ties, leaning forward because their hands were cuffed behind their backs.

As we walked in, Williston glared up at us, but Sinclair burst into a huge grin and said, "Ah, there you are! My God, Dick, I thought you'd never get here. Tell these people who we are and get us out of here. Get them to set bail, if need be. You'll be amply reimbursed, I assure you."

I looked him over carefully for a while, then shook my head sadly and walked back outside. Hampton came with me, asking who these guys were. Sandra lingered to help write a report. Sitting in the car with Hampton, I tried to explain how this all had come about, but found myself just too worn out to recount the gory details. "I'll fill you in later," I told him.

Sandra was worn out too, when she returned to the car. "What's the word?" I asked.

"They'll be booked and held and then extradited to North Carolina. The California people are going to help us retrieve the three other girls. They have a couple of Asians on that job. Then, I think, we'll have everything we need to put the whole mess of them away for a long time."

44

G ot out of that hospital three days later, after they inspected, injected and detected me up one side and down the other. I mean they went at me like they was sure I had AIDS or something, and fed me food worse than you'd get in a fast food joint on a work slowdown.

Dick and Sandra brought by a video of Sinclair and Herb being taken out of the motel room with their hands cuffed behind their backs, put into a couple of police cars. Sinclair had on his Sunday go-to-church clothes, looking like he was gonna plead clean behind the ears. Herb was in shirtsleeves, his suit coat over one arm. Dick said it was important for me to see the police had caught them so they couldn't do me no more harm.

Then there was all them cops coming by, asking would I testify about being raped, they had all the medical evidence, they said, and knew those guys beat me. One cop, the last one they sent—youngest and cutest and also the dumbest—I finally went and told him that I really wanted to kill both those sons of bitches and was sorry I only got to stick one.

Looks at me hard and says, Don't you know you could get put away for murder?

I look back just as hard at him and say, Don't *you* know I coulda got murdered by them?

Says, Oh!

Takes out a little notebook and pen and starts writing, says, Let's take it from the beginning and you tell me what happened.

By this time, I'd told Dick and Hampton and Sandra, told nurses and doctors and other cops. Was plain sick and tired of talking about it. Just wanted to get the hell out of that hospital.

But I went through it all over again, from hiding out in Dick's van to run, and how Herb Williston was gonna sell my ass, come after me and I shot him with Mace, how Sinclair must have hired those two maniacs to grab me, how they handcuffed me and raped me, and how I stabbed the one with that letter opener. This cop must have written pages in his notebook, even though he had a tape recorder running. You'll have to testify, he said.

No shit, I said. Testify's my middle name.

Later this same day, Sandra come up by herself to see me and told me she was going to be away for a while, but she'd be back. That didn't cheer me up. Where you going? How long you gonna be gone?

Says, I got to go back to North Carolina—and then Philadephia. But I'll be back to follow up on this case, your kidnapping and rape, and the conspiracy to force you into prostitution. And we're working on locating those other girls so we can get to the bottom of this horrible thing.

Then, the next day, the doctor who was seeing me the most says, Well, Jane, you'll be going home in an hour or so. How do you feel?

I say, Home? What home?

Says, You're to be picked up by your... eh, guardian, I understand. Mr. Richard Steel, I believe his name is. Yes, that's what it says here.

I was feeling pretty good when Dick and Hampton showed up. They brought a traveling bag full of new clothes, and what do you know—this time I got that pair of Jordache.

We all piled into Hampton's car and drove up the mountain, where I made sure I still had Mrs. Sweet's urn of ashes. Fed my puppy, and after that, things went by so fast it's a blur.

Hampton bought us this real nice house in a place called Westlake Village. My bedroom window looks out over this lake, and Mindy got a dog door so she can come and go whenever she feels like it. Out to the back yard, all fenced in. I got a bedroom with my own bathroom. Dick got the same and Hampton got a whole wing. He comes here a couple times a week to work. Says he got a real estate project in mind.

Dick hired a tutor to come in every day and work with me on reading and writing and numbers. All summer long. She's a soft old lady named Terry Riley and she says I'm smart as a whip and learning fast. Makes me feel upbeat to see her coming, she cons my self-esteem so good.

I been hanging out with a girl named Cindy. She's a few months older than me and knows her way around this neighborhood. We bike everywhere. She's nice, and even though we ain't knowed each other very long, we're best friends. Dick bought me this real hot dirt bike. Me and Cindy ride over to where I'll be going to school in September, where they're holding practice.

I ask Dick, How'd you like to be a soccer mom?

Says, What are you talking about?

Me and Cindy are trying out for the soccer team.

Oh, okay, sure, I'll be a soccer mom.

Me and Cindy want to start young so we can make the USA soccer team on TV.

A worthy goal, he says kinda sly.

Yeah sure, I know, it's pie in the sky but shit, Dick, it's fun to daydream.

Well, soccer is a whole world better than sexually acting out. Daydream your game and who knows, maybe you'll make it come true. Creative visualization.

You got it, soccer mom.

I'll buy you some books on the game.

You buy 'em, I'll read 'em.

Then, couple of weeks after we got settled in with furniture delivered, Dick says, It's time to hold that ceremony to scatter Mae's ashes on the ocean. And he gets on the phone and calls around to his two sons and their families, and sets the date for Sunday.

Come Sunday, we drive down to a place called Marina Del Ray, got more boats than you ever saw in one place. Park the van and walk out onto a dock to a big white boat, and here's Hampton on it, waiting for us.

We step onto this boat and while Hampton's taking me for a tour, here comes Kent and Anna and their three kids, and a while after that comes a lady I never met before. Hampton tells me her name is Charlene and she's his wife. She comes carrying something sorrowful, seems to me. Guess I'll find out later what this is all about.

Kent and Dick untie the lines and Hampton backs this big boat out of its dock, turns it, and heads it out to sea. It's a bright sunny day with big white clouds in the sky, the kind that give you a little shade now and then without blocking the sun all day.

It does something to you when you go out onto the real ocean. It's like the boat noses up and becomes real business-like. I'm carrying the urn and setting near the back of the boat, outside the main cabin. Dick and Hampton are up on what's called the flying bridge, looking at a compass and steering this monster boat. I'm with Anna and Kent and the kids, got the urn between my legs, and Charlene is inside the cabin so her hair won't get undone by the wind.

I say to Kent, What's wrong with that lady there, Charlene?

He says, Oh, she and Hampton are talking about getting a divorce. I'm surprised she came to this ceremony.

I hand Mrs. Sweet's ashes to Kent and say, I'm gonna go in there and talk to her.

Be careful, he says, and he's right, cause it's hard to walk with the boat going this fast.

Inside the cabin, I sit down beside this lady and say, Your name Charlene?

Yes, she says, and you're Jane.

I just want you to know I think you're real pretty and I'm sorry if you're feeling down.

Oh, she says, so nice of you to care!

Would you like to help me turn over Mae's ashes to Dick? I got 'em held hostage till he's ready to scatter.

She thinks this over awhile, then smiles big and says, Sure! What do I have to do?

Be the go-between, I say. I'll hand the urn to you and you hand it to Dick. When the time comes.

I can see that makes her feel better. It's a trick I learned back at Grandmother's Home. When someone new comes into group, you get them involved by turning them into a go-between.

When the time comes, Hampton slows the engines way down and the boat's nose kind of settles back down in the water, and pretty soon we're just riding up and down on swells.

Charlene comes out of the cabin and Dick and Hampton come down from the flying bridge, and I stand up holding this urn of ashes. Dick walks toward me like he's gonna take the urn out of my hands, but I say, Wait. Charlene. And I hand the urn to her, and she turns and looks at Dick and hands the urn to him. They stand there looking at each other for quite a spell, like they ain't sure who the other is.

When Dick turns back around, I see he's got tears coming down his cheeks and his hands are trembling so bad he can't get the stopper out the top of the urn.

Hampton takes a try at it and gets the stopper out, then hands the urn back to Dick.

His hands are still trembly, though he's wiped away the tears. He holds the urn up toward the sky and says, Mae, you were a wonderful woman and a wonderful wife. And now, as was your wish, we scatter your physical remains on the waters of the Pacific. I know you're out there somewhere, watching, knowing, still with us in some way we don't yet understand.

Then Kent and Hampton both say, We love you, Mom, wherever you are. And Dick up ends the urn and lets Mae's ashes blow away in the wind.

Then all the grownups start crying and push into this big hug around Dick, and I take the three kids inside the cabin and look in the refrigerator to see what there is to eat. We find colas and snacks and help ourselves.

After the grownups stop crying, Hampton revs up the engines again and we head back to shore. I go and sit beside Dick on the flying bridge, with Hampton on the other side of him, steering. Dick says, That was a sweet thing you did, Jane.

Which?

Involving Charlene.

Oh, that. Guess that's one good thing come out of the system, how to get new people into group. Then I looks past Dick at Hampton, who's smiling at me, so I wink back at him.

This puts a big frown on Mr. Sour's forehead and he leans over near my ear and says, You reach for Hampton's private parts and I'll cut off your hand.

I say real loud over the engine noise, Dick, don't get your shorts in a twist! Why would I do a thing like that? I'm way too busy working on my self-esteem to get into any more sexual acting out.

He looks like he don't believe me at first, then breaks a grin and gives me a hug. Makes me feel like I'm radiating inside, like Mrs. Sweet must have felt when he put his arm around her.

Yeah, I knew it all along, Mr. Sour loves Sweet.

The End

About the Author

Robert Gover grew up in an endowed orphanage (Girard College in Philadelphia), received a BA in economics from the University of Pittsburgh, worked as a journalist, became a best-selling novelist at age 30, lived most of his life in California, and now lives in Rehoboth Beach, Delaware. *On the Run with Dick and Jane* is his ninth novel. His previous book, *Time and Money*, explores economic and planetary cyclical correlations. His first novel, *One Hundred Dollar Misunderstanding*, a satire on American racism, remains a cult classic.

www.ingramcontent.com/pod-product-compliance
Lightning Source LLC
Chambersburg PA
CBHW020828260626
47169CB00003B/881